ALL I WANT

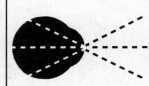

This Large Print Book carries the
Seal of Approval of N.A.V.H.

ALL I WANT

JILL SHALVIS

THORNDIKE PRESS
A part of Gale, Cengage Learning

GALE
CENGAGE Learning·

Farmington Hills, Mich • San Francisco • New York • Waterville, Maine
Meriden, Conn • Mason, Ohio • Chicago

GALE
CENGAGE Learning®

Copyright © 2015 by Jill Shalvis.
Thorndike Press, a part of Gale, Cengage Learning.

Thorndike Press® Large Print Romance.
The text of this Large Print edition is unabridged.
Other aspects of the book may vary from the original edition.
Set in 16 pt. Plantin.

LIBRARY OF CONGRESS CATALOGING-IN-PUBLICATION DATA

Shalvis, Jill.
  All I want / Jill Shalvis. — Large print edition.
    pages cm. — (Thorndike Press large print romance)
  ISBN 978-1-4104-8634-9 (hardback) — ISBN 1-4104-8634-6 (hardcover)
  1. Large type books. I. Title.
PS3619.H3534A78 2016
813'.6—dc23   2015036252

Published in 2016 by arrangement with The Berkley Publishing Group,
an imprint of Penguin Publishing Group, a division of Penguin Random
House LLC

Printed in the United States of America
1 2 3 4 5 6 7 20 19 18 17 16

ALL I WANT

ONE

Zoe Stone had tried on everything in her closet and not only did her room now look like an explosion in a mattress factory, not one single item of clothing had worked for her.

She was still standing there eyeing the carnage when her sister, Darcy, appeared in the doorway, arms loaded with clothing. "Got your 911 freak-out text. Here's all the stuff I've ever borrowed from you."

"You mean stolen?"

"Tomayto, tomahto." Darcy dumped the entire pile of loot in the only space available — on top of the slightly tubby Bernese mountain dog snoring in the center of Zoe's bed.

"The pretty little black dress of yours is in there," Darcy said. "You should absolutely be wearing that for your date instead of the granny dress you've got on. Seriously, how old are you, eighty-five?"

She'd just had her first anniversary of turning thirty, thank you very much, but Zoe looked down at herself. Her floral print dress was soft and clingy, fell to just past her knees, and hid a multitude of sins — such as the fact that she'd been stress-eating her feels all week. "It's not that bad."

"Zoe, you could walk into any Denny's before five o'clock and get a discount."

"I like this dress," Zoe said, "and so does Oreo."

Oreo, the aforementioned Bernese mountain dog, cracked open an eye and looked up at Zoe with love and adoration. "See?" she said, ruffling the dog's big head. "And not that I have time to change anyway, but I don't see what's wrong with this outfit."

"Absolutely nothing," Darcy said, "assuming that you don't care if you ever get laid again. And for God's sake, stop taking fashion advice from a dog who rolls in bear poo and thinks he smells good."

Panting happily, Oreo smiled up at the both of them.

Through the open window came the sound of a vehicle pulling up. Darcy moved to the second-story window and peered out. "Looks like your blind date's here. What's his name again?"

"Newman Taylor."

"Well, Newman's in a black Jeep with the top off. Not his top, the Jeep's top, but still very nice — Whoa."

"What?"

Darcy's nose was glued to the window now. "Holy crap on a stick — he's hot for a guy named Newman. *Way* too hot for that dress you're wearing. Quick," she said, waving a hand at Zoe. "Exchange it for the LBD."

"I'm fine in this," Zoe said. Maybe because she *couldn't* wear the LBD; she hadn't shaved her thighs — her own little insurance policy against making any rash decisions tonight such as getting naked. No way would she be tempted knowing she had hairy thighs. "And get away from there and stop spying on him." But then she moved to the window next to her sister and sucked in a breath because Darcy was right, Newman was hot. Dark hair, a little wavy, a lot wind tousled. Black shirt that fit him well enough to define broad shoulders. Dark jeans. An easy gait that said *confident male.*

Butterflies took flight low in her belly and she pressed a hand to it. "Oh boy."

"And I bet he's got a six-pack, too," Darcy whispered. "Maybe even an *eight*-pack. I'm going to need you to remember every detail for me."

For Darcy, abs were a requirement in a man.

But Zoe had learned a lot for a woman who'd just had her thirtieth birthday — again. She had a completely different list of requirements. Honesty and kindness. That was it. Easy to remember and simple. But she'd also learned that nothing about men was simple.

"I wonder what color his eyes are —" Darcy broke off as the guy stopped on the path to the house and unerringly looked up at the window where the two of them stood staring at him.

With a commingled squeak, they dropped to the floor.

Afraid he was missing some fun new game, Oreo barked happily and leapt off the bed and right on top of them.

"Oomph." Darcy pulled the silly dog in for a hug. "You big lug. You need a diet."

Zoe pushed Oreo's tail out of her face. "Think he saw us?" she asked, panicked.

"Nah," Darcy said.

Zoe let out a relieved breath. "Really?"

"No." Darcy grinned and sat up. "He totally saw us."

Oh for God's sake. *The guy's a dentist,* she reminded herself. By definition, that meant he most likely was a people person, right?

Right, she decided. And him being a people person was a good thing since one of them needed to know what they were doing.

She and Darcy — and Oreo — crawled away from the window and stood.

"Feels a little like old times, doesn't it?" Darcy asked, dusting herself off. "Remember when we sneaked out of the house to do that midnight full moon climb up White Eagle with the Connelly brothers? We climbed out the window and got caught by Grandpa and were grounded for the rest of the summer."

"That was you and Wyatt," Zoe said. Their brother had always been able to find trouble. "I never got grounded."

"That's right. Wyatt was way more fun than you."

Zoe slipped into a pair of flats and Darcy rolled her eyes.

"What's wrong with the flats?" Zoe asked. "You wear flats all the time."

"Yes, because I have a spinal injury that makes me want to drop to the floor and curl up in a ball whenever I wear heels," Darcy pointed out. "You don't have such an excuse. Plus you have legs a mile long that look amazing in heels, which makes me hate you just a little bit."

"Flats," Zoe insisted.

"Fine. So what do we know about this guy?"

"He's a dentist from Hennessey Flats," Zoe said. "Karen set me up with him. He's her neighbor."

"The Karen who does your hair, the Karen who's been married and divorced three times?" Darcy asked.

"Yeah, so?"

"Sooooooo," Darcy said, "don't you think if her neighbor was hot, she'd date him herself, if not make him husband number four?"

Well, crap. She hadn't thought of that.

"Plus . . . a *dentist*?" Darcy asked doubtfully.

"What's wrong with him being a dentist? At least he's gainfully employed."

"Nothing's wrong with it," Darcy said reasonably. "If you want to sleep with a guy whose hands have been inside other people's mouths all day long. Do you know how many germs that is? A million. A million trillion."

Zoe shuddered. "Great. Thanks for that. Don't you have somewhere to be?"

"Yep," Darcy said, but moved back to the window. "You got a reprieve; he stopped to take a call."

Zoe grabbed her purse and turned to

12

Oreo. "Hold down the fort for Mommy, okay?"

Darcy snorted. "If a bad guy showed up, he'd hide in your closet."

This was probably true but the big, goofy dog was the only home security system she had right now. In the past few months both Wyatt and Darcy had moved out, Wyatt to live with his fiancée, Emily, and Darcy to live with her boyfriend, AJ.

Zoe had told herself she was good with that. Sure, she missed bossing them around as she'd been doing since the dawn of time because one, their foreign diplomat parents had never seemed to notice that they'd had children, and two, well, Zoe kind of just loved to boss people around. But she wasn't going to complain. Not when she'd seen just about every corner of the world and knew exactly how good she really had it right here in Sunshine, Idaho, alone or not.

Besides, with her newfound freedom she had a lot planned for herself. She wanted to fix up the house, although she admittedly had very little talent in that area. She wanted to learn to bake, even though she had even *less* talent in that realm. She wanted to date — where she had absolutely *zero* talent.

It might seem silly, but to a woman who'd

been uniquely unlucky in her love life, Zoe had never gotten the hang of dipping her toes into the wading pool, especially with the audience of her siblings.

But now, with the house empty, it seemed like a perfect time.

Hence blind date number one. And she was ready. She wanted this. She totally almost did.

"He's off the phone," Darcy reported, back at the window.

Oh God. "I changed my mind," Zoe whispered.

Darcy turned to her. "No."

"Yes!"

"Then why did you tell everyone to set you up with blind dates so that you could get laid?"

"I never said that! I really wish you'd stop saying it."

"What?" Darcy asked. "That you want to get laid?"

Zoe shot Darcy a look that went completely ignored. "And that's not why I wanted to go out. I just wanted . . ." She trailed off, because what she wanted was much more complicated than her short list of man requirements.

She had a job she loved: being both a pilot-for-hire and giving flying lessons out of the small regional Sunshine Airport. Sunshine was a sleepy ranching town at the base of the heart-stopping Bitterroot Mountains and didn't see a lot of action, but she managed to keep busy enough to eke out a living.

She had Wyatt and Darcy, whom she loved fiercely even though on any given day she felt like strangling and/or smothering them, but she was working on that.

And then there was the ancient — and some might argue dilapidated — 150-year-old Victorian house that her grandparents had left the three of them, which she loved with the same fierceness she loved her annoying siblings.

Not to mention Oreo, whom she'd rescued not all that long ago and who'd quickly become her favorite family member.

So yeah, her life was good and she was happy, blah blah blah.

But something had been missing for a while now.

Joy.

She'd never given that particular emotion much thought before. She'd always been too busy keeping things together. But now that she had an empty nest, so to speak, she'd decided she was due. Past due —

At the knock on the front door downstairs,

she nearly leapt out of her skin.

Startled, Oreo gave a loud bark and farted at the same time, and then as he did every single time this happened, he whipped his big head around to stare at his own hind end in surprise.

Darcy grinned. "Killer protective instincts, this one." She rumpled Oreo's fur. "I'm going to sneak out the back door, okay?" At the door, she blew Zoe a quick kiss and then smacked her own forehead. "Oh, almost forgot! Wyatt told me to remind you that his friend Parker could be showing up any time over the next few days. And change your dress and shoes!"

"I'm not going to change!"

Darcy sighed the put-upon sigh of a sister who thought she knew everything. "Fine. But do me a favor?"

"Anything if you'll leave."

"For once," Darcy said, "just once, act spontaneously, okay?"

"Spontaneously?"

"Yeah, like if when you open the door and he's even hotter up close, step outside your comfort zone and kiss him. Right up front, you know? Set the mood."

Zoe just stared at her. "Are you completely nuts?"

"Well, obviously," Darcy said. "But what

does that have to do with anything?" She laughed, but then her smile faded. "Listen, most people spend a first date filled with anxiety, obsessing over the good-night kiss. Will there be one, won't there be one . . ."

"I don't obsess," Zoe said.

"Are you kidding? You're the queen of obsessing. So just get it out of the way, okay? Act spontaneously. And then relax and go with the flow."

"I always go with the flow," Zoe said.

Darcy laughed. "You go with the flow never. Try it my way? Just this once? Trust me, if there are sparks, you'll thank me."

"And if there aren't?" Zoe asked.

"Then you don't need to worry that that dress makes you look like a grandma."

And then the whirlwind that was Darcy was gone.

Zoe took one last look at herself in the mirror. Okay, so maybe the dress didn't scream *sex,* but that was okay. She wanted a guy to want her for *her,* right?

Right.

The knock came again. Solid. Firm. And the butterflies in her belly once again took flight.

Oreo's, too, given that he gave another ear-piercing bark and scrambled to hide under her bed. All he could fit under there was his big, fat head, which left the rest of him sticking out.

She thought about joining him, but she'd never been much for hiding her head under the bed. So she made her way down the creaky stairs, her dress catching on her legs. Dammit. Darcy was making her doubt the choice, but it was too late now. Still, if the dress wasn't going to make a statement, then she'd have to make do with her personality.

No pressure or anything . . .

Oreo followed her, hiding behind her legs as she opened the front door and got her first look at her blind date and . . . stopped breathing.

Damn. He was even better looking up close. Tall, and that leanly muscled build of his spoke of a man who worked with his body, not a guy who sat on a stool with his hands inside his patients' mouths all day. He had sharp, light green eyes that crinkled in the corners, like maybe he spent a lot of time in the sun or, better yet, smiled a lot. A scar bisected his left eyebrow, giving him a dark and mysterious air. His square jaw had a slight shadow of growth, shown off when his mouth curved at her scrutiny, and this time her heart kicked hard because he also had a killer smile.

"Hey," he said in a deep, warm masculine voice.

"Hey," she mirrored back as Darcy's words flashed in her head. *Act spontaneously. Step outside your comfort zone. Kiss him.*

Heart pounding, Zoe let out a breath and moved forward, having to go up on her tiptoes to brush her mouth across his.

His lips were warm, firm, and yet somehow giving at the same time. She could have easily lost herself in him, but sanity returned and she stepped back.

His smile got a whole lot warmer, but he didn't speak.

"Thought I'd get that out of the way," she managed. "It's nice to meet you. I've never met a dentist without having to be in a dentist's chair." Great, and now she was rambling. She bit her tongue to keep it from running off with the last of her good sense.

"Nice to meet you, too," he said. "Who's the dentist?"

Zoe's smile congealed and her heart stopped, just completely stopped. "Uh . . . *you,*" she said, "You're the dentist."

Still smiling, he shook his head. "Not me."

Oh God. "You're not Newman Taylor," she whispered in horror.

"No," he said. "But if your next guess is

Parker James, you'd be right."

Oh God. Wyatt's friend, to whom she'd agreed to rent a room for the few weeks he was in town. She'd had mixed feelings about it, but Wyatt had vouched for the guy, and Zoe could really use the money for some desperately needed renovations. "You're my brother's old friend."

"Not all that old, really," he said, and looked at her mouth.

The mouth she'd kissed him with. *Good God, I kissed him.*

He grinned.

And . . . she'd said that out loud. Perfect. She covered her face. "I'm sorry, I —"

"Don't be sorry," he said. "That kiss was the best thing to happen to me all week."

Behind her fingers she moaned a little, and he laughed at her. "Wyatt didn't mention the welcoming committee," he said. "He did say you might be grumpy. I like this better."

She was going to have to kill her brother, but since he was out of town for the weekend at a vet conference, that pleasure would have to wait.

Maybe she could just move to Iceland. Iceland *might* be far enough to escape the humiliation, but probably not. Dammit. She'd kissed a perfect stranger, just accosted him on her doorstep. And . . . now her chest hurt. Maybe an impending heart attack would explain her behavior. Holding her chest, she used her other hand to point at him to stay. "I just need a minute," she said.

And then slammed the door in his face.

Behind her, in the living room, a brick fell from the ancient old fireplace. It did that every time she slammed the door. She'd tried to get someone out here to fix it but the contractor had wanted her to promise her firstborn, so she'd just decided not to slam the door anymore.

But she kept forgetting. *Note to self: Stop kissing strangers, and stop slamming the door.* She ran to the kitchen, where she'd left her cell phone, and pounded out her brother's number.

"Yo," Wyatt said in greeting. "Hear you're going out with some dentist guy tonight. Watch where he puts his hands. You don't know where they've been."

Oh, for God's sake. Her siblings gossiped like a pair of old ladies. "You're a veterinarian," she pointed out. "God knows how many worse places your hands are all day long. Maybe I should tell Emily to watch where *you* put *your* hands."

Wyatt just laughed. Since Emily — the love of his life — was also a vet, it had been an idle threat and they both knew it.

Zoe sucked in a deep breath. "Listen, about your friend, the one who's coming to stay —"

"Yeah, Darcy told you he's coming early?"

"Uh-huh," she said with what she thought was a perfectly even voice.

But Wyatt had been seeing right through her for years. He was the only one who could. "Zoe," he said in his most annoying brother voice. "You're going to be nice. You promised. At least until I get back to Sunshine."

"Yeah," she said, and grimaced. "About that . . ." She closed her eyes. "I might be a little short on nice as it turns out." *Try hoochie-mama on for size . . .*

"Shit, Zoe. He's there already? What did you do?"

"Hey, I didn't do anything." *Well, except kiss him.*

And then slam the door on his nose . . .

Crap. "So . . . just how good a friend is this guy again?"

"Very," Wyatt said. "We met in college when we were bartenders at the same place. On my first night, we got jumped at closing by five drunk assholes. Parker saved my ass. Haven't gotten to see him in years, though, so don't chase him away before I get home."

She grimaced again. "Gotta go."

"Zoe —"

She disconnected. "Oops," she said. "My bad." She glanced at herself in the microwave glass door. "Go make nice," she told her reflection. She turned to do just that, stopping to grab one of the cooling chocolate chip cookies she'd baked earlier. She was a great cook but she'd never been much of a baker. Determined to change that, she'd used one of her grandma's recipes — Zoe's first-ever batch that wasn't from the grocery store's frozen aisle. She took a bite . . . and nearly gagged. They tasted like baking soda.

She spit the disgusting thing out in the sink and rinsed it down. Okay, so her baking needed a lot more work.

And maybe your attitude.

Brushing the crumbs from her hands, she went back to the living room. She let out a heavy breath and once again opened the front door.

Parker was crouched low, chuckling over Oreo, who'd stayed outside with her new roommate and was sniffing at the guy's proffered hand.

"He's not much for new people," Zoe warned. "And especially not much for men. He's a rescue and —"

And nothing because Oreo jumped into Parker's arms and licked Parker's chin.

Traitor.

Parker winced as he lowered Oreo back to the ground, but the pained expression vanished so fast Zoe wasn't sure if she'd imagined it. "Are you hurt?"

"Cracked a few ribs a couple of weeks ago," he said lightly. "Still a little sore, that's all."

"How did you do that?"

"Wrangling some big-game poachers."

She stared at him. "Is that code for *none of your business*?"

"I don't talk in code." Mr. Mysterious rose to his feet, Oreo in his arms like he weighed nothing instead of one hundred pounds of tubby Bernese mountain dog.

"Careful," she said. "You'll hurt those ribs."

"I'm fine."

The statement was so alpha male to the core that she laughed. "Of course, you're fine. You're a man. Good to know you're all equally pigheaded."

Not insulted in the least, he grinned. "You have us all figured out, then?"

"Not that much to figure out," she said.

Those sharp green eyes held hers. "Maybe I'll surprise you."

The words brought a quiver to her long-neglected lady parts, but she was pretty confident he couldn't surprise her. But then he let Oreo lick his face again.

"A real watchdog you've got here," he said fondly, and set Oreo down with one last body rub.

Well, damn, she thought reluctantly. She had to give him at least a few brownie points for loving up on her big old silly dog. "Yeah," she said. "He's a real killer." She slid the killer a long look.

Oreo pretended not to see it, which only served to prove her point about men . . .

"So," Parker said straightening. "Can I come in yet or do you want to slam the door on my nose again?"

She felt her cheeks flush but met his gaze.

He held it prisoner with his warm, patient one and waited her out.

Great, he was also a man who knew the value of silence. She'd never met anyone like him, that was for sure. "You can come in," she said, deciding to pretend that the past few moments had never happened, hoping that he'd already forgotten them.

Denial wasn't just a river in Egypt . . .

TWO

Parker James followed the pretty — and crazy — brunette into the house, his lips still tingling from the touch of hers. He wondered about the missing dentist and why she'd kiss the guy if she'd never even met him — not that it mattered to him.

He'd reaped the benefits. And now he was left to wonder if his insta-attraction to her was thanks to the surprising welcome, or the universe's way of messing with him since she was his old buddy Wyatt's sister. Hell, maybe it was just one of life's little mysteries.

"Help yourself in here," Zoe said when they'd entered the kitchen. She turned to face him and for the briefest of beats her eyes flicked to his mouth and he knew she was thinking about the kiss, too.

"Thanks," he said. "But I probably won't be around much."

"Wyatt said you're on vacay. What brings

a guy to Sunshine, Idaho, for a vacation?"

Much more than he was willing to share, starting with the fact that *forced leave* would've been far more accurate than *vacay*. "Peace and quiet," he said.

She looked at him from fathomless light brown eyes that appeared to be as good at hiding her thoughts as his own were. Good for her. She was interesting, his temporary landlord, he'd give her that.

And she tasted good, too.

"Wyatt also says that you work for the U.S. Fish and Wildlife Service," she said, watching him carefully. "And that you travel around a lot."

Close enough, he supposed, even if it was an understatement on all counts. He was actually a supervisory special agent, or RAC — Resident Agent in Charge. It was his division's duty to enforce the many federal conservation laws in place to protect endangered species and other forms of wildlife. He did so by investigating and infiltrating wildlife trafficking rings, illegal guiding operations, and all matter of assorted other criminal groups.

Since that often meant going undercover for cases that ranged from a simple buy-bust transaction to multi-month undercover stings, it was his usual MO to leave out the details. "Yep, I'm at the USFW service," was all he said. Besides, this was just small talk, casual chatter. She might as well have said, *Nice weather we're having.*

Except that he didn't feel casual with her and he suspected it had something to do with the way she was still looking at him with those honey-colored eyes that inexplicably drew him when he didn't want to be drawn.

Did she feel it, too?

Did it matter? No, he decided, it didn't. Whatever the odd tension between them, nothing was going to happen. So he met her gaze calmly and coolly, usually a pretty clear indication that he didn't want to be engaged in further conversation, but his heart wasn't in it.

And it didn't matter anyway, because unlike most everyone else, she completely ignored the look, pushing for more information. "So you what?" she asked. "Keep hunters and fishermen in line, making sure no one exceeds their license quota, that sort of thing?"

He could appreciate her nosiness. He really could. He himself was nosy as hell, but he never spilled his guts, no matter how good a woman tasted. And she smelled good, too, like chocolate chip cookies, so he made some vague sound of agreement to her assessment of the job she'd described, a job that was genuinely important.

It just wasn't *his* job.

"What about poachers?" she asked, not giving up. "People are always getting arrested for poaching in Idaho." She paused. "You mentioned wrangling some big-game poachers."

So she tasted good *and* she was sharp.

He made another low hum of vague agreement because she was right, poaching was a problem. In fact, the man he was currently hunting had started out poaching and had made millions on his illegal gains.

Not that he was going to share with the class.

"You Fish and Wildlife guys have a reputation for being real hardasses," she said. "You a hardass, Parker?"

"The hardest," he said.

That got him a smile. "It's a good thing, the job you do," she said, surprising him. "We'd lose a lot of species to extinction without you."

Aw, hell. Now he felt like a dick for misleading her, but he still kept his silence. She didn't need to know that he had a reputation for being one of the toughest wildlife criminal investigators in the country

— something he'd proven the hard way with his badge and gun. Officially he worked out of the D.C. office, but the truth was he was actually rarely there.

He'd arrested people who'd smuggled ivory, skins, rhino horns, parrots, and rare reptiles from all over the world. Big-game poachers had become his trophies in federal court. In one case he'd arrested a cheetah poacher who'd smuggled illegal hides from Africa into the United States. He'd located and stopped eagle poachers who were using traps, bullets, and poisons to kill the birds for their feathers. His cases had halted illegal use of endangered-species body parts in Chinese medicine from New York to San Francisco.

Fact was, over his career he'd worked hundreds of cases for wildlife — each of them unique, all-consuming, and dangerous. As a result, he'd lost more than one decent relationship with a woman to the job, and most of his family. And this latest job hadn't proved to be any different — none of which he wanted to talk about.

Zoe looked at him for a long minute and then blessedly changed the subject. "So when you *are* around," she said, "do you cook?"

He smiled at the hopeful tone in her voice.

"Yes, but only when I'm trying to get laid."

She snorted and then turned away, clearly over him.

He told himself that worked for him. Completely. Socializing wasn't high on his list of priorities. Hadn't been for three weeks now. Getting hit by a truck full of big-game poachers making their getaway had put a real kink in his life plan. But since it had nearly put a kink in his life period, he wasn't complaining.

Much.

And he'd caught the bad guys. Or some of them anyway, though their ringleader, Tripp Carver, aka the Butcher, had eluded him — which the slippery son of a bitch had been doing for three long years now.

A fact that infuriated Parker beyond reason.

Around him, the kitchen smelled delicious, and his gaze locked in on the plate of cookies on the far counter. Homemade cookies. He couldn't remember the last time he'd had homemade anything, and like Pavlov's dog he migrated over there, passing an open laundry room on the way. In the doorway hung the only thing that could have taken his eyes off the cookies — a row of enticingly lacy and silky things in all colors and textures.

Damn. They were hot as hell, especially when he pictured them on the leggy brunette trying to ignore him every bit as much as he was trying to ignore her.

But then she caught where his gaze had gone and gasped in clear horror at the sight, as if she'd completely forgotten the things were there. To his dismay, she started snatching down the panties and bras, shoving them into a basket.

"Sorry," she said, grabbing something black and lacy. "It's been a hectic week."

"No apologies necessary." His voice sounded rough and husky to his own ears, but his brain was very busy picturing her in that black and lacy number and it was messing with his entire equilibrium in a big way.

"It's laundry day," she said, her cheeks red as she hugged the basket to herself. "The dryer's harsh on delicates."

"I'll remember that. I'll be sure to hang all my delicates," he said.

He couldn't remember the last time he'd felt like laughing so much in such a short period of time. Not surprising as the entire first part of the year he'd been on a joint task force between the Department of Justice and the U.S. Fish and Wildlife Service, stuck in a courtroom testifying on a case for two months. For most of that time he'd alternated between wanting to bash his head against the wall in frustration at the snail's pace of the case and yearning to get back in the field, back to doing what he did best — sniffing out the asshats of the animal world.

Which was why he'd landed here in Sunshine. But all that had been set aside in his brain at the sight of the hot undies.

Now that they'd been stuffed away, he was back to the cookies. Mouth watering, he snagged one. "These smell amazing."

"Wait!" she cried, and then froze because it was too late, he'd popped the cookie into his mouth.

He froze, too, because it was possible he'd never tasted a worse chocolate chip cookie, not even in the history of ever. He managed not to choke on it, barely. Normally he didn't care much what people thought of him, but Zoe was kind enough to let a perfect stranger stay in her house simply because her brother had asked.

And also, she was hot and so were her undies, so he very carefully chewed and swallowed manfully when what he really wanted was to spit that crap out. And it *was* crap. Bad crap.

"So, what do you think?" she asked.

Ah, shit. He hated when a woman asked

him that, or anything to do with his opinion, like did her pants make her look fat, or was her haircut okay, or did her cookies suck . . . because deep down she already knew the truth.

He could lie. He was good at lying, real good. But though he couldn't have explained why to save his own life, he didn't want to lie to Zoe. "Too much baking soda," he said.

She tightened her lips.

"You want me to go now, right?" he asked.

She let out a low laugh. "No, I want to throw away the cookies."

He laughed, too. "Probably a good idea."

"Yeah." She eyeballed the tray. "I just wish I'd done that before you ate one and found out I suck at baking."

"Your secret's safe with me," he said.

"I swear I'm an excellent cook. I just never mastered baking, is all."

"Okay."

"No, really."

"Hey, whatever you say."

She laughed again. "You're . . ."

A dick. An asshole. He'd heard it all before.

"Honest," she finally settled on.

He met her gaze and there went that odd thing in the air again. Animal magnetism,

34

he thought.

Or maybe not. Maybe it was just him. He had no idea. His woman-radar was off, way off, at least according to his little sister Amory, who was forever after him about "dating" the wrong kind of woman. He'd never had the heart to tell her that he wouldn't exactly describe his relationships as *dating,* and he liked it that way. "Don't have any reason to lie," he said.

Zoe chewed on that for a moment and then headed through the archway back into the living room. "C'mon, I'll show you your room now."

She walked him through the rest of the house, which had clearly been lived in long and hard but, in spite of showing its wear and tear, was just as clearly well loved. The living room was classic Victorian with fantastic original antique moldings and lots of nooks and crannies, all filled with comfy chairs, bookshelves, pictures, and other knickknacks.

Parker followed Zoe up a narrow set of stairs, watching her ass as they went. It was a very sweet ass, one that even her oddly old-lady dress couldn't hide, and he went back to picturing some of her pretty lacy things beneath it. Black? Pink? Sheer?

At the top of the stairs she opened the

first door on the right. Inside the bedroom was a full-size bed, a dresser, and a comfortable-looking club chair in a corner.

"There's a bathroom down the hall," she said. "I'm sorry, but the other two bathrooms in the house are out of commission until I hire a plumber, so we have to share. I'll need the shower at seven tomorrow morning to get to work on time."

While he was picturing her standing in her shower, freed from that dress and wearing nothing but suds, she went on.

"The rules," she said. "We should go over the rules."

This got his attention. "Rules?" he asked, wondering if one of them was going to be no weapons. If so, they'd have a problem as his job required him to be armed. And since he lived the job, he was always armed.

"No overnight shenanigans," she said.

He waited for her to smile, indicating that she was kidding, but she didn't. "Understood," he said. "Though it's a damn shame given our smokin' chemistry."

She stared at him for a full beat. "I wasn't referring to you and me," she finally said. "I was referring to you and any dates you might want to bring home." She paused. "Smoking chemistry?"

"You denying it?"

She blushed yet again but held his gaze. And her silence. Finally she said, "Also, no dogs."

Nice subject change. They both looked at Oreo, who'd followed them and was sitting at her feet, panting and looking up at her adoringly. She patted him on the head.

"He's a rescue," she said. "And he was neglected and abused by some asshole, so he doesn't like men. And also there were a lot of mean dogs where he lived. Other dogs terrify him. Actually, everything terrifies him. He's a nervous Nelly and I want to move slowly with him."

"He doesn't seem all that nervous to me," Parker said.

Oreo farted audibly.

Zoe fanned the air. "See? Nervous."

Parker laughed. "My guess would be he's eaten some of your cookies."

"Ha-ha," she said. "But don't be fooled. He can be a real killer."

At this, Oreo slid bonelessly to the floor and rolled to reveal his belly, presumably for a good scratching.

Parker couldn't help it; he laughed again and bent to oblige the dog.

Above him, Zoe sighed. "It's probably because in comparison to him, you smell really good."

Parker tilted his head back. "Ah, so you *do* feel it."

She grimaced. "Look, sometimes things spill out," she said around her fingers. "Ignore it."

"Yeah, not really good at that," he said.

"Then it's a good thing I am." And with that she hightailed it out of the room.

Oreo looked torn for a moment but then huffed out a sigh and got up and followed after his food provider.

Huh. He'd come to Sunshine for a boat-load of complicated reasons that had absolutely nothing to do with a real vacation or enjoying himself, but he was doing just that.

THREE

Parker went outside to retrieve his duffel bag, and while he was out there he received a text from his sister.

Thanks for the pretty mountain pics! You meet your wife yet? I wanna be a sister-in-law!

Parker shook his head. She never gave up. At age eighteen, Amory was a romantic, wanderlust spirit tied to their hometown and their parents in a way he'd never been. She claimed to be okay with that. She was sweet and naïve and overprotected for good reasons, by both his parents and himself, but she lived for the daily pics he sent from wherever in the world he happened to be. She also lived to try to domesticate him, or at least get him to find a woman to marry.

He put his phone away and went back inside to find a set of legs sticking out from beneath the kitchen sink. Zoe, flat on her back.

He crouched at her side. "What are you doing?"

"Napping," she said, voice muted since her head was in the cabinet. Her dress had ridden up to midthigh. She had a set of really great legs to go with her great ass.

"Need some help?" he asked.

"It's just a slow leak, but it's driving me crazy." Her voice was strained, like she was trying to work a wrench. "I've got this."

In direct opposition to the words, the sink began to drip faster.

"You're making it worse," he said, and bit back his grin when she swore beneath her breath and climbed out from beneath the sink, her face and hair wet.

"What did you say?" she asked.

"Absolutely nothing." He grinned. "I have a question."

She straightened her shoulders and met his gaze warily. "What?"

"Do I get a key?"

She seemed to relax marginally and moved to a drawer so full of junk he had no idea how she found anything, but she pulled out a key and slapped it into his palm.

He closed his fingers around hers. He waited until she met his gaze to ask the question he knew she'd been expecting before. "Do you greet all of your tenants with a kiss?"

"No." She looked away. "And you're my first tenant."

"Setting a new policy, then," he said with a nod. "My lucky day. So who's the dentist?"

She stared at him as if just realizing something and whirled, eyeing the clock on the wall next to the fridge. "Oh my God."

"What?"

"He never showed!" she said.

"Your dentist?"

"No call, nothing." She snatched a cookie from the plate and shoved it in her mouth. She chewed once, grimaced, muttered *"Dammit!"* and then spit it out into the sink.

He grinned, and she narrowed her eyes at him. "Are you laughing at me?" she asked.

"Wouldn't dream of it."

She pointed at him. "Now *that* was a big, fat lie."

"Never said that I couldn't lie," he said, "only that I choose not to." Mostly. "So the dentist . . . he was a blind date?"

She blew out a sigh. "Yes. I've been stood up by a guy who hasn't even met me yet." She looked down at herself. "Which means it isn't the dress's fault. Ha!"

When he didn't respond, she lifted her

head, eyes narrowed. "You think there's something wrong with this dress, too? My sister, Darcy, said it was a granny dress."

Parker fought a smile. "I was thinking bingo night. But it wouldn't have stopped me from taking you out."

They stared at each other until his phone buzzed. Pulling it from his pocket, he looked at the screen. Oh shit, not good — a Face-Time call from his boss. "I'm sorry, but I've got to take this," he said, and walked from the room and into the living room before hitting answer.

" 'Bout time," Sharon Morton said. "Where the hell are you?"

He'd purposely answered with his back to the living room wall, a blank off-white color that could be anywhere in the world. "On leave," he said. "As you well know."

She gave him a steady look. "You can't blame me for checking in on my most prized special agent."

Uh-huh. Granted, there were only two hundred USFW special agents nationwide, and maybe he'd been touted as cream of the crop, but he knew damn well there were others every bit as good as him. "We both know you say that to all your men."

Her mouth curved. Sharon, the SAC, special agent in charge, reported directly to the chief officer in Washington on each of the eight field regions of the United States. Most hated her because she ruled with an iron fist, but Parker had never had a problem with her. She was direct and tough as nails and knew how to let her team do what they did best: catch criminals.

She was also a curvy bombshell who, if you didn't know her, looked like an actress playing the part. If you *did* know her, you knew better than to dismiss her as only a hot chick because she'd put your balls in a vise for even thinking it.

"I'm going to assume you're at home," she said. "And not directly disobeying orders not to follow the leads from your informant on the Carver case."

Since that wasn't a question, Parker said nothing.

"Because," she went on in that same I-eat-puppies-for-breakfast voice, "if I thought you were in Idaho after all that happened —"

"You mean after the case was dropped?"

She gave him a long look. "That, too."

The case was the bane of Parker's existence. Tripp Carver was still on the loose, left free to continue his reign of terror on endangered big game. He was out there right now, bringing illegal gains into the

43

country, things like rhino and elephant tusks, and tiger parts, among other things — all highly valued by antique dealers. These goods were then distributed and sold at high dollars.

As in millions of dollars, annually.

Last year alone thirty thousand elephants had been slaughtered for their ivory, which sold for $1,500 a pound. Illegal rhino horns commanded prices as high as $45,000 a pound, roughly equivalent to the price of gold.

They'd knocked out the dealers directly beneath Carver, but that wouldn't slow the asshole down for long.

Parker and his team had been closing in on him, and in fact had located him at one of his storage warehouses in Oregon three weeks ago, when in the ensuing scuffle one agent had been killed and another injured.

Parker rubbed his ribs. A major setback, yeah, but he and the team had laid out a new sting — only to be one hundred percent shut down by Sharon. She'd pulled the plug on the entire operation, saying that they'd spent enough money on this case, that they had what they needed for now — twelve dealers in jail — and that there were other open cases that needed their attention, newer and shinier cases.

Parker disagreed with the stand-down order. His informant, Mick Diablo, an ex-smuggler for Carver — furs, skins, anything that commanded money — had heard a rumor that there was currently $4.5 million worth of rhino horns and elephant ivory sitting in storage that would soon be sold off — if the cache wasn't located first.

Parker intended to locate it. *And* Carver while he was at it.

One week ago, Mick had slipped Parker a solid tip, a sighting of Carver in Rocky Falls, an isolated, out-of-the-way county in northern Idaho, some town named Cat's Paw.

Parker hadn't been able to locate Cat's Paw on any map, but he'd found Rocky Falls. When he'd pushed back on their stand-down order, thinking he had a real shot at finding the Butcher once and for all, he'd been told in no uncertain terms to drop it.

Parker had said that he could do a lot of things pretty damn well, but dropping it wasn't one of them.

In return, the powers that be had suggested that since he was so recently injured and all, not to mention grieving the loss of fellow agent Ned Force, now would be a great time to take some of his thirty-two saved vacation days. Or all of them. Maybe

45

in the South Pacific.

Parker had thought Idaho a better fit. He wasn't exactly sure what outcome he was hoping for, but he just had a feeling that somehow Carver would screw them and vanish. He couldn't let that happen. "We are an inch away from nailing Carver," he said to Sharon, watching her face carefully. "Why not go after him with all we've got?"

"You realize no one else in the entire office questioned me on this," Sharon said.

"That's because they all kiss your ass."

"You should try it sometime," she said dryly.

Yeah, maybe when he was dead. "We're closer now than ever. Give me one good reason to back off."

This garnered him another long look through the phone. "It's not your job to question why," she said. "It's your job to get back into lean, mean fighting shape for the next case."

"I told you, I'm fine."

"Jesus, Parker, would you please knock that chip off your shoulder?" she griped. "You had a close call. Nearly bought the farm in fact. And we lost Ned."

Parker did his best to keep his expression even, though it was possible he was grinding his back teeth into powder.

"The case was dropped and you're taking some well-deserved time off," Sharon said. "Go heal and grieve like a normal person. Learn to relax."

He *was* healed. Mostly. The grief sucked, but he was handling it. "Maybe I *am* relaxing."

"Why do I doubt that?" she asked, and shook her head. "Do you have any idea what I'd do with a month off?"

"Go stir-crazy?"

"Go to a deserted island," she corrected. "With nothing but my loaded e-reader and a cabana guy to feed me grapes. Make that *two* cabana guys."

"Yeah," Parker said dryly. "That's exactly what I'd want to do on vacation."

She stared at him, the stare of a woman who knew how to bring a man to his knees. "Just tell me you're not going to do something stupid and use your considerable skills to let me and this office down."

He had no intentions of being stupid. As for his skills, he didn't plan to share his plans or any of the details of his "vacay," at least not at this time.

Hence his temporary housing. Wyatt had said his older sister had this big old house and would welcome the chance to earn some extra money. Parker had heard *older sister* and imagined her to be middle-aged, in possession of no less than five cats, and maybe a little wrinkly to boot.

Zoe was none of the above . . .

Which meant that, as a supposed investigator, one of the best of the best, he'd just broken one of his own rules — assuming *anything.*

Guess that made *him* the ass. Because Zoe couldn't be much more than thirty and was deliciously curvy, with honey-colored hair that fell in loose waves to her shoulders and matching eyes. The-girl-next-door pretty even if she was dressed like a grandma in a long, floral print dress.

Not that it mattered. Not only was she the sister of an old friend, but also he didn't mix business and pleasure.

Ever.

Even if she owned a goofy, wonderful big old dog that was currently drooling on his foot.

"Parker," Sharon said impatiently.

"Have I ever let the office down?" he asked.

She swore and shook her head. "You're a *serious* pain in my ass, you know that?"

Ditto, he thought grimly. "Love you, too," he said, very aware of the soft footsteps that had come down the hall and stopped in the doorway of the living room behind him.

"*And* a smart-ass," Sharon added.

"Aw, now you're just trying to sweet-talk me," he said.

She shook her head and ended the call.

Parker shoved the phone back in his pocket and turned to face Zoe, who was unabashedly eavesdropping.

She had the good grace to look apologetic, nibbling on her lower lip, which reminded him of how sweet that lip was. He'd enjoyed her kiss, short as it had been, but it was messing with his head in a very different way than Sharon ever had.

Work had been his priority for so long he'd neglected his own personal needs. It had been months since he'd been with a woman. He'd have liked to say that would change now that he was on "vacation," but he knew it wouldn't.

At least not until he caught Carver. All his concentration was going toward catching that fucker, and maybe then he'd take a badly needed *real* vacation. Maybe somewhere in the South Pacific after all, for some surf and turf.

Maybe Alaska for some fishing.

Hell, maybe he'd actually go home.

But he knew the truth. He'd do none of those things. He'd jump into a new case, like always. Because his life was his work.

"Sorry," Zoe said. "Thin walls. Sound carries in this old house."

"Something to remember."

She stared up at him, her eyes somehow both sharp and yet vulnerable at the same time, her sassy mouth slightly curved.

Damn. He loved a sassy mouth and was a complete sucker for sharp yet vulnerable eyes.

Not interested. You're not interested, you don't have time to be interested . . .

And maybe as long as he kept repeating that to himself, it might actually have a chance at being true.

FOUR

The next morning Zoe opened her eyes and blinked blearily at the clock. Seven thirty. "Oh crap!" she gasped, and leapt out of bed.

She'd forgotten to set the alarm.

That was what she got for staying up late working on the damn kitchen sink — which she'd only made worse. Even more demoralizing was the fact that Parker had stayed up just as late, working at her kitchen table on his laptop, a witness to the whole debacle.

He'd been watching when she'd pinched her finger between a pipe and her wrench. He'd offered to play doctor and patch her up *and* fix the sink.

She'd declined both offers with far more reluctance than she'd ever admit to.

He'd been watching when she'd broken a pipe and had ended up with a gallon of water in her face — and though he'd made a clearly superhuman effort not to laugh, she'd caught the small smile around the mouth she couldn't stop thinking about.

Which really ticked her off because he'd been talking to a woman on his phone yesterday, one he was clearly close to. For all she knew, she'd kissed another woman's man. *Good going, Zoe.*

So she'd again refused his help with yet another terse "I've got this," which if anything seemed to amuse him all the more. He'd still been watching when she'd finally sworn the air blue, shoved clear of the sink, and stalked off to bed.

Now she was late for work on top of grumpy. She was giving a flight lesson and then had a flight scheduled. Kicking it into gear, she raced out of her bedroom. Oreo was right on her heels with an excited bark, hoping the rush was to breakfast. They both ran down the hall and straight into the bathroom, belatedly realizing the shower was running.

She'd forgotten she was sharing a bathroom with her houseguest.

She'd never forget again. He stood in her shower, the glass steamed but still plenty clear enough to see him — every single inch of him as his hands ran over his lean, hard body, water and soap sluicing in their trail.

Good sweet baby Jesus . . .

Slow and calm as you please, Parker turned his head, those deep green eyes meeting hers where she stood frozen in place.

"Need something?" he asked, casual. Calm. Like it was an everyday occurrence to have a woman walk in on the middle of his shower.

God. God, he was so beautifully made, and now that the soap had vanished into the drain at his feet, she could see him even more clearly. His entire right side was a bloom of fading bruises, the colors of a kaleidoscope. Heart pounding in her ears, she took a step back and right into the doorjamb, hard enough to scramble her wits.

Or maybe that was just him; maybe *he* scrambled her wits. "Sorry," she managed, covering her eyes. "My alarm — I'm late — The door wasn't locked."

"The lock's broken," he said.

"Right." She knew that. It had been broken forever. "I'll get it fixed right away," she said, nodding like she was a bobblehead. "I'm really sorry. I . . . forgot."

He smiled. "Just remember, paybacks are a bitch."

Oh God. She took another step back and tripped over Oreo. Catching herself, she whirled and ran out of the bathroom. For a minute she stood there in the hallway, torn between horror and another emotion that took a second to process.

Sheer, unadulterated lust.

"Woof," Oreo said, nudging her toward the stairs, reminding her that he believed he was starving, wasting away to nothing.

"Okay," she whispered. "We can recover from this." She had no choice. Running back into her room, she shoved herself into clothes and raced downstairs, needing to get out of the house before Parker came down. She hurriedly fed Oreo and then stopped and stared at the kitchen sink.

It wasn't dripping.

She'd actually fixed it?

"Woof!" Oreo had gobbled up his food in about a nanosecond and wanted more.

"Sorry, Wyatt said I had to put you on a diet."

From upstairs she heard the shower go off. Oh shit. She shoved Oreo out the back door. "Hurry! Do your business!"

Oreo stared at her.

"You know what I'm saying!"

Oreo looked out at the yard. There were no adventures in the yard. No mailmen to terrorize. No new bushes to anoint. He let out an unhappy whine.

"We don't have time for a walk," she told him. "I'll make it up to you later, I promise, just hurry!"

With a huge doggy sigh, Oreo loped off to do his morning constitutional.

Zoe grabbed a bagel and a Slim Jim left over from Darcy's stash and deposited them in her purse for later, got a bummed-out Oreo back inside, and left.

She went straight to Wyatt's empty house, let herself in, and used his and Emily's shower, the whole time picturing how Parker had looked in hers. Which was amazing. Gah. She stole a new toothbrush from Wyatt, dressed from a go bag she kept in her car for unexpected overnight flights, and left for work.

And still, every other second or so she felt her face heat up as she remembered walking — no, racing — into her bathroom, interrupting Parker's shower.

Which meant she had a semipermanent blush on her face. Not that Parker had seemed all that bothered — unlike her; she was very bothered. As in hot and bothered.

She hoped he'd been kidding about payback. Maybe he would laugh it off. Maybe he would forget it.

And maybe pigs could fly.

She didn't know much about Mr. Mystery

yet, but she doubted he forgot much. Still, she'd talked herself into feeling slightly better by the time she parked in the airport lot.

The fixed-base operator she flew out of had three hangars. One for the business front, one for maintenance, and one for plane storage. Services provided at the FBO were the usual located at such regional airports; fuel, charts, maintenance, hangar services, lounges for pilots between flights with TV, WiFi, comfy recliners, and even a private room with a bed if needed.

What made the Sunshine Airport different from most of the other small airports around the country was the altitude and the fact that the airport was situated in a mountainous bowl surrounded by the rough and jagged Bitterroot Mountain peaks. Unique wind and weather patterns created a challenge for all types of aircraft and required special skill and training — which she taught.

"Looking real good today, babe." This from Joe Montoya, operations manager of Shell Corp., which owned and operated the FBO.

Zoe wore her usual flying uniform — black pants and blazer over a white cami. Nothing special and certainly nothing even remotely va-va-voom, so she gave him a knowing look. "What do you want, Joe?"

"Now that hurts," he said, clapping a hand to his heart. In his midthirties, he ran a tight ship. This was most likely thanks to his two tours overseas, courtesy of Uncle Sam. The guy could bark orders like a drill sergeant. And the airport wasn't the only thing that was run tight. Joe was so cheap he squeaked when he walked, and was known for under-staffing and then getting everyone to work harder than they should have had to.

So if he was complimenting her on a day when she knew she looked rough, then he most definitely wanted something. She went hands on hips.

He grinned. It was the I'm-irresistible smile from his repertoire of a wide variety of smiles including his two personal favor-ites: the gotta-have-me-now and you're-going-to-do-this-for-me-cuz-I'm-cute.

Long immune from five years of working together, she arched a brow.

"Tough crowd this morning," he said. "You forget your Wheaties?"

"Spit it out, Joe. I've got a lot to do today."

"All right, all right. I need a little favor, that's all. I need you to go out with me."

She stared at him. "What?"

"Yeah," he said, and grimaced. "My sisters signed me up for this stupid online dating

service. Have you ever tried one of those?"
He lowered his voice. "Those chicks are
scary as shit. But then my sisters got my
mom and grandma in on it, so I lied and
said I didn't need a dating service because I
already had a date for Friday night. So now,
I need you to go out with me."

"Why me?" she asked.

"Because you're looking for dates, right?"
At the look on her face, his smile widened.
"Yeah," he said. "Word's going around that
you want to be set up. So I'm setting us
up."

This was all her own fault.

"I'll pick you up at six," Joe said.

"No way."

"Oh come on, I'll even splurge for dinner," he said. "Fair warning, they're going
to spy on us, I can guarantee that, so all
you need to do is look like you're really into
me."

She blew out a sigh. "For how long?"

"An hour tops."

"And you're buying dinner?" she asked
dubiously. "You never buy anything."

"This will be worth the price. And after,
you can dump me if you're not having a
good time. But I gotta warn ya . . ." He
flashed a trouble-filled grin. "You're going
to have a good time. You like steak?" he

asked. "Most women like steak, right? The bar and grill does steak. I'll even do the whole bring-you-flowers bit, whatever you want, just please do this for me."

"So this is a pretend date, right?" she asked.

"Well, I'd rather it be a *real* date but I'll take what I can get. You're a hard one to catch."

This caught her off guard, which after the morning she'd had was really saying something. "What does that mean?" she asked.

"It means you wear a sign on your forehead that says *back the fuck off.*" Joe laughed a little. "Don't get me wrong, I like it. You're tough as hell, babe, and it's good for business. It's just hard to get inside you. And I don't mean it in a dirty way — well, unless you want me to," he said with a brow waggle. "So . . . whaddaya say?"

"I say I've got to get going."

"So that's a yes, right?" he called out as she headed down the hall toward the side exit to get to the other hangars.

She stopped and turned back. "Joe, I've got a bunch of paperwork to finish, weather to check, flight plans to file, and I need to check on the Cessna Caravan. I've got lessons and a flight."

"Actually, you've got *two* flights," he cor-

59

rected. "And the Caravan's still grounded."

It had been grounded for a month for repairs and maintenance, way longer than either of them had expected, but she'd been told it would be done today. "Still?"

"Yeah. You've got the —" He flipped through the schedule. "— Cardinal today."

"How much longer on the Caravan?" Zoe loved the sturdy single-engine Cessna.

Joe shrugged. "I've lit a fire under maintenance."

Dammit. There was nothing wrong with the Cardinal, which was also a perfectly capable single-engine, but the Caravan had a turbine engine, so it had more oomph and was way more fun to fly. "And what do you mean two flights?" she asked. "There's only one on the books."

"I added a new one last night and moved your schedule all around, delaying your lessons. Sorry, I forgot to text you." He flashed his smile again. "Okay, so I guess I need *two* favors. But hey, you're going to get paid for the flight."

She hated when he messed with her schedule. She actually made more money on the flight lessons she gave, which helped her pay off her loans. Getting a pilot's license and keeping it was incredibly expensive. "You do remember the last time I did you a favor?" she asked. "I ended up flying your mother to Breckinridge and we got snowed in? Do you have any idea what it's like to spend three days with your mother?"

"I'm familiar," he said with a shudder. "Which is why I paid you to do it."

"It was her seventieth birthday," Zoe said, "and she was meeting — and I quote her here — her *boy toy.*"

Joe laughed. "Yeah, you probably deserved double time on that one."

Zoe looked around, suddenly worried. "She's not my additional flight today, is she?"

"No. He is." Joe gestured to the man walking in the front door, his long legs eating up the space, his every movement exuding an easy confidence.

Parker James.

Completely of its own volition, Zoe's gaze ran over him from head to toe. He was of course fully dressed now, but that didn't matter. She could still see him as he'd been in her shower earlier, the room steamy and humid, his long, lean, hard body slick with water and soap running in rivulets down it.

She stared at him, doing her best to hold back all the tumbling mass of emotions hitting her at once. Normally she was good at that, really good, but naturally her one really good life skill deserted her, leaving everything she felt all over her face. Annoyance. Embarrassment.

And let's not forget the very reluctant lust.

Parker stared at her right back. Not annoyed. Not embarrassed. As for what he *was* feeling, he kept his own counsel.

Damn him. And then Joe's words sank in. Parker was her first flight?

"Zoe," Joe said. "This is —"

"You," she said to Parker.

He smiled. She didn't know all of the smiles in *his* wheelhouse yet, but she labeled this one *The Big Bad Wolf.*

FIVE

Joe divided a look between Zoe and Parker. "You two know each other?"

"Little bit," Zoe said.

Parker said nothing.

"So . . . old friends?" Joe asked.

Zip from Parker. A silent alpha. One more thing to add to the list of reasons why Zoe was *not* going to like him, despite what he looked like naked.

"Not old friends," she said.

"New friends?" Joe asked. He was speaking directly to Parker now, but Parker didn't appear interested in defining their relationship.

Or lack of one.

Zoe sighed. "He's living with me," she said, and Joe, who'd just taken an unfortunate sip of coffee, choked, and snorted coffee out his nose.

"Goddammit," he muttered when he could talk.

"Parker's a friend of Wyatt's," Zoe said. "It's a favor. Apparently I'm just full of favors today," she added.

Joe was mopping up the coffee he'd spilled with some papers on the counter. "Dottie's going to kill me."

Dottie was his office manager, and even though she was married to Devon, their other pilot-for-hire, she terrified Joe.

Not Zoe's problem. She turned to Parker. "Where are we heading?"

"Rocky Falls," he said.

"There's no airport up there."

"I need to see the layout, no landing required."

Rocky Falls was the northernmost county in the state. It was mostly open, rugged, isolated, nearly uninhabitable forestland, bordered by a few far-reaching ranches. Just past those, the growth was so thick, seeing anything from the air but a blanket of green sliced with the occasional blue ribbon of rivers and tributaries was all but impossible. "I thought you were here on vacay," she said.

"Yep. I'm sightseeing."

Uh-huh. "There's nothing to sightsee out there except trees."

"I like trees."

She laughed. "That's ridiculous. There are

64

far cheaper ways to see trees."

"Jeez, don't tell him that," Joe said, and looked at Parker. "She's not much of a saleswoman. Don't listen to her. I gave you a really good rate for your two hours."

Zoe kept her gaze on Parker. She had a good bullshit detector and it was going off now. Blaring, in fact. But if he wanted to pay a small fortune to "sightsee," what did she care? "I've got to get the weather, file a flight plan, and perform a flight check." She eyed her watch. "Wheels up in forty-five."

With that, she about-faced and exited the glass door opposite the front desk, heading across the tarmac to the Cardinal tied down there. She was already busy running through her preflight in her head: tire pressure, oil and fuel levels, flight controls, cowlings . . .

"Zoe."

She stilled in the early-morning sun and slowly turned to face Parker, who'd followed her out. He wore his clothes with the same ease he'd worn nothing at all. And dammit, she really needed to stop thinking about that.

"Do we have a problem?" he asked.

Other than she knew that the promise his body made in clothes was kept when he was out of them? "No."

"Is it about this morning?"

"What about this morning?" she asked, going for an innocent tone but ruining it by flushing.

Because she knew *exactly* what about this morning.

His eyes revealed his amusement. "If it would make things less awkward, I'll be happy to walk in on your next shower."

"I didn't mean to!"

"Is that why you stood there staring for a full three minutes?" he asked. "Drooling?"

"I . . . it wasn't three minutes!" She put her hands to her hot cheeks. "And you're the dishonest one. You said you weren't hurt that badly, but your ribs —"

"Are healing," he said. "And that's not what you were staring at."

True story.

He smiled. "And you liked what you saw."

Oh God. She had, she really, really had. She closed her eyes and wished for a big hole to swallow her up. "I hardly even noticed you were naked."

"So much for honesty."

"You don't get honesty privileges," she said. "Not until it goes both ways."

"You don't think I'm being honest with you?"

"*Sightseeing?*" she repeated dubiously. "Sorry, but you don't seem like the type to spend thousands of dollars on a sightseeing trip just for the hell of it."

"Maybe it's not just for the hell of it."

She shook her head. "Why do I feel like we're playing some kind of game here, except I don't have a copy of the rules?"

His smile went a whole lot more real. "I irritate you."

"Yes," she said, and smiled grimly. "How's that for honesty?"

She didn't expect him to laugh out loud but that was exactly what he did, tossing back his head to do so. Finally, still grinning, he shook his head, his eyes lit with . . . affection? "I like you, too, and your smart mouth," he said.

"Are you saying I'm a smart-ass?"

He smiled. "If the shoe fits."

She thought of the woman he'd been talking to on his phone, who'd had a sure and confident voice as she called Parker out on his shit. Zoe didn't know what shit exactly, but there'd definitely been a tension there, one she assumed was sexual.

But he seemed to be flirting with her now, and Zoe didn't know how to take that. "And you . . . like smart-asses?"

"Yes."

"So you like women who are bitchy to you?" she asked.

He smiled. "Don't have much experience with that problem."

She could believe it. "Is that your way of saying women usually fall all over you?"

"Well, not all of them," he said with a false modesty that made her want to laugh. She tried to hold it back but couldn't quite manage it.

"See?" he said. "I'm irresistible."

"You're something," she agreed. "But I don't think irresistible is it."

"Admit it. I'm growing on you."

"That's one thing you're not going to do," she said firmly, and she meant it, too. At least her brain meant it, but her body didn't seem to be on board with the plan. After all, she'd been burned by a mysterious man before, badly, one who'd turned out to be a big, fat liar.

She wasn't going there again. Ever. Nope, she needed transparency from a man. And Parker, for all his bad-boy, cowboy 'tude and cocky swagger, wasn't anything close to transparent.

At all.

And that made him downright dangerous to her. He was the kind of man that messed with a woman's heart, so it was a good thing hers wasn't available to him.

But if she'd worried about living with him

and his knowing eyes and way-too-hot bod— now she also had to work with him.

Except the oddest thing happened when they got into the air.

He wasn't a know-it-all. He didn't try to flirt or drive her up a wall.

None of that. He asked her questions about Idaho as they flew, as though he'd done research on the area. He mentioned some of the other places he'd been — seemingly everywhere — and knew a lot about . . . well, a lot. He asked her about the wind patterns and the different techniques required for flying out of the high-altitude Sunshine airport, and she was fascinated in spite of herself.

He was driven, focused, sharp, and . . .

"Damn," he murmured softly beneath his breath, and pulled out a set of binoculars when they were at altitude, locking on something out the side window for a long moment.

He looked badass to the core. *Who the hell was he?* Because right now, focused and still, he sure as hell didn't look like a guy on a break from work. He looked like a guy who kept secrets, dark ones.

Another wolf in sheep's clothing . . .

At that thought, she panicked — inwardly.

Because outwardly she was cool. Cool as ice.

Or so she hoped. "Rocky Falls is coming up on your right," she said.

"What else is out here?"

"White Mountain," she said. "And Angel Lake."

He didn't react, and she knew she hadn't given him anything of interest.

"And then there's Cat's Paw," she said.

He turned his head and looked at her. "That's not on the map."

"No," she said. "It's mostly just national forestland, but years and years ago the locals called that specific area Cat's Paw and it stuck."

"Why the nickname?"

"Because mountain cats used to be so prevalent there — before poachers and too many people nearly wiped them out," she said.

"Can you circle around and fly over the same spot again?"

"Yes." She slid him a look. "Is there a reason?"

"Does a paying customer have to give you one?" He asked this with a casual, teasing tone, but his body language was anything but casual or teasing.

Nope, she thought, watching him pull a

camera from his duffel — an expensive one with a long-range lens — there was nothing flirty about the man at the moment, no matter what his words said.

She circled around and once again they flew over the area, nothing but forestland with the exception of an area that looked as if it had been clear-cut recently. Inside the clearing was a circle of vehicles. Hunters, she thought at first, but there were way too many cars for a usual group of hunters. "That's new," she said. "I was out here two weeks ago with another client and the landscape hadn't been touched. And I've never seen so many hunters in one spot before."

He took a few more shots and then slid the camera away and turned to her. "You're sure?"

"Very."

"You had a client who wanted to see Cat's Paw, too?"

"No," she said. "Well, I don't know, he didn't say what he was doing specifically. He was a land developer and I got the feeling he was looking to buy something out here. You, too?"

He spent a long moment zipping up his bag. "No."

She waited for more. Nothing came. "You

always a little mysterious?" she asked.

He leaned back, looking casual and at ease, but again, there was nothing casual about his sharp gaze as he took in the landscape around them with a care that was anything but sightseeing. "What is it you want to know?" he asked.

"I'm not sure exactly." She looked at him again. "I just feel like I'm missing something about you."

"We're strangers," he said. "There's a lot you're missing about me. No one's an open book."

She tried to read into that but couldn't. He was a stone when he wanted to be. Which brought some unhappy memories to the surface. "Maybe you're an ax murderer looking for a place to bury the bodies."

His sharp and definitely not-happy gaze met hers. Mr. Mysterious was insulted. "Do you really think your brother would put me in your house if I were an ax murderer?" he asked.

"No." One thing for certain — Wyatt trusted this guy implicitly or he wouldn't be in her house. "I'm sorry," she said. "That was a little rude."

"You could just trust I'm a good guy."

Nope. Been there, done that, still had the scorch marks on her heart, thank you very much. But she could at least be nice. "I'm not all that good at trust," she admitted.

"I've noticed."

She needed to not care what he thought of her. She had no idea why she did. She wanted to let it go and not speak again, but she couldn't seem to stop herself. "You're looking for something."

"Aren't we all?"

Okay, that was it. She would ask him another question never.

"Let's make one more pass," he said.

She eyed the time. "I can't. I've got other prior commitments today."

He didn't react to that, not outwardly, anyway. He was consistent on that but inconsistent everywhere else; focused and intense one minute, grinning and flirty the next. Zoe didn't trust inconsistent. It equated to dishonesty for her.

When they arrived back in Sunshine and landed, she went about her postflight checklist. After finishing the tie-down, she turned and nearly plowed right into Parker. "Oh," she said in surprise. "Sorry." Normally clients exited the plane right away and never looked back, either not paying attention or not caring that her job wasn't over.

But Parker hadn't gone anywhere; he stood there in his sexy mirrored sunglasses looking cool, calm, and utterly badass.

"What can I do to help you?" he asked.

"Nothing. I've got this."

He raised a brow.

"Really. I'm good."

Parker looked at her for a long moment. Then he nodded and walked away, heading inside.

By the time she finished up and poked her head into the second hangar to check on the Cessna Caravan and then made her way back to the terminal, it was empty.

"How was the flight?" Joe asked, coming from the hallway that led to the lounge and bathroom.

"Fine," she said, distracted, turning to look in the back, where there were a few tables and a small deli run by Thea, Joe's sister.

That area was empty as well.

"Who you looking for?" Joe asked.

"Nobody."

"You're a shitty liar," Joe said. "And he left."

"I didn't ask."

"No, but you wanted to. Who is this guy to you, anyway?"

"Renovation money."

"Okay." Joe paused, searching her expression for she had no idea what. "He went back up with Devon. Paid a pretty penny for it, too."

This didn't surprise her, and she started to head back to the mechanical hangar.

"So about Friday night," Joe said. "You never said yes."

"Joe —"

"Just one night," he said, sounding unaccustomedly desperate.

She blew out a sigh.

"Unless of course I can talk you into more." He waggled a brow.

"Don't push your luck," she said. "Fine. Dinner on Friday. And nothing more."

"Sure, we'll start with that," he agreed readily.

Start *and* end because she wasn't looking for a one-night stand with Joe. She wasn't looking for anything with anybody.

Liar, a small voice in her head said. *You'd be more excited if it were Parker . . .*

Shaking that off, she gave herself a lecture. She had a long day ahead of her and she didn't have time to daydream about Parker.

So of course she spent the rest of her day doing exactly that.

Six

The next afternoon, Parker sat up and got licked from chin to forehead for his efforts. "Thanks, dude."

He and Oreo were both on the floor in the shower of the second upstairs bathroom, where Parker was working on fixing the faulty drain. Just like he'd fixed the leak in the kitchen sink the night before. Of course he'd had to wait until the stubborn-as-all-hell Zoe had gone to bed to do so.

He pulled half a loofah from the drain, shook his head, and started the water. Drained perfectly now. "Done," he told the dog. Now he and Zoe could each have their own bathroom.

Not that he particularly needed any privacy. He just felt a little bad for his prickly landlord, who clearly had no idea how to accept help.

"She's stubborn as hell," Wyatt told him when Parker called to check in. "Always has been."

No shit, Parker thought.

"Something she'll never tell you," Wyatt said, "is that she's got some debt. Getting a pilot's license costs a lot of money and she's got loans to pay off. Now that I'm doing okay, I've tried to pay them off for her but she refuses to let me."

Sounded like Zoe.

"I've also tried to help her out with the house," Wyatt said. "But she always says she's got it and kicks me out."

"She told me the same," Parker said. "So I waited until she was gone to fix a few things."

Wyatt laughed. "Better sleep with one eye open. You're going to piss her off when she finds out."

"Maybe she won't realize it's me . . ."

"She's ornery, but she's not stupid," Wyatt said. "In fact, she's smarter than all of us put together."

"Yeah, well, I've already got the pissing-her-off part down. I seem to manage that without even trying."

"If that were true, you'd be dead and buried already and no one would ever find your body," Wyatt said.

Parker laughed.

"Hey, I'm not kidding. She's something

fierce when her feathers are ruffled, though to be fair to her, she's always had to be."

"Why?" Parker asked. He knew about their parents. They were foreign diplomats who spent most of their time in third-world countries. Growing up, Wyatt and his sisters had done the same.

"She'll murder me in my sleep for telling you this," Wyatt said, "but since you're living under her nose it might help you understand her. Our parents are great at their jobs but pretty shitty parents. They put it all on Zoe to watch out for us. Or not."

"She's only a year older than you."

"Eleven months," Wyatt said. "But I was clueless back then. She was the only grown-up. Like the time we were supposed to meet up with our parents in Budapest from our various boarding schools, but they got delayed. Zoe was maybe . . . twelve? And there we were, stuck in a strange country where we didn't speak the language and Americans weren't looked on all that fondly to say the least, and she still managed to feed us and keep us safe for the three days it took our parents to get to us."

Parker was impressed. "She's tough."

"More than you know. I don't know how many times she held it together under grim circumstances," Wyatt said. "But I do know

I'd be dead a few times over without her."

"You're her family."

"Yeah, but it's just how she's wired if she cares about you. Trust me, man, when shit's hitting the fan, there's no one you'd rather have at your six than Zoe."

Parker thought about that conversation long after he'd washed up from the plumbing work and sat at the kitchen table with his laptop studying maps of the Rocky Falls area where Zoe had pointed out Cat's Paw. Like him, she was a survivor and a caretaker. She'd do anything for her siblings.

Just as he would for his sister. He sent money back for Amory's care every month, but he knew the best thing he did for her was stay away.

After hearing Wyatt talk about Zoe, he couldn't imagine anything keeping her from being near her siblings. But then again, she didn't have a job where she chased after bad guys willing to sell their own mother for a buck.

He tried to concentrate on the map in front of him, but he was good at multitasking and a good portion of his thoughts stayed on Zoe.

Watching her fly had been a huge turn-on. She'd handled the plane like it had been an extension of herself, and he'd had trouble concentrating on his business when what he'd really wanted to do was join the mile-high club. Never mind that doing so with his pilot would've gotten them killed.

When he'd gone back up with Devon, he'd gotten a better feel for the area. This was more a reflection on the fact that Parker hadn't wanted to strip Devon naked and lick him from head to toe as he had Zoe.

He'd saved a lot of time by asking Devon to go directly to Cat's Paw, where he got a longer look at the vehicles in that mysterious clearing. With his high-powered binoculars, Parker had focused in on several additional fascinating facts. One, he could see two huge blinds, way too big for traditional hunting. More like the size that could be hiding vehicles that someone didn't want seen.

This was proven when he watched a tank being driven into one.

A tank.

In the woods.

And then a Humvee, filled with guys armed to the teeth.

A huge red flag to say the least.

And two, there'd also been a Humvee four-wheeling through the trees toward some low-lying buildings he'd missed the first time because they'd been as carefully camouflaged as the blinds.

And then there were the weapons. The kind that weren't necessarily for hunting animals — at least not the four-legged kind.

When he'd asked Devon to make a second pass, the pilot had refused, citing two reasons. One, he'd been booked for a direct there-and-back and he didn't want to tap into his reserve fuel. And two, apparently there were rumors circulating of militia taking over the property and he didn't want to draw any trouble by bringing attention to himself or the plane.

Militia.

Made sense. And if that was the case, Parker hoped like hell that if anyone down there was paying attention to aircraft in the area, they'd missed Zoe earlier.

Staring at the map now, Parker shook his head. What the hell was going on? He had some ideas and didn't like any of them. One was a niggling suspicion that he'd had for some time now, that a deal had been struck with Carver for his freedom. Pulling out his phone, Parker called Mick.

His informant answered with a gruff "What the hell do you want?"

"Answers," Parker said.

There was a pause. "I already gave you a shit-ton more than I should have."

"Which wasn't all that much."

"I gave you all I had."

"Now see," Parker said. "I doubt that."

"Ah, man, come on," Mick whined. "You know I can't talk to you no more if I want to keep breathing."

"Tell me enough to catch the Butcher and you have nothing to fear," Parker countered.

"Jesus, you're killing me. Did you go to the Rocky Falls area? Cat's Paw?"

"Yes," Parker said. "And why Cat's Paw? Only locals know about that place."

"Carver grew up there. He's still got connections."

"There's nothing there," Parker said. "Except a possible militia hideout."

"Yeah, his brother's militia," Mick said. "And that asshole's as mean as Carver."

Parker felt his temper stir. "And you left all this out before because . . . ?"

"Because you didn't ask."

"Or because you were trying to fuck up the investigation," Parker said. "A federal crime, by the way."

"No, I wasn't trying to fuck you up, I swear!"

"Or maybe you were trying to get me killed."

"No! Man, you're touchy. It's nothing like that," Mick rushed to assure him.

"Then why don't you tell me what it *is* like."

"You asked and I told you, he's there in Idaho. It got too hot with you guys, specifically *you,* so he went home to hide out until things cooled off. He knows that entire area inside and out. And it's a great place to lay low because it's tough to get to and nearly impossible to sneak up on him. Plus, having grown up on that mountain, he's got friends and relatives who'll protect him to the end."

"By friends and relatives, you mean the people he's now using as a screen for protection?" Parker asked.

"Well, it's not like they're innocents," Mick said. "His family tree belongs on the walls of post offices and cop shops across the country, if you know what I'm saying."

"What else am I missing?" Parker asked.

"Nothing! Now do me a favor and lose my number."

Parker disconnected. Then he called his only other contact in the area besides Wyatt. Kel was a local sheriff and a good one. If anyone knew anything about this, it would be Kel.

"Been a long time," the sheriff said when he answered. "You've been busy, I hear."

Law enforcement, *all* divisions and agencies, were like the quad at any high school.

Filled with gossip. "Little bit," Parker said. "And you?"

"I'm thinking you didn't call to chitchat."

Directness. Parker appreciated it. "I need to know what's going on up at Rocky Falls."

"Why?"

Fair enough question. "A few years ago we arrested what we thought was a small onetime-operation kind of guy for endangered species poaching. He worked the Pacific Northwest, selling skins and other illegal items to a bigger organization. Small fries, but we wanted the bigger cartel so we cut him loose under certain terms."

"Certain terms," Kel repeated. "You recruited him as an informant."

"To help us catch his former boss, Tripp Carver, also known as the Butcher."

"The guy who killed one of your agents," Kel said.

"Yeah, and now we've got rumors of four point five million dollars in skins and ivory being readied for sale."

"And you think this Carver is in Rocky Falls with the goods?"

"Specifically at Cat's Paw."

There was a beat of silence. "Thought you were on medical leave," Kel finally said.

Parker pleaded the fifth, and Kel laughed softly. "Okay, so that's not going to slow you down, I get it. You got anything more than rumors?"

"I've gone further on less. What can you tell me?"

"That you're not the only one with eyes on the prize."

Parker read between the lines on that one. "Local law's on it?"

"Bigger," Kel said. "We were told to stay out of it. I can nose around some if you need."

"I need." Parker heard Zoe coming in the front door, heard the sounds of Oreo scrambling off the spot on the couch he wasn't supposed to nap in and go skidding to the foyer with a welcoming *woof!* He thanked Kel and disconnected, and then ambled into the living room.

Zoe had dropped her things and crouched down to give Oreo a doggie treat from her purse. "Who's a good boy?" she murmured.

"Well, I don't like to brag, but I've been pretty good," Parker said.

She lifted her gaze to where he'd stopped in the doorway between the kitchen and living room, leaning against the jamb. "Do you want a cookie, too?" she asked.

"Depends," he said. "Did you bake them?"

She rolled her eyes and pulled Oreo in for a full body hug, giving him a loud smooch on top of his snout.

"I wouldn't say no to one of those, either," Parker said.

She ignored this, too, except for the flush that stained her cheeks. She looked beat to hell. Her hair was tousled and she had what might have been a grease stain across her jaw. At some point she'd ditched her blazer and wore just the white silky tank top, also sporting a stain across one breast.

Catching him looking, she shrugged. "Dougie, our mechanic, was moving too slow on the Cessna Caravan. I was giving him a hand."

"You can work on an airplane but you can't fix anything here at the house?"

"Yeah, well, I'm an enigma," she said. "An annoying one. Just ask anyone in my family."

Pushing off the jamb, Parker moved close to her, watching as her breath caught and her eyes locked on his mouth.

It was a relief, really, to know that he caused the same baffling reactions in her as she did in him. "I'm not annoyed by you," he said.

"No?"

He smiled. "No."

"What are you?" she whispered, still staring at his mouth.

"Lots of things." He pulled her up and rubbed his thumb over the stain on her jaw, feeling a surge of satisfaction when her breath caught again. "Including turned on."

Her gaze flew to his. "I turn you on?"

"Yes."

She stared at him some more. "We're not doing this. We'd be stupid to do this."

"I agree. But that doesn't seem to mean a damn thing to me."

She didn't say anything and he raised his brows. "Am I alone in this, Zoe?"

Appearing to wrestle with that, she hesitated, and he wondered if she'd lie.

"No," she finally said. "But that's only because I haven't actually . . . Well." She grimaced. "Let's just say it's been a while for me. With someone else. Together." When he smiled, she groaned. "You know what I mean!"

"And that's the only reason you want me, because it's been a while?"

She busied herself with gathering up her things.

But Parker hadn't gained his investigator skills by accident. He'd started as a teen trying to figure out how to get out of the life that had been set in stone long before he'd been born, and he'd only honed his ways of ferreting out the truth in the years since. He'd long ago learned the value of holding his silence, and sure enough his patience was rewarded.

"Okay, that's not the *only* reason," she finally said. "My current theory is that it's because you're sweet to my big, silly dog." She paused. "And also maybe a little bit because you have nice eyes." She closed hers.

He laughed. "I like where you're going with this."

"I'm not going anywhere." She fanned her heated cheeks. "Except to the shower." She popped open her eyes. *"Alone."* She headed up the stairs.

Parker was trying really hard not to imagine her stripping out of her clothes when he heard the bathroom door yank back open.

"Hey," she yelled down the stairs. "Why does this lock work?"

Oreo looked at Parker.

Parker put a finger to his lips, and Oreo seemed to grin at him.

The door slammed again.

And a brick fell out of the fireplace.

The next morning Parker found himself at the local gym being beat all to shit by Wyatt's good friend AJ. Wyatt had recommended the guy for PT, and AJ was putting

Parker through his paces when his cell buzzed.

Sharon.

"Sorry," Parker gasped to AJ. "Gotta take this." He moved aside for privacy. *"Hola."*

"I told you to back off," Sharon said.

Parker didn't pretend to misunderstand. "Backing off isn't a strong suit of mine."

"How about being unemployed?" she asked. "Is that going to be a strong suit of yours?"

"He's here, Sharon," he said quietly. "Carver's hiding out until the heat on him dies down."

"Have you seen him?"

"No, but —"

"Parker —"

"We can nail him."

"No," she said flatly. "We can't."

"But —"

"Listen to me very carefully," she said in her someone's-gonna-die tone. "Don't be stupid and jeopardize your career."

"You think this is about my career?" he asked in disbelief.

She sighed. "No. But this is bigger than us. Okay? That's all I can say. Now back the fuck off and walk away so I don't have to come out there and kick your ass myself."

And then she hung up on him.

Parker stared at his phone.

"Problem?" AJ asked.

"No," he said automatically. But yeah, there was a problem, a big one. Walk away? Kel had hinted that another agency was involved in this thing. The Bureau of Alcohol, Tobacco, Firearms and Explosives? FBI? Homeland Security?

And why?

And even more importantly, how the hell was he supposed to ever walk away from this case?

Very late that night, Zoe sat on the couch in some serious pain — and shame. As a rule, she ate fairly healthily but all bets were off during times of stress. Proving the point, she'd just polished off an entire bag of pizza rolls by herself and was covered in crumbs and questioning her choices in life. Plus, she'd screwed up another batch of cookies, burning this bunch, so the place was a little smoky.

Oreo sat with her, taking up more than his fair share of the couch, snoring audibly.

She hadn't turned on any lights. Not because she was trying to save money on her electric bill, although she could do with a little saving there. Earlier she'd attempted to change the lightbulb in the hallway and most of the downstairs had gone dark. Not all of it. She could, for instance, turn on a light in the living room, but she didn't need a light in here. She needed one in the kitchen to clean up her mess.

And to forage for more food.

But try as she might to figure out the electrical problem, she couldn't. It would have to get in line with all the other things that needed fixing.

In any case, the only glow came from the TV, where her *Friends* season ten marathon was coming to an end.

Until the lamp suddenly came on.

Gasping in surprise, she blinked up at Parker. "What are you doing?"

"Checking on the odd sounds of a woman sobbing at three in the morning," he said.

Oh God. She hadn't been sobbing. *Had she?*

Parker sniffed the air. "You burn something?"

"I think the oven's defective."

"Do you?" Parker asked.

She let out what she meant to be a laugh but sounded horrifyingly close to a sob. *Dammit.*

"Hey." Parker came close. "What's wrong?"

She swiped at a few residual tears. "Nothing."

"Zoe," he said softly, with far too much empathy.

"Just never mind! You won't understand."

"Try me," he said.

She sighed. "Rachel got off the plane for Ross."

Parker turned in a circle, casing the room. "Who's Ross?"

She let out a choked laugh and wished for a tissue. She also wished that she weren't in her beloved King's College sweats that were so battered and threadbare she might not be one hundred percent decent. Oh hell, who was she kidding? She was scrubbed free of makeup and had her hair piled up on top of her head and she was wearing Shrek slippers. She wasn't even close to decent. "Ross from *Friends,*" she said. "He and Rachel got back together and it was . . ."

Sweet. Sexy. *Romantic.*

Not one of which was in her life and hadn't been in a long time. And damn if her eyes didn't fill again. She did her best to blink them back, but that only made it worse.

Parker studied her for a beat and then turned and walked off.

SEVEN

Smart man, Zoe thought with a soggy sniff. She told herself she was actually relieved that Parker had walked away from her. He definitely shouldn't talk to the crazy lady —

The lights came on throughout the house with a hum of electricity.

And a minute later, Parker reappeared.

She stared at him. "You fixed the lights."

He looked around. "Were they broken?" he asked, his tone just a little too innocent.

She narrowed her eyes. "I tried to change a lightbulb and everything went out. I even changed the fuse but that didn't work, either."

"Huh," he said noncommittally.

Oh, she was so on to him. "And my kitchen sink isn't dripping anymore," she said. "And the shower isn't clogged."

He shrugged those broad shoulders. "Guess you're better at plumbing than you thought."

They both knew she wasn't.

But he was. "Thanks," she said quietly.

"I don't know what you're talking about."

She sighed. "And also, you're way too good at that."

"At what?"

"Lying."

"Here," he said, ignoring that comment entirely and dropping the roll of paper towels from the kitchen into her lap. She tore off a piece and blew her nose, expecting him to leave. Instead he crouched before her, grimacing as he did so.

"You're still hurting?" she asked.

"Nah."

"Right," she said. "And I can bake cookies like Martha Stewart. Lift up your shirt."

"Didn't you see enough the other morning?"

No, actually, she hadn't, and the truth was she could stare at him all day long and not see enough, but that was another thing entirely. "Your shirt," she said with an impatient *do it* gesture.

With another shrug, he lifted his shirt.

Momentarily stunned by his perfection, she had to work at finding her voice, and even then her mouth disconnected from her brain. "It's like you've been Photoshopped."

"See, you *do* like something about me,"

he said, and gave her a slow, slaughter-a-million-brain-cells smile.

She squirmed a bit but hell, she couldn't make much worse of a first impression, right? After all, she'd already mistakenly kissed him, slammed the door on his nose, and walked in on him in the shower. And now she was sitting here in her pj's and crumbs, no makeup, a tear-streaked face, and possibly also a snotty nose — not exactly at her best. She spent a lot of time letting people see only what she wanted them to — a hardworking professional woman on top of her game. And yet somehow in a matter of days she'd revealed herself to him, letting him see someone else entirely.

The real her, maybe.

In any case, she was so far outside her comfort zone with him, she couldn't even see her comfort zone. And that made her wonder about *his* comfort zone. Did he even have one? She doubted it. He seemed like the kind of guy who could find his zone anywhere, comfort or otherwise. "How are you even moving around?"

He'd let his shirt drop back down. "It looks worse than it is."

"Really?"

"Really." He was still balanced effortlessly

on the balls of his feet, looking up at her.

Really looking. This close up she could see the stubble on his jaw, which was an appealing mix of every hue of brown under the sun and made her fingers yearn to touch him.

Bad fingers.

In the low lighting, his eyes seemed to glow and she dropped her gaze to his mouth, which made her remember the taste of his kiss.

"I smell something burning," he said.

"It's the cookies."

"I'm pretty sure it's your brain. What's going on, Zoe? You're not upset over a sitcom."

Tomorrow night she was going to go with a harmless *Saturday Night Live* marathon. "It's nothing," she said.

"Nothing's got you wearing pizza sauce and crying over some guy on TV?"

"Not some guy," she said. "Ross. As in Ross and Rachel." When Parker just shook his head, clearly clueless, she sighed. "Never mind." Tipping her head down at herself, she eyed her sweatshirt and the stain on it. "And how do you know this is pizza sauce? Maybe it's blood from my last tenant who asked too many questions, you ever think of that?"

While he laughed softly, she rubbed a paper towel on the stain that was regrettably not blood but indeed pizza sauce. That was always the danger with perfectly cooked pizza rolls — they tended to explode all over you.

Not that it had ever stopped her.

"You told me that I was your first tenant," he said.

"You always remember everything?"

"Yes," he said. "But I also saw the empty pizza roll bag on the kitchen counter when I got the paper towels. That shit'll kill ya, you know."

"Hey, I eat healthy six days a week," she said in her defense. "And then I get one eat-whatever-I-want day. I just believe in making the most of that day."

His mouth twitched. "Not judging."

"Good. And I wasn't crying."

"Okay," he said so easily that she had to wonder who'd trained him on how to deal with a woman's tears so well because he'd navigated through her emotion and the aftermath with shocking ease.

"I wasn't," she said. "I just had something in my eye."

"Whatever you say." He rose to his feet in one fluid motion, wincing only a little.

She opened her mouth to say something

about being careful when she realized that he was fully dressed in the same clothes from earlier in the evening. "You weren't sleeping?" she asked.

"I was."

"You sleep in your clothes?"

"No," he said. "I sleep in nothing."

Oh boy. Images of *that* filtered through her head, really great images, too, because since the Shower Incident she didn't have to imagine him naked; she'd seen the real thing and it was now burned in her brain. The images effectively chased away some of tonight's odd and inexplicable melancholy, and remembering that, she closed her eyes and breathed for a moment. When she opened them, she was once again alone in the room.

For the best, she decided. The other night she'd apparently scared away the dentist before he'd even shown up. Tonight her tenant. Quite a roll, even for herself —

"Here."

Parker materialized in front of her, this time a bottle of vodka dangling from his fingers. "Made you some laced hot chocolate." He paused, flashed a smile. "Without the hot chocolate." He held out the bottle.

She let out a low laugh and tossed a sip back before she could think about it, and then promptly choked. It burned going down, but at least it had the consideration to leave a trail of delicious warmth in its path, completely eradicating the rest of her odd and inexplicable sadness.

Or maybe Parker had done that.

She offered him the bottle back. He took a pull, though he didn't cough or react other than to let out a breath, as if he were finally relaxing after a long time of being tense, reminding her she hardly knew anything about him.

"You make some pretty excellent laced hot chocolate without the hot chocolate," she said.

He flashed a smile and gave her back the vodka. "Told you I was good in the kitchen."

She had a feeling he'd be good in any room of the house, most especially the bedroom. That was when she remembered what he'd said on his first day here, that he was good in the kitchen when he wanted to get laid.

"You just turned beet red," he said. "Care to share?"

"No." She gulped another shot before once again handing the bottle over.

He just grinned. He knew, the ratfink bastard.

"So what happened to this new batch of

cookies?" he asked.

She sighed. She'd tried a different recipe of her grandma's, but this had been one of those done-by-memory things and she'd clearly done something wrong, which had made her miss her warm, funny, loving grandma like she'd miss a limb. "I don't want to talk about it."

"How about the dirt stains on your knees?"

She looked down at herself. "Turns out my talents don't lend themselves to electrical work, either. Besides the bad fuse, there's something wrong with the cable and Internet. I was outside looking in the cable box."

"I can take a look."

"No," she said. "I've —"

"Got this?" he asked, only slightly sardonic.

"Yes," she said. And she'd really believed it, too. Before the *Friends* marathon she'd watched an hour of YouTube cable and Internet troubleshooting tutorials.

Clearly they hadn't helped.

"Wyatt warned me you were stubborn," he said.

"Hmph," she said. "What did he say about our baby sister, Darcy?"

"That she's batshit crazy."

Zoe laughed.

"And amazingly brave," Parker added.

Zoe stopped laughing because this was true. After what Darcy had been through, anyone and everyone who knew her would describe her as amazingly brave. "What else did he say?"

"About you?" Parker asked.

"Yeah."

Apparently pleading the fifth, Parker just smiled.

"Come on, don't be shy now," she said.

He laughed, the amusement coming from his gut and . . . damn. It looked good on him. Especially since she got the sense that he hadn't laughed a lot, at least not recently.

"Been a long time since anyone called me shy," he said.

"Nice subject change."

His eyes turned dark and sultry. *"Fierce,"* he said.

Her heart skipped a beat at the heat in his gaze. "What?"

"Wyatt said you were fierce. Fiercely loyal, fiercely smart, and fiercely protective of those you care about. He said you'd always had to be, that even though you're only a year older than him, you were the only warm, caring authority figure he ever had."

She slid him a long look. "Wyatt said I

was warm and caring?" she asked, disbelieving.

Parker flashed white teeth, and she blew out a sigh. "He said bitchy, didn't he?"

"He said that without you, he'd be dead a few times over," Parker said. "It seems like you never really got a chance just to be a kid." He wasn't kidding or smiling now, and though his voice didn't hold pity — she might have had to beat him over the head with her empty plate if it had — he was very serious.

"He said your parents put way too much on your head with consequences you shouldn't have had to pay," he said, and suddenly she needed another sip of that vodka and held out her hand for it.

He obliged, and while she knocked back another shot, he gestured toward her sweatshirt. "So you went to King's?"

"Yes."

"A long way from Sunshine, Idaho," he noted.

"I was born in Paris," she said. "Which was an accident, by the way. My mother miscalculated. She meant to be back in Belize, where she was stationed at the time."

Parker nodded. "Wyatt once said something about living in fifteen different countries in as many years."

102

"We were children of foreign diplomats," she said. "It was life." A life that had been as vagabond and full of wanderlust as it could possibly be. As a result, Wyatt had been the kid who'd yearned to get to stay in one place long enough to join a baseball team and have a dog. Darcy had acted out, running away, going wild, and then as punishment had often been sent to boarding schools, far away from all of them.

Zoe had simply gone along with the lifestyle, unable to imagine anything else. That is, until she started coming here to Sunshine for the summers to live with her grandparents.

Suddenly she'd had normal hours and home-cooked meals and warm, loving authority figures in her life. It hadn't been until her grandma and grandpa had died within six months of each other a decade ago that she'd felt true loss and devastation and grief.

After college she'd come back here and found that as much as she'd loved being a child of the world, it was lovely, really shockingly lovely, to have a home base. "My grandparents were born and raised right here in Sunshine and never left," she said. "Not once." She shook her head. "I always had a hard time imagining such a thing."

"And yet here you are," he said.

She shrugged. "Turns out I like having a home base more than I could've imagined." She looked around at the warm, comfy living room that she hadn't changed much. "Though the home base is a little emptier than I'm used to."

Those sharp, assessing eyes of his met hers again, softer now. "You lonely, Zoe?"

"Nope." At least not that she was going to admit. "I have Oreo."

They both looked at the dog, snoring away.

"What about you?" she asked.

"What about me?"

"You know what," she said. "You've learned a lot about me in a short time. My job, where I live, my story . . ." Plus other things like how she'd been stood up, that she couldn't bake or fix anything to save her life, that she cried watching *Friends* . . . "And yet I know next to nothing about you."

He smiled, like that was good with him, and actually got up to leave.

"Are you serious?" she asked his back, feeling brave and daring thanks to the alcohol. "Give me something more than you're here for a vacation, in the middle of Nowhere, Idaho. Which, by the way, I don't believe at all. Time to fill in some blanks, Mr. Mysterious."

EIGHT

Zoe watched as Parker slowly turned to face her, his mouth twitching at the corners, no doubt amused by her curiosity.

"What do you want to know?" he asked.

Just about everything. "Where did you grow up, do you have family, how would they describe you, where do you live, what's your job like . . ." She trailed off, not wanting to scare him away.

"I'm not sure I imbibed enough vodka for all of that."

"I can fix that," she said, and offered him the bottle.

He came close again and took it slowly. Zoe got the feeling that in his world not a lot of people challenged him. And yet she couldn't seem to stop herself from doing that at every turn. She wanted to know more about him.

"My life's not all that exciting," he warned.

"I bet otherwise," she said, and added what she hoped was an enticing smile.

Again she got the almost-smile, but no words.

Was he being evasive on purpose, she wondered, or was he simply not into talking about himself? The alcohol hadn't changed him at all. Even though he'd had his share, his eyes were still sharp and assessing.

Evasive, she decided. Which put her on guard because unlike most red-blooded women, Zoe didn't like evasive, mysterious men. Or at least she didn't like evasive, mysterious men *anymore.* And honestly, this was almost a relief because it gave her yet another fail-safe reason not to get involved with him.

Not that she'd ever planned to in the first place.

"I grew up in a small copper mining town in northern Arizona," he said, surprising her. "If you're born there, you live and die there, working in the mines in between."

"Not you, though," she said.

"Not me." He paused, as if hoping that'd be enough for her.

Poor, delusional man; that had only served to make her more curious. At her *go on* gesture, he shook his head.

"My parents would tell you that I'm stubborn, too," he said. "And they'd add that I'm also an unfeeling, selfish son of a bitch."

"Because you didn't stay?" she asked, her smile fading. "But that's not a crime. Everyone deserves to live the life they want."

"The Jameses have always been miners," Parker said. "It's what we do, and tradition is tradition. My parents worked all the time; it was all they ever did. It was what was expected of everyone, me included, even though I never wanted to be a miner."

"So you left," she said, fascinated by the unexpected glimpse of what had created Parker the man.

"The day after I graduated high school, I hitchhiked to New York and bartended while putting myself through college," he said.

She thought that sounded incredibly brave. "What was your major?" she asked softly, wanting him to keep talking forever. They were in a little bubble here in the warm, cozy living room with Oreo snoring on the other end of the couch and the rest of the world asleep.

"Criminology," he said, and surprised her again.

"Impressive."

"Not really," he said. "I did it because it was the opposite of everything I knew, and I wanted to piss off my parents. Turns out I liked it so it stuck." He'd settled his long body into the leather recliner next to the couch and stretched his long legs out in front of him. Now he leaned back, like maybe he was as exhausted as she was.

Suddenly she felt bad about waking him up and keeping him up. "You don't have to babysit me," she said. "I'm fine down here by myself."

He didn't say anything.

Or move.

"Seriously," she said quietly. "Go back to bed. I'll keep it down."

"The sobbing, you mean?" he asked.

"Hey," she said. "It was a touching ending to ten seasons, okay? And I'll have you know, I never cry. Or very rarely," she corrected. "I can't even remember the last time I did."

But actually that was a lie because she did remember. It had been when Darcy had moved out three months ago, right on the heels of Wyatt doing the same. She'd been alone for the first time since she and her siblings had taken over their grandparents' family home.

That night she'd accidentally blown up her microwave while making popcorn. She'd gone outside to fumble through the electrical box to replace the fuse and had — in the space of five minutes — locked herself out of the house and sliced open her finger trying to pry open the breaker panel.

She'd sat on the front porch in the dark, head to her knees, and cried from loneliness. She'd allowed the pity party until she'd spent herself and that was that.

She got over it.

It was what she did.

And now she wasn't alone anymore — at least for as long as Parker stayed — and she didn't know how she felt about that. Suddenly chilled, she hugged herself and wondered how cold her bed was going to be.

"I could build you a fire," Parker said.

Did he notice everything? "Not until I get the fireplace fixed," she said.

"I could —"

"No," she said. "Thanks, but I've got it."

He looked at her for a long beat, saying nothing.

"What?"

"Just trying to figure out if you're an exceptionally stubborn person or if you've been badly burned."

"I've never burned myself on that fireplace."

"You know that's not what I meant," he said quietly.

Yeah, but she'd thought maybe he'd be a good guy and let her change the subject, but she should've known better. One thing she knew about him already was that he didn't let much slide. She stood up, not all that happy to find herself a little wobbly on her feet.

Parker stood, too, and she found herself disconcertingly close to him. He was tall and had a way of moving that made her think of a big cat.

A feral one.

She told herself that he was irritating and not at all sexy, but she was a big, fat liar. Or at least drunk Zoe was. "I'm working on getting myself a life," she heard herself say. "Learning to bake, going out on dates, *not* getting burned . . ." *Dammit, Zoe, this is why you don't drink, shut up.* "I think I should put myself to bed now," she said, and turned to leave.

"So the answer's yes."

Like a moth to the flame, she turned back. "Yes what?"

"Yes, you've been burned."

His hand came up and cupped her jaw, his long fingers sinking into her hair. "It's because we're all assholes," he said.

"The entire male race?" she asked, meaning to tease, but her voice came out soft and a little shaky.

"Every last one of us." His gaze dropped to her mouth as the pad of his thumb gently rasped over her lower lip. "Remember that on this new lease on life you're going for."

Since she doubted she could speak, she nodded. And then, before she could do something really dumb, like let the vodka talk her into kissing him, she backed away, turned, and headed up the stairs.

At the top, she moved to her bedroom door, looked into the cold, empty room, and then turned back and . . . tripped over Oreo, who'd followed her. "That's it," she said. "There're too many men in this house." She crouched low to love up on the sweet, sleepy dog. "And one of you is nosy, mysterious, and smarter than the average bear, yes he is."

Had she been burned by a man?

Hell yes. Not that she was going to talk about that.

Ever.

"We're not going to like him," she whispered nose to nose with Oreo. "You hear me? No more melting over him, either of us. I'd ask you to shake on it but you don't have opposable thumbs."

"Would you like me to shake on it?" came the low, amused male voice behind her.

She grimaced to herself and rose, turning to face Parker. "Okay, new rule. Wear a bell or stop sneaking up on me."

He smiled easily. "You've got a lot of rules. You should know, I'm not much of a rule follower."

"Try real hard," she suggested.

"I will if you will."

She stared at him. "What's that supposed to mean? *You* have rules for *me*?"

"Only one. And it's easy," he said. "No W's."

"W's?" she repeated.

"We're coexisting here in this house for the duration, right?" he asked.

"Right," she said slowly.

"So let's do just that, in the moment," he said. "No wondering, wishing, or worrying."

She stared at him some more. "I don't understand." But she did. She understood exactly even before he stepped into her, before her heart kicked into gear, before he gently pushed her up against the wall and then not-so-gently kissed her.

Heat swamped her because, holy cow, this was not like when she'd sweetly, chastely kissed him on his first day here.

Not. Even. Close.

Of their own accord, her hands slid up his chest and fisted in his shirt to hold on tight for the ride — and it was a ride. A helpless moan clawed its way out of her throat, but just as it was getting good, really *really* good, Parker broke away.

Stepping back, he looked deep into her eyes. Apparently he saw something he liked because he smiled. "I'd suggest rule number two be that you try to keep your hands — and mouth — off me," he said. "But as it turns out, I like both of those things very much."

It was official. She really was going to have to kill Wyatt for asking to let Parker stay in her home. And then Darcy just on principle. And then Parker himself.

Slowly.

Sure she'd go to prison for it, and she looked horrible in orange, but she felt it would be worth it. Especially when, with a soft laugh, he vanished into his room.

NINE

Zoe was still a little mad at herself when her alarm went off two hours after she'd finally crawled into bed. She stared up at the ceiling wondering what had possessed her to stay up until three in the morning on a workday.

Idiocy, that's what.

And okay, maybe a little misguided lust.

Misguided, because hot as Mr. Mysterious was, she wasn't going there, not with him — no matter how much she might secretly want to.

She blamed the vodka for that. Surely it had been the over-imbibing that had made him seem sexier than he really was, not to mention made that kiss seem like the very best kiss of her entire life.

Stupid vodka. Why couldn't the alcohol have made her *forget* the taste of Parker, the heat he'd generated, the way his hard body had fit against her softer one?

Instead, it was making her replay the entire scene every two seconds.

Don't think about it now, she ordered herself. Yeah, right. She'd have better luck attempting not to draw air into her lungs. Racing around her room to gather clothes, she headed to the bathroom, this time pausing outside the door to listen carefully before she barged in. The other shower had been fixed, so he'd probably be using that one. She still knocked twice to make certain before entering, rushing through her morning routine, forgoing makeup and hairstyling to be on time.

So she was doubly mad when she finally arrived at the airport only to find that her morning flight lesson had been cancelled.

Now she looked like crap *and* she had nothing to do for three hours.

Parker had tried to go to bed, but after that kiss with Zoe he was way too keyed up to sleep and gave up after an hour. Instead he changed into running clothes and hit the streets.

Running cleared his mind. Not that he'd been up to running since nearly being killed by Carver, but he thought today felt like a good day to get back to it.

A few minutes in he was doubting that

thanks to the fact that each step jarred his ribs and made him want to go crying to his mama.

The sun wouldn't rise for another hour. The air was high-altitude dry and a perfect-for-running fifty degrees. Probably later it would be a scorcher, but for now he had the cool predawn air and the world to himself, it seemed. The only sounds came from a high wind rustling the pines that were gently swaying like hundred-foot-tall ghosts and the sound of his feet hitting the pavement.

When he came to a bridge he stopped in the middle and pretended to look down at the river beneath moving slow and meanderingly. Breathing hard, hurting like hell, he gulped for breath. After a few minutes, still not ready to continue, he pulled his phone from his running shorts pocket. Accessing his camera, he focused it on the last of the moon seemingly sinking into the water with the blue glow gliding over the rocky riverbed.

He sent the pic to Amory, thumbing in a quick *miss you.* When he got a ping that told him the message had been sent, he shoved the phone back into his pocket and forced himself to keep going.

As Sharon had pointed out, he needed to

get back to lean, mean fighting shape for the job. He'd worked his ass off to climb the ranks. He wasn't going to let anyone think he wasn't able to get back to it. And if a small part of him realized that in pushing himself so hard to become something important, to make something of himself, he'd instead become a workaholic like the workaholic parents he resented, he ignored it.

His phone buzzed an incoming text. He was smiling as he pulled it back out of his pocket, already formulating his teasing response about Amory being up so early.

She loved when he sent her pics and stories. A late-in-life baby, she'd been born with Down syndrome when Parker had been twelve. Their parents had qualified for state funding and had gotten help, and they'd been lucky enough to have that help genuinely love and care for Amory. But this had created an unexpected problem. Amory had been overprotected and overshielded from normal life at every turn.

She expressed only contentment with her life, but Parker could only imagine how constricting it was. She had to feel closed in by perimeters of her quiet existence.

He hated that for her, and that more than anything else had him texting her pictures from wherever in the world he was as often as he could.

But it wasn't Amory on the phone.

It was Kel. "So," the sheriff said without preamble. "Interested in knowing that Cat's Paw is suddenly a hot topic around the water cooler?"

"Very," Parker said. "Although word got back to my boss that I've been digging."

"You up shit creek?"

"Without a paddle," Parker confirmed. "Tell me you got something concrete to make it worthwhile."

"I've got a buddy in the ATF. He couldn't confirm for certain, but word's out that your guy cut some sort of a hush-hush deal."

Parker had suspected this very thing, but goddamn, that asshole didn't deserve a deal of any kind. "Anything specific?"

"Nothing," Kel said. "Whatever's going on up there, it's above my pay grade. They still haven't included any local law enforcement. I've got a few feelers out for more intel. I'll keep you posted."

"Thanks," Parker said. "Appreciate it."

"Stay safe."

"You, too." Parker stared at his phone after he disconnected, torn by conflicting urges. He wanted to say fuck everyone and whatever they were waiting on and go in after Carver himself. But that was stupid

119

and selfish, and he tried very hard not to be either of those things.

He needed to play this safe but he wasn't exactly in tune with his safe side. He looked at the time, and knowing it was two hours ahead in D.C. and that his boss would be up and in the office chewing on the balls of her underlings for breakfast while simultaneously running her world, he called her.

"All I want to hear from you," Sharon opened with, "is that you're on a fucking island making your left hand jealous of your right."

"I have a theory," Parker said.

"Oh Christ. Is it that you're a pain in my ass? Because that's a fact, Parker, not a theory."

"I think Tripp Carver made a deal," he said.

Sharon's silence went glacial.

"I think he's giving information," Parker went on, "and in return he's got his freedom. How am I doing? Am I close?"

"We're not having this conversation," she said.

Yeah, he was close.

"Listen to me, Parker," Sharon said. "You're not able to see reason on this case because of Ned's death, and I get it. But I'm trying to protect your job here."

He blew out a breath and rubbed his still-sore ribs. "I know, and I appreciate that. But I need you to be straight with me on this."

There was another long silence, during which Parker heard rustling and then a door shutting, as if Sharon was getting herself some privacy.

"What did he have that made it worth keeping him in the wild?"

"I'm not confirming this, Parker."

But nor was she denying. "Shit," he said with disgust. "This is insane. To give him his freedom after all he's done —"

"You need to see the bigger picture here," she said. "The *much* bigger picture, which, trust me, makes Carver look like a saint. Something's going down and if you screw things up, I won't be able to help you save your career. You have to let this go, Parker. Now repeat that back to me. You'll let it go."

He got what she was saying. If he pursued this, he was risking the career he'd so painstakingly built, but Christ it went against the grain. "I want in on the take-down," he said.

"I can't promise that. We're not running the show."

Yeah, he was getting that loud and clear.

"You know I'll do what I can," she said. "But in the meantime, stay the hell out of Idaho because if Carver sees you, he'll run. He'll vanish like smoke, and then he really will get away with it."

"He's not going to see me."

"You willing to stake your career on it?" she asked. "Because right now he's getting comfortable, and that's right where we all need him to be. Comfortable. Cozy. Lazy."

Carver was a lot of things, but lazy wasn't one of them. And yet Sharon was right. He had to let it go.

For now.

He went back to his run, halfway to dead when he stopped two miles later and bent over at the knees, gulping in air like it was his job. He was still there sucking wind when a truck pulled over in front of him on the side of the road.

Wyatt got out. He was in cargo pants, a T-shirt that read *VETERINARIAN: Because BADASS isn't an official job title,* and a fading smile as he got a good look at Parker.

"I'm fine," Parker said, still wheezing.

Wyatt nodded as he came close enough to put his hand to Parker's shoulder and push.

Parker fell over onto his ass.

"You're full of shit," Wyatt said, and offered him a hand to pull him up. "Get in the truck."

Parker didn't take orders from very many people. But stick a fork in him, he was done. "Love it when you get all demanding," he said, keeping his whimpers to himself. "Gives me the shivers. You going to buy me breakfast first?"

"Maybe after," Wyatt said. "If you're very good."

"After what?"

"If you want to kill yourself with physical activity, I've got just the way to do it," Wyatt said.

Fifteen minutes later they entered the Belle Haven Animal Center, where Wyatt worked as a veterinarian. They were greeted by well over a hundred pounds of Saint Bernard. Gertie threw herself at Wyatt and then shoved her big nose into Parker's crotch, making him yelp.

Wyatt grinned. "Welcome to the insanity."

"Help!" screeched a feminine voice. *"HELP ME!"*

Parker whipped around, automatically reaching for the weapon that he didn't have at the small of his back because, oh yeah, he was in running gear with no place to hide a weapon.

But there was no woman. Just a huge

parrot perched on a printer at the front desk.

"Help!" it squeaked in a shockingly authentic woman's voice. *"I've been turned into a parrot!"*

"Peanut, play dead," Wyatt said.

Peanut sighed and tucked her head into her feathers.

"Good parrot." Wyatt looked at Parker. "She's a nut."

"Damn, shit, *farts,*" the bird muttered beneath her breath, making Parker grin.

Wyatt sighed. "Peanut's a mimic, and Jade, our office manager, has a bit of a potty mouth."

"Boner," Peanut said, head still tucked into her feathers.

"Peanut, dead parrots don't talk." Wyatt turned back to Parker. "Follow me."

Parker did, and found himself working his ass off for the next hour mucking out four horse stalls. It was late June and the day had heated up. He swiped an arm across his sweaty brow. "Why are we doing this again?" he asked Wyatt.

"Because we had to fire the maid," Wyatt said, swiping his damp brow, too. "And also because each of us here owns a horse and we take turns at this. It was my day and you were looking to punish yourself for God knows what. Just being a friend, man."

When they finished, Parker staggered to a fallen log and sat. And because that wasn't enough, he lay flat on his back in a patch of overgrown wild grass, sweating, shaking, and unable to move.

Christ, Sharon was right. He wasn't in lean, mean fighting shape yet. Not even close.

"Aw. Need a nap?" Wyatt asked.

Remaining still, not even opening his eyes, Parker flipped him off. He wasn't going to move, not a single trembling muscle, for a good long time . . .

The scent of coffee roused him and he opened an eye.

A feminine hand waved an iced coffee — God bless her — in front of his face. He opened another eye and met Zoe's sunglasses-covered gaze. "Marry me," he said.

"Huh, you're right," she said to someone over his head. "That did revive him."

"Told ya," Wyatt said. "And I bet vodka would've done the same thing."

Zoe's eyes were still on Parker, and he watched as the memories of the night before flitted through her mind, making her lips twitch.

"It's too early for vodka," Parker muttered. "You," he said, pointing to Wyatt, "are an asshole."

"Sticks and stones," Wyatt said, and walked off. "Dinner tonight," he called back over his shoulder. "I'll introduce you and your potty mouth to the woman I'm going to marry."

"Is she a sadist, too?"

Wyatt flipped him off, and Parker let out a low laugh. "Shit. She is, isn't she?"

"Ready?" Zoe asked him.

He looked at her, taking in her long, slim-cut black blazer and skirt — blessedly short and revealing her mile-long legs. Was he ready? Ready for what? Because several really great possibilities were running on repeat through his mind, none of which could be done in front of her brother. Not to mention he'd need a shower first. And maybe another nap. "For?"

"A ride." She narrowed her eyes. "What did you think I was offering?"

He just stared at her.

She flushed and squirmed a little bit. "Do you have to make everything sexual?" she asked.

"As much as possible. What are you doing here?"

"Wyatt called me. Said you needed a ride. Something about you being an idiot and . . .

some other things I'm not going to repeat."

He found a smile. "Aw, come on. Talk dirty to me."

She snorted. "You want a ride or not? My first flight was cancelled but I have a lesson later that I can't miss, so . . ."

Parker looked at the building, knowing her car was on the far side of it, both of which seemed like a million miles away. "How about you sit and talk to me for a minute?"

She huffed out a breath but sat right there in the wild grass next to him. Her long legs folded beneath her, she settled without a care for if she got dirty.

And he nearly fell in love with her right then and there.

Nearly.

Ten

"What do you want to talk about?" Zoe asked Parker warily, her eyes covered by her dark sunglasses.

That was Zoe, more afraid of trusting someone than of getting dirty. "Do you like teaching people to fly?" he asked.

"I like flying," she said. "And in the beginning, lessons were an additional way for me to get hours in the air."

"You needed so many hours for your license, right?"

"Yes." She paused, clearly carefully considering her words. "You can't accept payment for flying with a private license, but you can be paid to teach. In order to fly for a living, I had to get a commercial license, which is mind-bogglingly expensive. It required — at least in my case — loans."

"How expensive?"

She turned to the sun and tipped her face up to it. "I've got about a hundred K in student loans," she murmured.

He let out a low whistle.

"Yeah. And getting that commercial license required a minimum of two hundred fifty hours in the air. Teaching got me to those hours, and I didn't have to pay for plane rentals or fuel." She shrugged. "Win-win."

"Nice," he said, impressed. "And you kept giving the lessons after you got your license."

"Yeah, I still get more lessons than flights compared to say, Devon, who's been working for two years less than I have." She lifted a shoulder. "It's the twenty-first century, but female pilots are still few and far between, and not always a client's first choice. Even though women have been flying as long as men, it's still very much a boys' club. Jobs are a lot harder to find. I'm lucky to get to work so close to home, but I don't always get a fair share of the flights."

Reaching over, he pulled off her sunglasses and waited until she met his gaze. "I'd hire you over a male pilot any day of the week," he said.

She snorted. "Shock," she said, not taking him seriously.

Which was for the best.

"Anyway," she went on, "for now at least,

teaching brings in more money, and more money helps me to pay down my loans." She shrugged again, philosophically. "So I teach." She looked at him. "Now you."

"Me what?"

"Tell me something about you."

"Well, for starters, my world is a man's world, too. In my field, men outnumber women five to one."

"Would you work with a woman as a partner?" she asked.

"In a heartbeat," he said.

She smiled. "That was quick. You did realize I didn't mean *sexual* partner, right?"

He grinned. "Either way. Women are smarter, sharper, more interesting, and far more fun to be with. No matter what we're partnering for."

Rolling her eyes, she got to her feet. "You coming?"

"Think you can go get the car and bring it over here to get me?" he asked hopefully.

Some of the annoyance left her face. "That bad?" she asked, her voice softer, her eyes softer, too, as she offered him a hand up.

Liking that, not above using that, he accepted her help but then groaned at the movement.

"What the hell did Wyatt do to you?" she

murmured, slipping an arm around him. "Here, lean on me."

Hell, yeah, he'd lean on her. Slipping an arm over her shoulders, he turned his face into her hair — which smelled grade-A amazing — and let his lips skim her ear.

She jumped a little and whipped her face toward his.

Their mouths brushed.

He groaned again — not in pain this time — but she pulled back with a frown. "Why did you push yourself so hard?" she demanded.

"Gotta get better," he said. "Get back in the game."

"What game?"

"Game of life."

"That's ridiculous," she said. "Life's not a damn game. And you've got to give your body time to heal. What better time than now while you're on a break from work?"

A break indeed . . . They walked through the animal center. Peanut was undead and telling off a cat, who was sleeping through the whole thing, curled up next to the printer. Gertie was snoozing in a sunny spot, a puddle of drool beneath her face.

Out front, Parker slid into Zoe's passenger seat and set his head back. Zoe shoved her car into gear and hit the gas. Parker enjoyed

131

watching her handle the road, but mostly he enjoyed how when she worked the clutch, her long legs shifted, forcing her skirt up higher on her thighs.

"You ever going to tell me how you really got hurt?" she asked.

"I already told you."

"Fine." She shook her head. "You don't want to tell me, that's . . . whatever. But you don't have to make stuff up. No wondering, no worrying, no wishes, remember? Live in the moment?" She glanced at him. "Or was that all bullshit?"

He met her gaze, surprised to find her eyes flashing with temper and . . . hurt. Well, hell. "Not bullshit," he said. "That's how I live my life."

"Uh-huh." Her jaw was tight, her body language tense.

And he couldn't keep himself from asking. "Who was he?"

"He who?"

"The asshole who put you so on guard all the time. What did he do?"

She sent him another long look. "He lied to me." She turned back to the road before speaking again. "About everything."

And clearly she'd put him in the same category. "I haven't lied," he said. He'd just let certain assumptions stand.

"Right," she said. "Wrestling big-game poachers?"

"Hey, that's true," he said. "We were . . ." *Closing in on the ringleader of an international smuggling conspiracy . . .* "Going after a wildlife poacher, someone we'd been after for a long time. I had a team with me, but we got separated in the takedown." He could still feel the sweat breaking out on his skin as his instincts screamed they were all about to be fucked. They'd been outnumbered, but they might've been able to hold their own if the Butcher hadn't gone for his truck. "The guy came at us in his truck."

Horror was all over her face. "To run you over? Oh my God, what did you do?"

"Dove out of the way." Parker's stomach clenched at the memory of feeling himself get clipped, flying through the air, and landing next to Ned, who hadn't been as lucky as Parker. "But not fast enough," he murmured.

She gaped at him. "He got you. That's how you got hurt." She paused and her voice was low and shocked. "You were telling me the truth; you really did get hit by a wildlife poacher's truck."

"Me and another man on my team," he said, and rubbed his aching ribs. Shoveling horse shit had been a stupid idea. But hey, he was still breathing. "Ned didn't make it."

"Oh my God. I'm so sorry, Parker."

So was he. He still burned with fury, which was why he couldn't walk away from this knowing Carver might be at Cat's Paw.

"I had no idea that being a game warden could be so dangerous," she said softly.

Something twinged inside Parker.

Guilt.

She thought he was a game warden, but that was how it had to be. He told himself he was good with the deception. Working as he did, traveling at the drop of a hat, sometimes going deep undercover for weeks, his plan did not include falling for a cutie-pie pilot — albeit a pretty tough, fascinating cutie-pie pilot — no matter what.

But damn. Sometimes his job and life sucked.

Zoe pulled into her driveway and turned off the engine. Then . . . didn't move. Sensing she was debating with herself over something, Parker stayed still.

Staring ahead, hands on the wheel, Zoe spoke to the windshield. "I was engaged," she said, surprising him. "Kyle turned out to be . . ." She sighed. "Not the man I thought."

Ah, shit. He wasn't going to like this story, he could tell. "He hurt you?" he asked quietly, feeling anything but quiet.

"Yes," she said. "He hurt me. But not in the way you think." She shook her head. "I met him in college. For a girl who'd grown up a child of the world, I was . . . incredibly naïve."

Parker thought of Amory, how naïve she was, too, how he constantly worried someone would get the best of her. How he'd probably kill anyone who did.

He hoped like hell Wyatt had taken care of Kyle the Asshole.

"Kyle was as exciting as I could imagine," she said. "Tough and mysterious and . . . well. When I met him, he'd been investigating some thefts on campus." She paused. "He was an undercover cop so it was a while before he told me, and in the meantime, we fell hard and fast. He was going to change divisions, stop the undercover work. We talked about buying a farmhouse in the country and having a bunch of kids and the proverbial white picket fence." She paused, clearly lost in the memories. "We found the place we wanted before we could get married, but he didn't have the whole down payment. So . . ." She closed her eyes. "I liquidated a trust fund and borrowed from my grandparents. And then he . . ."

Ah, hell. Reaching out, he took her hand.

Her fingers were cold. "Zoe, you don't have to —"

"It was a scam," she said calmly, though she was still talking only to the windshield. "The whole thing," she said. "All of it, one big scam. He wasn't an undercover cop at all. And he didn't have *any* of the down payment. In fact, he'd had no intention of buying that house, or marrying me, or anything." She shrugged. "He took the money — hell, I gave it to him, really — and then he vanished. And that was that."

Parker squeezed her hand, hating how calm she was. He wanted to see her mad. "Tell me you caught up with him and ran him over with a big-game truck."

"No. I looked for him but he was long gone. I never heard from him again," she said flatly, showing no emotion at all. It was so unlike the wildly passionate Zoe that he was coming to know.

"Bet I could find him," he said, eyes on her face. "And I'll be happy to run him over for you." *Right after I beat the living shit out of him.*

A very small smile curved her lips, relieving him. She liked the thought of him helping her. Progress. "Just tell me what you know about him and it's done," he promised.

"Wait." She turned and stared at him, the smile fading. "You're . . . not kidding."

"Fuck no," he said. "At least Wyatt went after him for you, right?"

Something crossed her face. Guilt? "Why aren't you telling me that Wyatt went after him for you?"

"Because he didn't."

"Why the hell not?"

She squirmed a little and dropped eye contact. And he knew. "You never told anyone," he breathed.

"Well, it's not like I was in a hurry to let everyone know I'd been a complete idiot," she said grumpily, yanking her hand from his.

He took it back and squeezed it. "You should've told someone," he said, pissed for her that she'd gone through that alone, that in so many rough times in her life she'd been alone.

"My parents would've expressed profound disappointment," she said, "and then never let me forget it."

"But Wyatt —"

"Was killing himself to get through vet school at the time," she said. "I couldn't, *wouldn't,* take him from that. And Darcy . . ." She shook her head. "She had her own problems."

"What about your grandparents?"

She shook her head. "They would've been sympathetic and way kinder than I deserved," she said. "I couldn't do it."

"So you —"

"Took an extra job to earn back the money I'd borrowed. They never knew."

"Jesus, Zoe," he said, sick for her. "You shouldn't have had to go through that by yourself."

And he'd just lied to her. Just like that asshole. It was all he could think about and it was making him sick.

"It was a long time ago," she said. "I was young and stupidly naïve, and believed everything everyone said. I learned my lesson."

She still wasn't looking at him. Tired of that, he reached out to turn her face to his. "It wasn't your fault."

"Hmm," she said, like maybe she was used to such things. And then he remembered the dentist who'd stood her up and realized she was used to such things from men.

Dammit. And then there was him. No, he hadn't stolen money from her or specifically set out to screw her over, but he'd sure as hell lied by omission. "Zoe —"

"I swear, if you're feeling sorry for me *I'll* run you over."

He smiled in appreciation for the sass. He loved a woman who, when backed into a corner, came out fighting instead of giving up. But she was looking at him with those honey-colored eyes that somehow managed to reach right through him, and his smile faded quickly enough. Shit. Was he really going to do this?

She started to get out of the car, but he grabbed her wrist. When she looked at him, he said, "There's something you need to know about me."

Her eyes went shadowed and guarded, and he hated himself a little bit. "I'm not a game warden."

She continued to stare at him, still as stone now. Hell, he wasn't even sure she was breathing.

"I do work for U.S. Fish and Wildlife," he said. "But not as a game warden. I'm a supervisory special agent. We're law enforcement, too, authorized and equipped to perform a full range of criminal investigative activities including search warrants and arrests."

"So . . . you do chase bad guys," she said softly. "For real?"

"Yes," he said. "And occasionally they chase me with a really big fucking truck."

She didn't smile.

"Zoe —"

"Are you really on vacation?"

"I'm on leave," he said. "Supposedly recouping. But I'm really looking for the guy who killed Ned."

"The wildlife poacher."

"Actually, he's more than that. He's the ringleader of an international smuggling conspiracy and someone we've been after a long time."

"And you think he's in Cat's Paw," she said.

"I do." He paused. "And you should know, my being here isn't exactly USFWS sanctioned. In fact, it's the opposite of being sanctioned."

She blinked. "You weren't kidding that you're not a big rule follower."

He found a small smile. Reaching out, he stroked a finger along her temple, tucking a runaway strand of hair behind her ear. "We okay, Zoe?"

The question made her smile, though he wasn't sure why. "You mean the 'we' who are living in the moment?" she asked. "The 'we' with the three W's? The 'we' who need to remember that you're only temporary here in Sunshine to begin with?"

"Yeah," he said. "That 'we.' We okay?"

She stared at him. "To be determined."
Fair enough.

ELEVEN

When Parker got out of the car, Zoe let out a breath, trying to sort out her feelings. The man had misled her but then had come clean simply because she'd been open with him about herself.

She hadn't been open about herself with a man since Kyle, so she felt like she was in uncharted waters here. Had Parker been so frank with her out of pity? Or because he really wanted her to know the truth? And if it was the latter, then why?

And did it mean that they really had a little something going on?

You know the answer to that . . .

And then there was his job, which sounded thrilling, exciting, and dangerous as hell.

She supposed the argument could be made that her job was all of those things, too, but she didn't look at it like that. Flying was just what she did, what she loved to do. In the air her problems dropped away and she felt weightless and free.

A little bit like how she felt with Parker, actually.

Truth was, she had no idea what to think or how to react to him.

She watched him walk inside her house and realized she did know one thing for certain — he had a really great ass.

The passenger car door opened just as the front door shut, and then Darcy settled into the passenger seat and gave Zoe a once-over.

"What are you doing?" Zoe asked.

"Came by to con some food out of you. And also to hear how the dating thing's going. Imagine my surprise when I had to wait for Wyatt's hottie friend to get out of your car. Thought he was going to kiss you there for a minute."

Zoe opened her mouth and then closed it. "I don't have time to get you food," she said. "I've got flight lessons. And as for the dating thing . . . it's not really happening."

"Because you have a thing for Parker?"

Zoe slid her sister a look. The kind of look that quelled even the bravest of souls.

Darcy, who'd never been quelled a day in her life, just grinned. "He's got a great ass."

Zoe thunked her head to the steering wheel. "I know!"

Darcy laughed, and the sound was so genuine that Zoe lifted her head. For a very long time Darcy's life hadn't lent itself to fun or amusement of any sort. Too long. Wild and restless had been Darcy's MO at any cost. Then two years ago that wild-and-restlessness had led her to a terrible — and nearly tragic — auto accident. It had been a drawn-out, horrendous recovery, but Darcy had as much grit and inner strength as she did crazy, and though she'd probably always limp, she was back to some semblance of normal. "I love seeing you happy," Zoe blurted out.

Darcy reached for Zoe's hand. "Thanks, and it's nice to be happy, but that's not going to get you a subject change. I want to discuss your new roommate's fine ass."

Zoe couldn't help it, she laughed. "You do realize that this is Wyatt's friend you're talking about."

"Uh-huh. And I'm currently sleeping with and planning on marrying Wyatt's other good friend. Your point?"

"My point is . . ." What was her point again? "I don't have time to talk about Parker right now."

"Well, I do," Darcy said. "Let's talk about what I saw between you two."

"You saw nothing."

144

"Oh how wrong you are, my favorite sister. I saw some seriously smokin' chemistry." Darcy said this with great delight. She really loved it when she thought Zoe was wrong.

But for the record, Zoe was never wrong.

"When the two of you were talking, you were leaning into each other," Darcy said. "Full eye contact. We both know what that means."

Well, damn. Maybe she was a little bit wrong. Just this one time. "That maybe we both forgot our glasses and had to lean in just to see each other?"

"Liar, liar," Darcy said. "You have twenty-twenty vision *and* eyes in the back of your head. Also," she went on, lifting a finger like she was cross-examining Zoe on the stand, "he touched you. And when he did, you" — she poked that finger in Zoe's direction now, like there was any doubt who she was talking about — "smiled a dreamy smile."

Zoe choked on a laugh. "Please. I do not have a dreamy smile."

"You *so* have a dreamy smile. And that smile was saying to Parker, 'Oh yes, take me right now.' "

"You've hit your head again, right?" Zoe asked, reaching out to touch her sister's forehead as if checking for a fever.

Darcy grinned and smacked her hand away. "Fine, if you're going to be in denial, then you should know, Kel asked me to get you to go out with him."

Zoe blinked. "When did you have occasion to see the sheriff?"

"Worried?"

"Should I be?" Zoe countered, but hell yes she was worried. It hadn't been all that long ago when Darcy had been trouble-seeking, and she'd often found it. Kel was a patient man, and a very good man, and also extremely good looking, but — "Wait. Kel asked you to ask me out?"

"Took you long enough," Darcy said. "Ran into him at physical therapy, where he was sparring with AJ. And let me just say watching two really sexy, really hot guys go at it in the ring in the name of sport . . . Pretty damn sexy even if I think boxing is crazy."

"Focus, Darcy."

"Right," Darcy said, giving herself a visible shake. "Well, he heard that you were seeking blind dates, so —"

"Oh my God," Zoe said, and closed her eyes. "This is so embarrassing."

"And he wanted to know, if I set you up with him if it'd qualify for a blind date since you two know each other and all," Darcy went on. "And I said yep."

"You did not," Zoe said.

"I did. And he said Monday was his next free night, so . . ."

Zoe stared at Darcy. "I'm not going out with Kel."

"What's tripping you up, the fact that he's really good looking, or that he's also a great guy?" Darcy asked. "Or maybe it's that you do have a thing for Parker, after all."

Zoe took the fifth and held her silence. This didn't fool her sister.

"Aw," Darcy said. "It's door number two. You like him, you really like him." She said this in an annoying singsong voice. "You want to kiss him. You —" Suddenly she broke off and her mouth fell open. "Wait. Holy cow. You *already* kissed him?"

"I didn't say that!"

"It's true, you totally already kissed him," Darcy said in an accusatory voice. "You kissed him and didn't tell me?"

Zoe yanked down the sun visor and stared at herself in the small mirror there. "You can absolutely not tell that by just looking at me."

"Was it good?" Darcy dropped her voice to a conspiratorial whisper. "Are you sleeping with him?"

"No!" But she wanted to be . . . Oh God,

how she wanted those knowing hands on her. "Now you've gotta go away. I'm not making my snooping, meddling, eavesdropping sister any food right now." But then, because she loved Darcy every bit as much as she was driven to madness by her, Zoe softened. "But I'll make you breakfast this weekend. Bring AJ."

AJ was the man who'd helped bring Darcy back from the brink, and at just the mention of his name Darcy got a dreamy look on her face.

It made Zoe still for a beat and then yank down the mirror again. God. It was true! She had the same dopey expression on her face that her sister did. She immediately swiped it off, because she wasn't falling for Parker in the same way Darcy had fallen for AJ.

She absolutely refused to fall at all. "I mean it," she said. "Get out of my car. I'm going to be late for a lesson." She gave Darcy the *shoo* hands.

Darcy just looked at her, no longer being silly or pesty. "Just promise me one thing."

"At this point I'd promise you all the food in my fridge to stop talking and get out of my car."

"Promise me that if he's a good fit you won't chase him away or dump him because

148

he was breathing wrong or wanted to take a pole-dancing class," Darcy said.

This was a not-so-subtle reference to the time last year when Zoe had gone on a two-guy dating spree. The first one, Evan, had wanted her to take pole-dancing classes. Not with him but for him.

She'd declined.

The second guy, Mike, she'd seen a few times before calling things off. "He was a mouth breather, and a very loud one."

"You got scared," Darcy said.

No. Well, maybe. But while Mike had been nice and kind and even gainfully employed as a ranch manager, he hadn't been the right one for her — with or without the loud breathing.

"Zoe," Darcy said. "I'm not leaving this car until you promise."

Zoe crossed her fingers. "I promise."

"Good. Now uncross your fingers and say it again."

Dammit. Zoe uncrossed her fingers. "I won't chase Parker away or dump him because he's breathing wrong." Nope, in her heart she knew it wouldn't come to that. Because he'd be walking out the door far before she was ready for him to do so.

TWELVE

After Zoe had left for work, Parker got into the shower to wash off his run and several hours of slinging horse shit.

Oreo trotted into the bathroom behind him. The big dog liked to stick his head into the shower and slurp at the water. At first this had been disconcerting to say the least, but Oreo had turned out to be good company.

Still, Parker's thoughts didn't drift far from Zoe.

She wasn't a woman to trust easily, if at all. And up until today he'd have said no way did she trust him, not even a little.

But something had changed between them now that they'd shared. And then there was the way she looked at him, like maybe she was torn between wanting to run and wanting to kiss him again.

He could admit to being torn between the same two things.

There was chemistry, more than he'd expected. More than he'd felt in a very long time. But his leave was by no means a vacation, and now that Sharon had made him, his ass was on the line.

His job had been hard on more than one relationship, including the tenuous one with his family. His parents had never approved of his career, pretty much leaving him out of the loop of their world. He had Amory and that was about it. He didn't think about it much, but when he did, he consoled himself with the knowledge that he didn't have room for more, anyway. He was gone for long stretches at a time, sometimes without much warning, and he couldn't always tell people where he was.

What woman would deal with that in a man?

No woman he'd ever met. No one wanted to be in a relationship where she had to give such blind trust.

Especially not Zoe.

He knew that much all too well now that she'd told him about Kyle the Asshole. He dunked his head under the hot water, letting it beat down on his sore muscles. When the water turned cold, he got out, dressed, and went to the kitchen table with his laptop. There he studied the images he'd

151

taken with his camera from twelve thousand feet.

Putting his trust in the system wasn't easy, but he'd promised to lay low. In his mind, laying low equaled not being seen.

He had no intention of being seen. The area wouldn't be easy to watch in person. So he wouldn't do it in person. He'd set up motion detector cameras and rely on the feed. Because trusting the system was one thing. Letting Carver get away scot-free was another.

That wasn't going to happen. He'd seen some interesting things in the air with Zoe, one of them being a ranch that had piqued his interest. He went shopping for what he needed and made the three-hour drive up to Rocky Falls. It took longer to find Cat's Paw. He was going off the pics he'd taken, matched up to his GPS, and found the ranch he'd wanted to take a better look at.

He didn't get close, not wanting to be made. Instead, he left the car in the woods and went in on foot, avoiding the roads and clearings, managing to outmaneuver the few guards he caught sight of at the fence lining the ranch.

For a long time he just watched and realized there were only two goons. Though they were armed to the teeth, they were bored and spent a lot of time talking to each other instead of paying attention to their surroundings.

This left Parker free to stealthily place his equipment without getting caught. Which wasn't easy, as it involved a lot of tree climbing, and his ribs hurt like a bitch.

On the way home he made a stop at the county recorder's office to see who owned the land, but they were closed. He consoled himself with the knowledge that with the cameras in place, he could now watch what was going on at Cat's Paw.

He was supposed to meet Wyatt and Emily for dinner, but he went back to Zoe's place first to shower and change. It was six o'clock on the dot when he pulled into Zoe's driveway and parked next to a car he knew wasn't hers.

A guy got out at the same time as him.

Joe, from the airport.

He'd nearly forgotten her date with the guy. He'd told himself it was absolutely none of his business what she did with her free time. None at all.

He almost believed it, too.

Joe wore jeans and a polo shirt with the airport's logo on a pec. His sole concession to the night's date appeared to be that he'd tucked the work shirt partially in.

Joe nodded to Parker and they both headed up the walk. Joe stopped on the porch.

Parker didn't. *Look at that,* he thought with a grim smile. There was a benefit to not being The Date, after all. Resisting flashing Joe a smug smile, Parker let himself into the house and found Zoe in the kitchen eating French toast. It smelled so damn good that for a minute he completely forgot what he'd come in here to tell her and just inhaled the cinnamony, buttery scent of the room.

Zoe smelled good, too, like syrup, and she looked pretty fucking sexy in a white tank top and . . . well, he had no idea what else because Oreo was in her lap.

The chair appeared to be straining.

She fed Oreo a bite of French toast and met Parker's gaze. "Don't judge me," she said.

"Are you kidding? I'm about ready to steal that plate from you. It smells amazing."

"It's my secret ingredient."

He dropped his duffel bag on a chair. Playfully, he moved in behind her, scooped her hair away, and pressed his face to the nape of her neck to smell her. "Is the secret ingredient you?"

"No," she said, elbowing him with a laugh.

But goose bumps broke out on her skin and she shivered. He actually thought maybe she moaned, too, but that might have been him. Unable to help himself, he took another big sniff of her.

"Cinnamon," he said with a hungry sigh.

"Told you I could cook." Her voice sounded a little shaky as she dragged a piece on her plate through a river of syrup and stuffed it into her mouth. "It's just baking that keeps defying me. But no worries."

He grinned. "Because you've got this."

"Well, yeah." She smiled.

He stared at the gorgeous, resilient, tough-as-nails woman and felt a mixture of pride, hunger, lust, and, most surprisingly of all, affection.

"So what's that stuff?" she asked curiously, pointing to his opened duffel bag on the chair. Inside was the one extra camera he hadn't placed up at Cat's Paw.

"It's for surveillance."

"Like . . . a nanny cam?" she asked.

"Sort of. Except it's not a continuous feed. It doesn't roll until it detects motion. You can watch the feed from an app. I drove up to Cat's Paw and put some in play today."

"And you have a leftover camera."

"It's a spare. In case one malfunctions."

"Huh." She ran a finger over it. "Think I could borrow it?"

He stared at her as all sorts of really erotic thoughts vied for first place in his head. He wondered if they were on the same page.

"I've always wanted to put one here in the house to see what Oreo does all day long," she said.

Nope, he thought, laughing at himself. Not on the same page. Not in the same book. "He sleeps on the couch," Parker said. "He snores. He occasionally farts and wakes himself up. He trolls the kitchen in case the elves have brought him food and then he goes back to the couch. That's about it, but sure, have at it." He pulled the camera from the bag and set it on the table. "You'll need to load the app on your computer." He rattled it off, expecting her to say never mind, it was too complicated, but she didn't look intimidated in the least.

In fact, other than when she was attempting to bake, Zoe never looked intimidated at all. And damn if that wasn't attractive as hell.

She went back to her French toast, taking another bite before moaning.

And Parker went hard. "Damn, woman." He looked to the pan on the stovetop hopefully — yes, there was a God, because there were two more pieces in there. "Can I —"

The doorbell rang.

Oreo barked and farted.

Zoe rolled her eyes and pushed the dog off her lap. "Wonder who's here?"

"Oh yeah," Parker said. "It's your date."

She blinked and then her mouth opened in an *Oh!* of surprise.

Parker stared at her for a beat and then tipped his head back and laughed. He'd been feeling pissy about the date with Joe, and she'd not even remembered. "You really forgot?"

She put her hands on her hips and appeared to fight for words, which gave him a moment to take in the rest of her. Her hair was piled up on her head, but much of it had escaped, brushing her bare shoulders. She was wearing sweat bottoms that were way too big for her, but that was okay because they'd slid dangerously low on her hips, leaving a strip of her stomach bare.

She had a belly ring piercing, a twinkling pale blue crystal. He wanted to put his mouth to it. A little surprised at the force of the urge, he took a step back and shoved his hands into his pockets on the off chance they decided to act without his brain's permission and toss her down on the table so he could pillage.

"Shit," she said. "I really did forget." She blew out a breath and looked down at herself. "I've got to change. And also pretend I didn't just stuff my face."

Parker grinned.

Zoe pointed at him. "Shut it. And let him in?" she asked, heading to the stairs. "Tell him I'll be just a minute."

Parker eyed her hair. And the syrup drop on her left breast. "Maybe you should take two minutes. Or you know . . . more."

She made a sound of great exasperation and left. She raced up the stairs and slammed her bedroom door.

A beat later it whipped back open. "Hey!" she yelled down. "Why didn't a brick fall out of my fireplace?"

Parker, halfway to the front door, stopped and eyed the fireplace. A brick hadn't fallen out because he'd fixed it with one trip to the local hardware store for a mortar patch. But Ms. Prickly I've-Got-It wouldn't want to hear that. "A brick totally just fell out," he said.

There was a pause, and then she was at the top of the stairs, staring down at him. "You just lied to me."

"It was a white lie," he said. "And everyone knows white lies don't really count."

She blinked and then pointed at him.

"Stop fixing my life!"

He laughed. "This house is not your life."

The look on her face told him that he was wrong. She thought that the house was her life. "Hey," he said. "I —"

The doorbell rang again.

"Just get the door!" she said, and vanished.

Parker had to fight the urge to go up those stairs and make Zoe forget all about Joe. He could do it, too. This wasn't ego but fact. She looked at him every bit as much as he looked at her. But again, it was a massively bad idea so he opened the front door.

" 'Bout damn time." Joe stared and stopped at the sight of Parker. "Is this going to be awkward?"

"Not for me," Parker said, and gestured him in. "She's not quite ready."

Joe nodded and hunkered down before Oreo, who'd come into the living room behind Parker. "Hey, boy. Hey, buddy. What's your name?"

Oreo growled low in his throat and hid behind Parker's legs.

Joe pulled his hand back in. "No? We're not friends yet?"

"He's a rescue," Parker heard himself say. "He doesn't like men all that much."

Oreo poked his head around Parker's thigh and glared balefully up at Joe before licking Parker's hand.

Joe laughed a little. "So what does that make you?"

Parker ignored this and picked up the silly oaf, who weighed as much as a mountain.

Oreo set his big head on Parker's shoulder and sighed trustingly.

It was possibly the best thing that had happened to Parker all day. He loved dogs. He loved all animals. He'd certainly saved enough of them. But in his line of work, moving around as he did, being gone for weeks at a time on a case, he'd never gotten to have a pet of his own. He'd never realized how much that bothered him.

"Sorry I'm late," Zoe said, rushing down the stairs. She'd put on that same long, flowery old-lady dress as on Parker's first day, and for some reason Parker felt a whole lot better. Especially when he saw Joe's face.

Grinning, Parker said to Zoe, "A minute?"

"Oh," she said. "Um, sure." She followed him into the kitchen, twisting her hair up as she went.

She still smelled like syrup.

Parker did his best not to lean in and lick her like a Tootsie Pop.

"What is it?" she asked, smoothing down her dress. "Do I look okay?"

"Sure. If you're going to that bingo night

we talked about."

She stilled and stared at him, and then looked down at herself. "I just figured since this dress never went out on the date with the dentist that it was okay to wear again. Some people like this dress, you know."

He watched Oreo sniff at the dress, leaving a fairly significant drool stain. "You're absolutely right," he said. "You should wear that dress."

She glared at him. "You don't want me to look good on my date."

Give the woman a prize.

"I'll have you know that I wore this dress to Wyatt's birthday dinner last month and he liked it," she said defensively.

"Because he isn't interested in banging you."

She stared at him. "I *really* hate it when she's right."

"Who?"

"Darcy. Argh, I don't have time to change."

"Yes, you do." This was Joe's voice, coming through the double doors to the living room.

Zoe crossed to them and yanked them open, revealing Joe standing there, bent a little, like maybe he'd been peeking in the crack.

161

He straightened quickly, but apparently Zoe had bigger fish to fry. "You don't like the dress, either?" she demanded.

Joe hesitated.

"Well?"

He grimaced. "If I say no, are you going to back out of the date?"

"Do you want to bang me?" she asked instead of answering.

Joe's eyes slid to Parker. "Uh . . ."

"Oh, I'm sorry, is that a difficult question?" Zoe asked him.

Much as Parker was enjoying this, he was actually starting to feel a little sorry for Joe.

"Okay, yeah," Joe said manfully. "Sometimes I want to bang you. When you're not being mean."

Zoe sighed and picked up her purse from the table. "Let's just go."

"So . . . you're not changing?" Joe asked, a little crestfallen.

She narrowed her eyes at him.

"It's just that I really like your jeans," Joe said. "Especially the ones that kinda slide down a little bit when you bend over. Maybe you could —"

"We leave right now or not at all," she said.

Joe blew out a breath and gestured her out ahead of him.

Zoe started to go and then glanced back

at Parker, her expression a little . . . regretful?

No, that couldn't be right. And besides, why would she feel bad about leaving him behind? They had no dating in their future, and he would be leaving soon enough, going back to his fast-paced, crazy world. He smiled at her. "Don't drink and drive," he said. "Use your seat belts, and text if you're going to be out past curfew."

Worked like a charm. The regret vanished from her eyes as she turned away, flipping him off behind her back as she left.

Thirteen

Parker had laughed at Zoe's good-night finger gesture, but once she'd left, the house seemed . . . quiet. Empty of its life force. At his feet, Oreo plopped to the floor and huffed out a crestfallen sigh, setting his head on Parker's foot with a thunk.

Oreo clearly felt the same way.

Parker cheered them both up with the leftover French toast. Then he opened his laptop to check the cameras, even though if he'd caught any action, he'd have been alerted via his cell phone.

Nothing. No action at all.

Giving up for the night, he took Oreo out to do his business, stopping short at the end of the driveway when he heard the sounds of someone crying softly. Turning, he peered through the dark and found a little girl sitting on the next door porch.

She couldn't have been more than five. Her dark hair was long and crazy wild around her face. Her eyes were dark and drenched with tears, and the sight stabbed him right in the heart.

She looked so much like his sister Amory had at that age: sweet, guileless, and able to take down grown men with a single devastatingly vulnerable gaze.

Shit.

Don't do it, man. Just keep walking.

Instead he moved to the edge of Zoe's property line and called out to her. "Hey, you okay?"

She just cried harder. The front door opened behind her and a woman stepped out into the pool of light created by the porch lantern hanging above them. "Kaylie," she said with obvious relief. "There you are — Oh honey, I told you we couldn't keep them when Socks came up pregnant. One cat, baby, that's all we can handle right now."

"But the babies, Mama," Kaylie cried. "The babies are so cute."

The woman looked up and saw Parker standing there. "Are you a friend of Zoe's, or do I need to call the police because you're stealing Oreo?"

Oreo stopped anointing every single bush lining the driveway and sat on Parker's feet. Parker patted the dog's big head. "Friend," he said. "Parker James."

The woman looked at Oreo.

Oreo leaned on Parker, nearly knocking him over, and the woman laughed. "Okay, so you *are* a friend. I'm Manda. Can I help you with something?"

"I heard crying," Parker said. "Just wanted to make sure she was okay."

"I'm not okay!" Kaylie sobbed. "I don't want the kittens to go! They're not ready, Mama!"

Manda sighed and crouched low by her daughter. "When you found Socks in the yard a few months ago, I let you keep her on one condition. Do you remember that condition?"

"No more strays," Kaylie said. "But —"

"No *but*s," Manda said gently but firmly. "You've had six weeks with the two kittens, baby. They're old enough to be adopted at the humane society."

Kaylie sniffled noisily, still clutching the kittens. "But how will we know if they go to good homes?"

Parker remembered the sign he'd seen at the animal center where Wyatt worked. "There's a kitten adoption next Saturday at Belle Haven," he said.

Manda shook her head. "I can't keep them another week."

"Mama!"

"I'm sorry, Kaylie, but when the gray kitten climbed into the venting system yesterday, I lost the whole day of work. They're too rowdy."

Parker looked into Kaylie's wet eyes and felt his heart roll over in his chest and expose its tender underbelly. "I can keep them until adoption day," he said.

Kaylie immediately stopped crying and smiled brightly. "And then I can come visit them!"

"You don't have to do this," Manda told Parker.

"Mama, he already said he would!"

"You don't," Manda repeated to Parker.

"It's okay," he said, and channeled his inner Zoe. "I've got this."

Twenty minutes later he was the proud new temporary owner of a gray girl kitten and an orange tabby boy kitten, and a bag of supplies. The both of them could easily fit into the palm of one of his hands and maybe weighed half a pound soaking wet.

They immediately set to exploring their new world, both getting stuck behind the TV shelf in the living room in less than three minutes.

Parker rescued them and set them up in the bathroom to corral them. Oreo whined to get in but when Parker opened the door, Oreo took one look and took off. Parker snapped a few pics of the kittens and texted them to Amory, who immediately called him.

"I want one!" she yelled enthusiastically into the phone.

Balancing the kittens in his lap, he laughed at the sound of her voice, happy to have something take his mind off Zoe, who was still out on her damn date. "You know Mom and Dad would kill me."

"I turned eighteen last month. I get to make my own decisions now."

"I know," he said. "And I'm happy for you." He'd hoped she would take the opportunity to stretch her wings a little. Maybe get out more, travel — albeit very carefully — something, anything, to expand the four walls of her life.

"Henry wants a kitten, too," she said.

Henry had been her best friend since the fifth grade. He had Down syndrome as well and worked at the Home Depot right next to the florist where Amory worked. They spent a lot of time together and for the past few years Amory had referred to Henry as her boyfriend. Lately she'd made noises about wanting to marry him.

Parker wasn't sure she understood the

meaning of being married, but regardless, there was no way he wanted to see her go from being under their parents' thumb to being married. He wanted so much more for her, wanted her to get out and see the big world and all that was out there for her.

But he was alone in this. Their parents, Lowell and Tess James, had always been severely overprotective with their younger child, sheltering Amory from everything. Including him.

"These kittens are a long way from Arizona," Parker told her. "How's it going? What are you up to?" he asked, trying to get her off the subject of the kittens. The last thing he needed was to further alienate his parents by giving his sister a pet. "How's school?"

She was in a year-round school. The current plan was to keep Amory enrolled until she could get her GED. After that, she hoped to graduate from cleanup girl at the florist shop to actually making floral arrangements.

"School is stupid," Amory said. "But work's good. They let me make an arrangement last week!"

"Yeah?" he asked, smiling at her excitement. In his world, he often operated from a place where he was knee deep in the garbage of the world. Amory had always been his happy spot. This past week he'd added Zoe and Oreo, and now a pack of two kittens to that happy spot. Look at him, expanding his world without getting on a plane to do it . . .

"I made it for Tiffany," Amory said. "She works at the rec center. It was her birthday and I got to put it together all by myself!"

Parker could practically hear her beaming. "That's great, Am. Did you go on that rec-center-sponsored camping trip last weekend?"

"No," she said. "I had a cold. Mom thought I should stay home."

Parker rubbed the tension between his eyes. "I'm sorry to hear that. I know how you wanted to sleep under the stars and stay up late, and go on that full moon hike."

"It's okay. I mean, I'm sorry I didn't get to go. I know you paid for the trip, but me and Henry got to sit in the backyard. Mom made us hot chocolate."

"How's Henry?"

"Great! He got moved from the gardening department to *inside*! He gets to sweep the store every night before it closes! The whole store! He's got the best job ever. So when will you bring me a kitty?"

Parker wanted her to get everything her

heart desired. She deserved it, but he wasn't going home again anytime soon, and when he did, he wouldn't bring her a kitten unless it was parent-approved, which it wouldn't be.

"Please, Parker?" she asked. "Please come to see me. It's been like a year."

"It's been two weeks," he said with a laugh. He'd slipped into town and visited her at work, and then vanished again like smoke just before coming to Idaho. Although, granted, it had been six months before that since his last visit.

The truth was, his parents made visiting difficult and uncomfortable, and selfishly he let that keep him away from Amory. He'd have loved to show her the world in person instead of through pictures, but that wasn't going to happen. For years their parents had said she was too young, but more recently, after he'd brought danger to their front door, the subject had been dropped completely.

And he got it. He got it all too well. It had been a year since someone — Parker suspected Carver — had shown up on his parents' doorstep asking for Parker.

With a gun.

The police had never figured out who it was, and it hadn't happened again, but it was yet another reason to stay away. Zoe might call him Mr. Mysterious, but the truth was he was just extremely cautious. Borderline OCD cautious. He had to be.

He got that it kept people from getting too close to him, that it was a big turnoff to Zoe and just one more reason not to get involved.

But he'd already opened up to her much more than he should have, certainly more than he'd ever intended. More than he'd ever done with another woman.

"I've texted you every day, Amory," he reminded her.

"Not the same thing, Parker!" she said, imitating his tone and making him smile. "Oh!" she said suddenly. "I can do a free throw now, just like you taught me! You need to come see it!"

His chest ached at the beseeching tone in her voice. She missed him. Yeah, she had Mom and Dad, but they'd continued to hold the reins just a little too tight. Their hearts were in the right place and they operated from fear for her, that she'd get hurt or worse, with absolutely zero intentions of abuse or neglect, but Amory was starting to chafe under their constant supervision.

Or at least Parker would be chafing. Hell, he'd be going insane by now. "I'll come by soon as I can," he promised.

"Today?"

"No," he said, wincing when she let out a sound of distress.

"Tomorrow?" she asked.

"Soon as I wrap up this thing at work I've got going on, okay?"

"But that could be a very long time," she said. "Right?"

"Right," he said. "But hopefully not."

"But maybe!"

He sighed. Amory didn't have a good sense of time; she never had. Last year he'd bought her an iPhone and had taught her how to schedule in all her work shifts and anything else important so that she wouldn't miss anything.

She'd put in her entire life on that calendar, and his. She was forever texting him asking about his upcoming appointments so that she could program them into her calendar. "Maybe," he conceded. "I'll tell you when ahead of time and you can put it on your phone then. You'll be the first person I come see, okay?"

"Promise?" she asked.

"Promise."

"Pinkie-swear and hope to die?" she pressed.

"Never hope to die, Amory."

"It's a saying! And it means you have to keep your promise!"

"Fine." He caved with her. He always did. "Pinkie-swear and hope to die," he said dutifully, wincing again at the happy squeal that nearly pierced his eardrums. "Gotta go, Am."

"Love you, Parker."

"Love you back."

"See you next week!" she yelled.

"Am —"

But she was already gone. Parker slid his phone away, the movement causing the kittens to get a second wind, mewling and climbing on top of each other to try to get up his body. He set them back on the floor, where they immediately once again began to try to crawl up his legs.

With their claws.

He nabbed one in each hand before calling Oreo back in.

Oreo came sliding into the bathroom, panting in happiness at being needed. At the sight of the kittens still there, he suddenly stopped short, skidding on the linoleum, eyes wide in terror even though they were smaller than his paws.

"They're just silly little babies," he told Oreo.

He whined unhappily and tucked his tail

between his legs.

"They're not going to hurt you," Parker said, and set the kittens down in front of him to sniff. "See? Harmless."

The tabby stalked underneath a mistrustful Oreo and stopped between the dog's legs, eyeing the long tail with a curious eye. Then the kitten crouched low, wriggled his butt, and . . . *pounced.*

And missed Oreo's tail by a mile.

Still, Oreo cried.

"It's okay," Parker said. "I promise they're not going to hurt you —"

Too late. Because Oreo lifted his leg and . . . peed on them.

FOURTEEN

A half hour later, Parker had bathed the kittens and calmed Oreo down with a big bowl of food and some hugs, and the four of them were trying the meet-and-greet thing again.

Oreo lay on the floor, still wide-eyed but allowing the kittens to crawl all over him. The gray one climbed up the big dog like Oreo was Mt. Everest, ending up on top of his head.

Oreo's eyes rolled up and they eyeballed each other, scaredy-cat dog and mountain-conquering, fearless kitten.

Parker's cell rang. "You forget dinner?" Wyatt asked.

Shit. "Yeah," he said, "sorry."

"No problem. Hightail your ass to the bar and grill; we'll meet you there."

"Which bar and grill?"

"The only one in town — Pete's."

Parker trusted Oreo with the kittens but

he didn't trust the kittens with Oreo, so he set the two troublemakers up in the bathroom with kitty litter, water, and food, and shut them in. "There," he said to Oreo, who was watching from the hallway. "You'll be perfectly safe until I get back."

Oreo yawned, and Parker patted him on the head before heading out.

At Pete's, Wyatt introduced the beautiful brunette standing next to him as Emily, his fiancée. The three of them sat and shared a pitcher of beer, Emily listening in avid fascination as Parker and Wyatt told stories.

"Remember our bar brawl in college?" Wyatt asked.

Emily gasped. "Bar brawl?"

"Not our fault," Wyatt told her. "We were jumped."

"How could I forget?" Parker asked. They'd been jumped because Wyatt had smiled at the wrong girl. "I still have the scar." He ran a finger along his left eyebrow, which the scar bisected.

Wyatt grinned. "Good times."

"How about on your twenty-second birthday?" Parker asked. "When you decided to give everyone free shots from the bar, started a wet T-shirt contest, and got us both shit-canned."

Emily stared at her fiancé. "You started a

wet T-shirt contest?"

"Yep," Parker answered for him.

"Thanks, man," Wyatt said. And then to Emily, "You heard the part where I was twenty-two, right?"

Emily smacked him upside the head. "That was for the twenty-two-year-old girls."

Parker laughed. It felt good to do so. He'd been so busy for so long he couldn't even remember the last time he'd done this. Had fun. Relaxed.

They ordered food, and when they started eating, the talk turned to Parker's stint in Sunshine.

"I'm so sorry you couldn't stay with us," Emily said. "My sister's just back from her honeymoon and they're in our only spare bedroom."

"No worries," Parker said. "Zoe's house is great."

"And Zoe?" Wyatt asked.

Parker smiled. "Just as you described her."

Wyatt grimaced. "Uh-oh."

Emily smacked Wyatt on the arm. "How did you describe her? As warm and caring and lovely as she really is, right?"

Wyatt slid a look to Parker. "Right."

Emily narrowed her eyes on her fiancé, and it was fascinating to watch Wyatt grin at her with unabashed love and affection as he leaned in and kissed her on the end of her nose. And then her mouth. "Don't look at me like that, sweetness," he murmured. "Zoe's all of those great things on the inside, but we both know she's stubborn as hell and easily irritated on the outside."

Parker laughed at the accurate description. "No worries, it's been great."

Wyatt did a double take. "Great?"

Shit. Redirect. "Have you had her French toast?" Parker asked.

"She made you French toast?" Wyatt asked. "She won't make it whenever I ask, says if she did then I wouldn't appreciate it as much."

"I only got her leftovers," Parker said, hopefully coming across as harmless. Because that was what he intended to be — completely harmless.

Sure, he'd never been harmless a day in his life, but there was a first time for everything.

"Where is she tonight?" Wyatt asked. "I thought she'd come with you."

"She's on a date."

"Oh yeah," Emily said. "With that really good-looking dentist from Hennessey Flats."

When Wyatt looked at her, she laughed.

"Hey, I'm engaged, not dead," she said. "I Googled him because Zoe refused to do so. I wanted to make sure he wasn't a wanted felon or anything."

"Tonight's date isn't with the dentist," Parker said, leaving out the part where she got stood up. That was Zoe's tale to tell. "It's Joe."

Wyatt choked on his beer. "Joe, the airport manager Joe? What the hell is she doing out with that horndog?"

Back at the house, Parker had managed to shelve his frustration about the date. For one thing, Zoe hadn't dressed like a woman planning on getting any action. And for another, he'd sensed absolutely zero chemistry between her and Joe.

But after Wyatt's comment, he realized it didn't mean that Joe wouldn't try . . .

Fuck. He stood up and tossed some money down on the table. "Gotta go."

Wyatt narrowed his eyes. "Gotta go where?"

"Work," Parker said.

"At . . ." Wyatt looked at his watch. "Nine o'clock at night?"

"My job's twenty-four-seven."

Wyatt cocked his head. "You're on vacation."

Shit. "It's a working vacation, as it turns out."

Wyatt only stared at him, but Emily laughed. When she realized Wyatt wasn't amused, she nudged him. "Wyatt Stone, he's your friend and a good man. Be happy for them."

"Whoa," Parker said with sudden understanding. "There's nothing going on between me and Zo—"

"Why, don't you think she's good enough for you?" Wyatt asked.

"No — I mean yes!" Jesus, Parker was starting to sweat. "She's . . . amazing. I just meant we're not going anywhere with anything. We're not . . ."

Emily patted him on the hand. "It's okay," she said, still smiling. "You're going to survive this. Tell him, Wyatt. Tell him he'll survive it."

Wyatt just continued to stare at Parker.

"Would you rather she end up with Joe?" Emily asked Wyatt. "Or some dentist?"

Wyatt grimaced and scrubbed his hands down his face. "I'm half tempted to let him go storming into her date," he muttered. "But knowing Zoe, she'd marry Joe just to spite me."

"I'm telling you, it's not like that," Parker said again. And Christ, now he was protesting too much.

"Just sit," Wyatt said looking resigned. "Because trust me, I'm doing you a favor stopping you from going after her tonight. If you bust open her date, she'll bust your chops. Zoe likes to make her mistakes on her own. No one can tell her what to do."

Emily beamed at Wyatt. "Aw. You're so sweet."

Parker sighed and sat back down.

And then to prove a point to all of them — especially himself — he stayed out as late as possible so he wouldn't have to see Zoe return from her date and possibly invite Joe in and upstairs to her room.

Or not return at all.

He wasn't sure which would be worse.

When he finally pulled up to the house, it was dark and still. He looked at his phone.

Midnight.

Damn . . . The implication of Cinderella not being home wasn't wasted on him. He heaved himself out of the vehicle and headed up the walk.

He let himself in and out of habit did a quick search of his surroundings.

Definitely alone.

Halfway back through the living room toward the kitchen, he became aware that someone was watching him. Reaching for the gun tucked into the back of his jeans was second nature.

So was checking his surroundings without looking obvious. He heard a sound on the other side of the front door, but either his instincts were seriously off or he was just that fucked up in the head at the moment because he didn't check the peephole before whipping the door open.

He had a flash of Joe pulling back from Zoe, who fell backward into Parker's arms. He shoved the gun into the back of his pants and gripped her arms until she gained her balance.

He was ridiculously happy to see her because if she was here, it meant she was not in Joe's bed.

Joe stood facing them both. Clearly Parker had just interrupted something because the guy was looking frustrated and Zoe was looking . . . relieved?

"Well," she said quickly, flashing her fake smile — yes, Parker knew each and every one of her smiles and this one, the brittle fake one aimed at the man who had clearly just pressed her up against the door to kiss her, was most definitely Parker's new favorite.

"Thanks for opening the door for me, Parker," she said brightly. "Night, Joe!"

"But —" Joe started, taking a step toward her.

Zoe backed farther into Parker, forcing him to take a step into the house or have them both fall to their asses. She waved at Joe and . . . slammed the door.

Parker laughed. "Good to know you do that to every guy and not just me."

Zoe whirled around to face him, her eyes a little wild as she put her hands on her hips. "What was that?"

"You slamming the door on yet another man's nose?"

"Not that." She gave him a look that said she was contemplating trying to kick his ass. She wouldn't be able to, not even close, but it would be fun to have her try . . . Not that he was stupid enough to say so.

"You followed me," she accused without preamble. "You followed me on my date."

"What are you talking about?"

"We were at the bar when you got there," she said. "What the hell was that about? Why would you follow me?"

Like he was so hard up he'd actually follow her on purpose?

Shit, okay, yes, he was totally that hard up. "I didn't follow you. I was meeting Wyatt and Emily for a late dinner."

At this, she made a sound that conveyed

volumes on what she thought of him regardless. "If you saw us, why didn't you stop by and say hi?" he asked, putting the ball back in her court.

She crossed her arms. "Because . . . because it was a date," she said. "I didn't need to hang out with my brother on a date."

Or you, were the unspoken words.

"How did it go with Joe?" he asked, wondering if he was a complete ass for hoping it had sucked.

She didn't answer. Which meant it hadn't gone well. He tried to feel bad about that but he didn't. Not even a little bit. "We made it an early night," she said.

"Because of your dress?"

"Oh my God," she snapped and brushed past him, shoulder-checking him as she went through the living room ahead of him. "You're impossible. I don't know why I even try to have a conversation with you."

He had no idea, either. He was a complete asshole.

"What was that in your hand when you opened the door?" she asked.

"My hand?"

"You tucked something into the back of your jeans," she said. "Was it . . . a gun?"

"I don't know what you're talking about."

She rolled her eyes, pissed at the world and most definitely him, too. She stalked off.

Then suddenly she stopped short, stared down at her feet for a beat, and then turned back. She came toe to toe with him, hands on her hips, to stare at him.

He met her gaze. She was clearly seriously ticked, and since he had some strong self-preservation instincts, he held his silence.

Finally, she sighed. "Listen," she said. "I need to do something. Like, to you."

"Should I be worried?"

"Just go with it." And she fisted her hands in his shirt, hauled him down to her level, and kissed him.

WTF, his brain said. *Oh yeah,* his body said, taking all of one nanosecond to get on board. Somehow he managed to hold himself perfectly still because this was her show. But Christ, she'd taken him straight to heaven, pressing her soft, beautiful body in close, murmuring something that sounded like, "Dammit, no man should smell so good, ever . . ." before deepening the connection and kissing the living daylights out of him.

He moved then; he couldn't help it. His arms came around her, one of his palms sliding to the nape of her neck to hold her in place. The kiss detonated: a hot, intense tangle of tongues and teeth, one of those raw hot kisses that was so real, so in the moment that he lost every single thought in his head. Well, except one, which was *Holy shit hotness, Batman.* "Zoe," he heard himself growl, and in response she shivered in his arms and tightened her grip on him before slowly pulling back. "What?" he managed to ask.

"Your phone's ringing."

He hadn't even noticed. He was hard as a rock and yep, his phone was indeed ringing, although not as loudly as they were both breathing. Pulling back, he glanced down at the ID screen just as the phone stopped ringing. He'd missed a call from Amory. He blew out a breath and met Zoe's gaze.

"You get a lot of calls," she said. "From women."

He could have told her Sharon was his boss and Amory his sister, but he didn't. For one, his equilibrium was off and he never dealt with that well. And maybe it would be best if she thought he was a player. No way would she fall for a player.

His own personal insurance policy.

He always kept his worlds all carefully compartmentalized, each division in its own little box. His family and all that went with them in one box. Work in another.

He needed a whole new box for Zoe . . .

She took a step back from him. "Not that I'm keeping track or anything," she said. "Your life's your life. The three W's and all that, right?"

He suddenly wished he'd kept his mouth shut about the three W's. "Why did you kiss me?" he asked, his voice unintentionally thick and husky.

"I was trying to figure something out."

"Yeah? And what was that?"

She stared at him and slowly shook her head. "Never mind. My fault. I muddied the waters." She started to walk away and then turned back. "No, you know what? This is all *your* fault. You and your stupid sexy smile."

"Wait — What's all my fault?"

She blew out a breath. "Everything!"

"Perfect," he said. "Thanks for clearing that up for me."

"Hmph," she said, and vanished upstairs.

FIFTEEN

Zoe lectured herself through her nighttime routine. That was stupid. Stupid, stupid, stupid . . . Kissing him had been so stupid. Because she'd started out in perfect control but he'd wrenched that from her with ease as he'd taken over her kiss . . . God.

What had she been thinking?

Nope, scratch that. She knew exactly what she'd been thinking, that she'd needed to compare Joe's perfectly nice — and very short — kiss to Parker's perfectly *not*-nice kiss. Granted, Parker's kisses were a lot of things — panty-melting, heart-attack-inducing, sensually charged among them — but "nice" wasn't one of them.

And she'd been very glad for that.

She went straight to bed and lay there, absolutely refusing to relive the feeling of being in Parker's arms or having his mouth on hers. She was over that and over him.

She was trying so hard to get that life she

wanted, and it didn't include falling for the likes of the mysterious Parker James — a man she couldn't read, couldn't boss around, couldn't walk all over.

Couldn't anything.

Well, except kiss him, as it turned out. She seemed to manage *that* feat just fine.

But he wasn't for the likes of her. His job was dark, his life was dark, and in spite of all the things he'd told her she was pretty sure he had a few more secrets up his sleeve. But one thing that wasn't a secret was that he would leave. He'd walk away and go off to his next adventure, and she didn't see him looking back.

Which was fine. Totally fine. It just meant she needed to move on, too, because otherwise he was dangerous to her mental health. The three W's were one thing when she didn't care so much.

But not so good when she did.

And she did . . .

She purposely turned her mind to other things. The date tonight with Joe had been both enlightening and interesting.

He'd told her he was going to buy the FBO from the parent company and wanted to know if she wanted in. He wanted her as a business partner.

She'd have to buy in and that would take

more loans, but she'd have a stake in the business, one that was profitable right now and by all indications planning on staying that way.

And yet she hesitated. It was a big step, a huge commitment . . .

So what was holding her up? Not anything she wanted to admit out loud, but the truth was that while she talked a big game of settling down, her vagabond early years had stuck with her. If she was a partner, she wouldn't be able to take off on a whim and go . . .

And again, where are you going? You love Sunshine. Everything you want is here and you get the wanderlust fix by the very nature of your job . . .

She sighed and gave up, kicking off the covers to pad downstairs to find something to eat. What she found was Oreo, paws up on the counter, licking the tile, snuffling as he made his way along the length of it from sink to the toaster.

"Oreo!" she said, horrified.

Not looking all that sorry, he got down and slunk to his bed. She stared at him. "The other day an entire loaf of cinnamon bread went missing. Was that you?"

Oreo crossed his paws, set his head on them, and closed his eyes.

"You're a big faker," she said.

He huffed out a sigh.

Zoe made herself a small plate of cheese and crackers. Relenting, she shared it with Oreo and went back upstairs.

On her nightstand, her phone buzzed an incoming text from Kel.

You up?

She stared at the phone and debated with herself. On the one hand, she'd made a promise to herself to go out and have fun dating. On the other hand, the man she wanted to date wasn't exactly available beyond his "vacation."

Which meant chin up, she needed to move on.

She texted back: The answer is yes.

There was a pause and then Kel's response. Is that a blanket yes, because that could cover a lot of ground?

There in the dark, she laughed. And laughing was good, right? She thumbed her response: Just the date for now.

When her phone buzzed again she was expecting more from Kel, but it was her brother asking how she was doing. She responded that she was good because she'd long ago learned that if she said *great,* Wyatt would call bullshit — and in this case he'd be right. But if she said *shitty,* he'd come over and demand to know what was wrong.

Two seconds later he responded. Saw Parker tonight. Something going on?

Damn. She loved Wyatt more than she loved just about anyone with the exception of Oreo and — sometimes — Darcy, but her brother had a nose for sniffing out when she was troubled.

And Lord was she troubled at the moment. Not that she was ready to share *that,* so she thumbed in an innocent: Like what?

Wyatt's answer was simple. Shit, Zoe.

Yep, she was in deep shit. And she had no idea how to explain. Maybe she should have Parker tell Wyatt what was going on between them.

Hell, maybe she should have Parker explain it to *her.*

She took a moment to imagine that. Parker seemed more like a "show, don't tell" sort of guy, so naturally it would be a very hands-on explanation. Hands on, clothes off . . .

A moment later she had to physically shake herself out of the fantasy. A little hot and bothered, she texted Wyatt back. No worries, I've got this.

Wyatt's response didn't take long: Of

course you do . . .

She closed her eyes and then woke up what seemed only moments later, discombobulated. The color of the sky outside her window suggested she'd slept for a few hours at least, since dawn was arriving. She sat up, rubbed her eyes, and then stilled at the odd noise that sounded like . . . kittens crying? Shaking her head at herself, she rolled over and smiled at Oreo. "Kittens," she said with a laugh. "As if. You're terrified of cats."

She flopped back and closed her eyes again, and woke up at her usual seven o'clock. Sitting up, she looked at the other side of the bed, where Oreo usually was stretched out snoring and hogging the covers.

No Oreo.

Confused, she tossed back the covers. "Oreo?" He never got out of bed before her; the lazy lug could sleep all day. Chilly, she grabbed her blanket, wrapped it around herself, and staggered down the stairs and into the kitchen, where she stopped short.

Parker was in one of the chairs, Oreo sitting at attention at his side, the both of them staring down at what Parker held in his lap.

Two wriggling, mewling kittens.

Dog and man looked up at her in unison.

Dog smiled.

So did the man. Parker's gaze made her heat up from the inside out. She could stare at him all day, at that latent energy, the lean muscles, the smile . . . Of course he wasn't exactly the sweet, gentle sort of man she'd dreamed about, but then again, he was holding kittens — *Wait.* "Why are there kittens in my kitchen?" she asked.

"Interesting hair," Parker said.

Good. This was good because it was a sharp reminder that he was not sweet or gentle at all. Period. But she still reached up and felt her hair. Yep, definite bed head. Yikes. Possibly when he'd said "interesting hair," he'd actually been sweet and gentle there for a second.

And had she taken the time to remove her mascara last night? She glanced at her reflection off her toaster. Nope. She had raccoon eyes. She was quite the catch. "Don't change the subject," she said.

"I wasn't aware we were in the middle of a conversation."

"You have two kittens in your lap," she said. Except they weren't in his lap. They were climbing up his chest. One, an adorable gray ball of fluff, had made it to his shoulder and stopped to lick his ear.

Zoe understood that. She wouldn't mind

doing the same.

The orange tabby one leapt off Parker and landed on top of Oreo.

One-hundred-plus pounds of Bernese mountain dog froze in place while the kitten nonchalantly padded along the dog's back and sat on top of his head.

Oreo blinked, and the kitten leaned forward and batted his nose.

Parker laughed, grabbed the kitten by the scruff of its neck, and set it back in his lap. "Stop terrorizing the poor dog."

"He doesn't like cats," Zoe said, and then shut up in shock when Oreo leaned in and licked the kitten's face, leaving it drenched.

"Mew," the kitten said, staring up at Oreo adoringly.

"Woof," Oreo said softly. Gently. And then nosed the kitten, who fell over in Parker's lap and exposed its belly.

Oreo licked that, too.

And then the sound of little kitty purrs filled the room.

Zoe was boggled. "Okay, someone needs to explain what's going on here."

Oreo looked at Parker.

Parker snorted and met Zoe's gaze. "The cute little girl next door has big eyes and was crying over the kittens she wasn't allowed to keep. And, apparently, I'm a sucker."

"For big eyes or crying girls or kittens?" she asked.

"All of the above."

Dammit. That was sweet and gentle, too. But this thought took a backseat to the realization that he hadn't shaved and had stubble on his jaw. She wanted to feel it on her skin.

Everywhere.

And then he rubbed his hand over that jaw and the ensuing scraping sound made her good parts quiver. "So you're just a closet softie?" she asked dubiously, and damn she sounded all breathless.

"No." One corner of his mouth quirked as if he knew where her mind had gone. "Well, maybe a little," he said. "Don't tell."

He was teasing her. Because no way was he a softie, in any sense of the world.

And yet the proof was crawling all over him.

"One of my rules was no pets," she reminded him, having to fight the urge not to pick up the adorable gray kitty.

"Actually," Parker said, "you said no dogs."

Crap. He was right. Since when was everyone but her right? "What are their names?"

Parker shook his head. "Kaylie didn't

name them; her mom wouldn't let her because she wasn't going to be allowed to keep them."

She looked down at their adorableness. Manda was a sharp woman. Zoe wouldn't name them either or there was no way she'd be able to get rid of them. "What are you going to do about them?"

The gray kitten had been chewing on one of Parker's fingers, her entire body fitting in his big hand. He stroked her tiny head with his thumb, her rumbling purr filling the room.

Zoe's ovaries actually ached.

"I'm going to get them adopted at Belle Haven's adoption clinic next Saturday," Parker said.

Okay, so that was a good plan, and he was a good guy for helping out Manda and Kaylie, both of whom could use the help. But why was it that every single time Parker not only toed her line but stepped over it, she liked him even more? How ridiculous was that? What was her problem? All she needed to do was remember the things about him that drove her crazy and she'd be okay. Her heart would stay safe.

Still holding one of the kittens, he leaned over and kissed Oreo right on the tip of his nose.

Oh, for God's sake. How the hell was she supposed to keep her heart safe when he was nice to her silly dog *and* he saved kittens *and* he fixed the things in her house that were broken while pretending not to in order to save her own damn pride?

He sat there, rumpled from sleep, like maybe he, too, had just rolled out of bed, seeming very comfortable in her kitchen.

Like maybe he belonged there.

And then there was the fact that all he had on was a pair of sweats, dangerously low slung and showing off his abs and those sexy cut muscles on his lean hips, the ones that made women stupid with lust . . .

And never mind his eyes and how they seemed to heat when he looked at her. She'd never experienced anything like it, really. She'd enjoyed the men she'd been with and knew they'd enjoyed her back, but not a single one of them had even looked at her like Parker did. "You knew what I meant regarding the no-animals thing," she said. "You keep breaking the rules on purpose."

He smiled a little to himself at that and gently set the kittens on the floor, where they immediately cuddled up to Oreo.

Then he stood up and stepped into Zoe. "Not true. You only had two rules, the other one being no overnight guests. Haven't broken that one."

She took a step back and found herself up against the counter.

He set hands on the tile on either side of her hips and dipped a little to look into her eyes. "You've got a lot of rules."

"For good reason," she managed, trying not to stare at his mouth and failing miserably. His lips were somehow both firm and soft, and he always tasted good. So yeah . . .

At her scrutiny, those sexy lips curved. "I bet you have all sorts of rules in bed, too," he said.

She had no idea how in the world he managed it, but with him she always felt a whole lot aroused and just a little bit pissy at the same time. It was a special talent of his.

"Yeah," he said, sounding amused and not at all surprised. "You do. You have rules in bed."

"I don't." She hesitated. "Well, maybe a few," she admitted. Hey, it was just common sense to have rules.

He laughed softly, the sound sliding through her belly and heading directly south. *Dammit.*

"Maybe that's why your dates aren't working out," he said.

"My dates are working out just fine, thank you."

"Yeah?" he asked. "Did you get laid last night?"

She squirmed. Joe had made it clear that sex was absolutely on the table and up for discussion. She'd made it just as clear that it wasn't going to happen.

But she did want to be with someone. She wanted that quite badly. Just not with Joe.

Parker grinned. "I rest my case."

"Hey," she said. "I could have . . . with Joe. If I'd wanted to." But the amused doubt on Parker's face really did her in. "I could call him back right now even," she said.

He slid his gaze over her blanket — The Little Mermaid — from her head to the tips of her toes and smirked.

"Well, I wouldn't be in this blanket," she said. "I'd change. And not into the bingo dress, either. I'm retiring the bingo dress."

"What have you got instead?"

"Plenty," she reported. "I have a little black dress, for one."

"Yeah," he said. "That and some fuck-me pumps would do it. You've got great legs."

She did her best not to flush with pleasure because she did not care one bit that he liked her legs. Correction: She didn't *want* to care. "It's not *all* about physical attraction," she said.

"No kidding," he said with a self-

201

deprecating laugh as he looked her over again.

She narrowed her eyes. "And what's *that* supposed to mean?"

"Babe, you're covered in that blanket from head to toe, and I bet beneath it your pj's are flannel and baggy. That should be a turnoff but I'm not even close to being turned off."

She stopped breathing. "You're not?"

"Nope." He lowered his head so that his breath warmed her neck. He stayed still for a beat, ratcheting up the anticipation within her so tight that when he finally spoke, just the brush of his lips moving against her throat made her damp.

"Back to your bedroom rules," he murmured.

She huffed out a laugh that sounded nervous even to her own ears. Probably because she suddenly was.

And unbalanced.

So very, very unbalanced.

To try to ground herself she leaned into his solid chest.

"Tell me one," he said, those lips of his still ghosting over her throat with each syllable. "Slowly and in great detail."

She stopped a helpless moan from escaping. "No."

He rubbed his jaw to hers like he was a cat, a big, sleek cat. "Want me to guess?" he asked.

She meant to give him a shove, but her hands were still entangled in her blanket. "You don't know me well enough to guess."

"You don't want anything too intense," he said, ignoring that. "Get in, get out, and if you get an orgasm out of it, you consider yourself lucky."

She'd be totally insulted if his words weren't deadly accurate. "I'm not *that* uptight," she said.

He gave a soft, sexy laugh.

"You were wrong when you said *I* had the smart mouth," she said. "You're the one with a smart mouth."

"Maybe kissing it would help contain the sarcasm," he suggested, and this time his mouth was at her ear, drawing a shudder out of her. Somehow her hands had separated from her brain and dropped the blanket.

He looked down at her tiny boxer shorts and thin white cami.

"I stand corrected," he said roughly.

Smug, and also unbearably aroused, her hands slid down his chest.

And then back up.

Unable to handle the onslaught of all the

emotions — hunger, desire, need, and a yearning that weakened her knees — she couldn't hold back her moan this time.

"You're sweet," he murmured.

"No, I'm —"

"Shh," he said, and kissed her just beneath her ear. "You're also fierce," he went on. "Loyal. Tough . . ."

She heard another moan. Still her.

Parker sucked her earlobe into his mouth and then gently sank his teeth into her and gave a little tug.

She gasped and would've slid to the floor if he hadn't lifted her to the counter. He did it casually, easily, and then with a palm on each thigh, he pushed open her legs.

And then he made himself at home between them.

"But one thing you're most definitely not," he said, "is uptight." And then his mouth covered hers.

SIXTEEN

The kiss blew Zoe's socks off. It was so easy to get lost in the promise of what he offered: no wondering, wishing, worrying . . . Wrapped up tight in him as she was, she felt tempted. She also felt feminine and powerful and oh so ready for whatever came next . . .

But then he pulled back.

Reflexively she tightened her hold on him, and with one hand in his hair and the other spread wide over a deliciously bare pec, she stared up at him, confused. "Are we stopping?"

His gaze shifted from her mouth to her eyes, and the corners of his sexy mouth tilted up into a wolf grin that dripped with pure male sex appeal. "Your choice," he said, and cupped the nape of her neck as he brushed his lips against her temple. Then her jaw. The corner of her mouth. "Whatever you want, Zoe."

Whatever she wanted? She wanted him, now. "The kittens," she murmured.

"Fell asleep."

She craned her neck to see around him. Oreo had fallen asleep on his bed in the corner of the kitchen, and unbelievably the two little kittens had done the same, cuddled up next to him like he was their mama.

Tilting his head, Parker began a new assault on her senses as he worked his way along her jaw.

"So what is it you want?" he asked, lightly sinking his teeth into her earlobe.

His low voice rumbled from his chest through hers, and she sucked in a breath trying to take it all in. The warmth of his touch on her skin, the hunger in his voice, the invitation in his words . . . He stood between her spread legs, his tough body hard against all her soft spots. *What did she want?* A man-made orgasm would be a good start . . .

"Tell me," he said, voice low and just a little rough.

She lifted her head and met his gaze.

He flashed a smile. "Me," he said. "You want me."

God help her, she did. But she could delust her brain enough to roll her eyes at his ridiculous cockiness. "A little sure of your-self?"

He laughed softly, and she was just about to clock him for it when he said, "Babe, with you, I'm more unsure than I've ever been."

The confession, uttered with a hint of bewilderment and one-hundred-percent honesty, had the knot loosening in her chest. Were they really on equal ground here?

"Say it," he said with soft command, holding her gaze prisoner.

"I want you," she whispered.

He didn't gloat. He just let out a breath of what she chose to believe was relief before pulling back enough to look at her, really look at her. Clearly he wasn't into instant gratification at the moment because he didn't move, just appeared to really enjoy his view.

But *she* was wanting some instant gratification, bad, and reached for the tie on his sweats. With a groan, he captured her hands, spreading them out at her sides to look his fill as if he needed to memorize her every inch.

Impatient with that, she tried to pull him back into her, but he wasn't a man to be directed. Instead he let go of her hands to grab the hem of her cami and drag it up her body until it got caught on her arms. Now she had a problem. She had to let go of him if she wanted skin on skin.

But she didn't want to let go of him.

Ever.

She had no idea where that terrifying thought came from, so she shoved it deep and lifted her arms.

Parker tossed the cami aside and let out a rough breath at the sight of her bare breasts. "Damn, Zoe. You're so beautiful." Curling an arm low on her hips, his other hand cupped a breast, letting his thumb rasp over the tip. Back and forth until she rocked up into him. Bending his head, he used his mouth. And oh, goodness, his mouth. She was so distracted by his wicked tongue that she cried out in surprise and need when his warm, work-roughened fingers slid into the boxers and between her thighs. She'd fantasized about this with him, but the reality far exceeded any dream. His fingers seemed to know her body, understanding what she needed before even she knew, stroking her in a rhythm that had all cognitive thought put on hold. "Parker," she managed, clutching at him, her hips rocking of their own accord.

"Let go, Zoe," he said, his mouth working its way to her other breast. "I've got this."

She choked out a laugh at how he'd used her own words against her, and melted for him. The morning air was cool and should have chilled her bare skin, but Parker had his torso pressed into hers, and heat poured off his large body. Threading his fingers in her hair, he tipped her face up so he could kiss her as thoroughly as he wanted.

And apparently that was very thoroughly.

She was breathless in seconds, clinging to him, panting, whimpering for more as she explored his arms, his chest, everything she could reach.

He continued to do the same, kissing his way over her shoulder and collarbone, and then back to a breast where he once again drew a nipple into his mouth, sucking hard, and her eyes rolled back in her head a little. Realizing she had her hands fisted in his hair pulling hard, she tried to let up. "Sorry," she gasped.

She felt Parker's lips curve, and when he shook his head, silently telling her no worries, the gentle rasp of the stubble along his jaw made her moan for more.

This time his soft laugh huffed against a breast.

"Not funny," she managed, wanting to give back as good as she was getting, her hands skimming over the smooth muscles of his back, her fingertips searching out every ridge, every dip and sleek line of sinew. When she'd made it to his hips, she kept going into the back of his sweats, grabbing his very fine ass as she spread her legs wider and rocked into him.

At that same moment, he slid a finger into her and groaned along with her. "I've been waiting for this," he rasped.

"For me to grab your ass?"

"For you to be ready for me."

She'd been ready for him at first sight, not that she was about to admit *that*. "Well, you've got it now," she whispered, and then nipped at his throat. "What are you going to do about it?"

"Plenty." He kissed her hard and long before pulling free. When she mewled in protest, he flashed her a smile and hooked a foot in one of her chairs, dragging it toward him.

"What —"

"Shh," he murmured, and dropped into the chair and then leaned in to run his mouth up her inner thigh. When the material of her thin boxers thwarted him, he merely scooped them to the side. "Oh Christ, Zoe. You're so wet." Then he put his mouth on her and in less than two minutes she was nearly to that orgasm she'd been hoping for, so . . . very . . . close . . . as he held her there on the very thin precipice . . .

And then . . .

Her cell phone rang.

As it was plugged in on the counter right behind her, the ring nearly startled her heart right out of her chest.

"Ignore it," he said against her, and did something especially wicked with his tongue that made her forget the phone and cry out.

And then he did it again and just like that she was back on the very edge, her toes curled, her muscles trembling, her entire body tight and —

The house phone rang this time, obnoxiously loud, and she lost her place. "Dammit!" She pulled him up and let out a breath when what she really wanted to do was cry.

But ignoring a phone call went against the grain. She didn't get all that many calls, and some of the ones she'd received in the past few years had been life-changing. The news of the car accident that had nearly killed Darcy, for one. "I'm sorry," she said, breathing like a lunatic — or like a woman who hadn't gotten lucky in far too long. And damn, she'd been *sooooo* close. "I have to at least look."

Parker pulled back, his hair tousled from her fingers, his eyes liquid jade, torso bare,

211

sweats untied and sagging low thanks to her wandering fingers, his breathing not any more even than hers.

She wanted to jump his bones, but instead she slid off the counter and pulled her top back on before pointing at him. "Remember where we were," she said.

He smiled and swiped his forearm across his mouth. "I'm not going anywhere."

Damn. He was the hottest thing she'd ever seen. She looked at the ID screen on the phone and it was like a bucket of ice water. "Hi, Mom," she answered.

Parker slid her a look.

She turned her back on him. "Everything okay?"

It was a valid question. Her parents didn't check in often, and when they did it was always for a specific reason.

"Everything's fine," her mom said, sounding tinny and far away. Luckily she didn't respond in kind to ask Zoe how she was because the answer was *an inch from coming.*

"We're on the road and got an e-mail notice that our security deposit box payment has come due," her mom said. "We've always paid in cash, so I don't have an online account set up for it. We need you to go pay that for us from our account."

"Sure," Zoe said. She often handled their financial affairs when something needed to be done from here in the States. "You okay? And Dad?"

"We're both good, darling, thank you. We're traveling for the next few days. Be sure to tell Wyatt happy birthday for us."

"His birthday was last month," Zoe said, trying not to lose patience, but the woman got their birthdays wrong every single time. How hard was it to keep track of the three children she'd borne herself? "I got him a card from you."

"Time seems to go by so differently over here," her mom said. "Give him a kiss for me. And Darcy, too."

"I know they'd love to hear from you yourself," Zoe said. "Darcy especially, she's —"

"You're breaking up. Zoe?"

"I'm here," Zoe said. "Darcy's engaged. To AJ."

"Well, damn," her mom said, presumably to Zoe's dad. "I can't hear her at all, do you think she's still there?"

"Yes, I am," Zoe said quickly, louder now. "Mom? Can you hear me now? We miss you —"

"Can't hear a damn thing. Zoe," her mom yelled into the phone. "E-mail me when you make the payment, okay?"

"Okay, will do," Zoe yelled back. "Love you!"

There was no response. *"Mom?"*

But she'd already disconnected. Zoe stared at her phone and sighed.

"Hey." Parker came up behind her and set her blanket back on her shoulders. "You okay?" He ran his hands up and down her arms, making her realize she was chilly. Then those warm hands compelled her to turn and face him.

"Yeah," she said. "Thanks. I'm fine."

His fingers lifted her chin so he could look into her eyes. "Liar."

"No, really," she said, and mentally shrugged the call off. "Where were we?"

"Right here," he said. "With you talking to me."

"Now who's lying?"

He sat in the chair and pulled her into his lap, where she blew out a sigh and set her head on his shoulder. "I keep wishing for something that's never been." She realized this was probably cryptic, but she knew talking about it wouldn't change a thing. "Never mind me, it's silly. Stupid."

"It's not either of those things if it's bugging you," Parker said.

Something in his voice had her taking a

closer look at him. "Your parents forget your birthday and never tell you they love you, too?" she asked.

He let out a low laugh. "They don't forget my birthday, but yeah, *love* isn't a word they throw around very often. My dad's a miner to the very bone, which is synonymous with tough and impenetrable. Talking about his feelings isn't his strong suit — unless he's disagreeing with you on something. Then he doesn't hold back."

She'd talked herself into believing that she didn't want to know about him, what made him tick, what had molded him into the man he'd become, but she really did. She wanted to know more. Hell, she wanted to know everything. "And your mom?"

"She worked in the elementary school's cafeteria before she retired a few years back," he said. "She's very proud of my dad and all his years of hard work. Having a son who not only didn't want to do the same but yearned for an entirely different life confused her."

"Did she try to understand?" Zoe asked.

He shrugged. "Not a lot of communication went on. I didn't want to hurt them, but I knew I had to go. I owed it to myself to at least explore the life I wanted."

"Were they okay with that?" she asked.

He laughed. "No."

Her heart squeezed. Five minutes ago she'd had her thighs wrapped tight around his head and been close to singing the Hallelujah chorus, but now all she wanted was to have him keep talking to her forever. "Do you have any siblings?"

"A sister," he said. "She's twelve years younger than me." He smiled grimly. "An 'oops' baby that turned into my parents' entire world."

"Tell me she didn't go into the mines," Zoe said, hoping not.

Parker was quiet for a long beat. "No," he finally said. "She didn't."

Zoe could tell there was a lot more that he wasn't saying, but he had on that blank face of his, the one that said he didn't want to discuss it further, and she didn't know how to push without butting in where she didn't belong. She clutched the blanket to her, thinking that by now they should've been naked on her kitchen floor. The image was hot as hell, because though she wasn't used to these feelings, there'd been something so freeing about having his hands on her, knowing that they were both in the same place and looking for the same endgame.

An orgasm.

Period. Well, in her case it was more of a comma, with a whole bunch after that, but it didn't matter. The moment had passed and she knew it. "I should get ready for work," she said reluctantly. "I've got a long day ahead. I won't be back until late tonight."

He nodded and gave her a little smile, and damn if she wasn't sorry that she'd ever answered her phone.

Seventeen

Parker sat at the kitchen table with his laptop, the tabby kitten asleep on his lap and Oreo on his feet. The kitchen floor was in shambles thanks to the crazy gray wild-woman kitten who had attacked a roll of paper towels and spilled Oreo's food and was currently batting a pen across the floor.

Parker supposed it was fitting. He had a certain brown-eyed brunette currently wreaking such havoc on his life and heart as well. The kitten was just taking after the best.

She batted the pen past the dog.

Oreo, trying to sleep, sighed for the fifth time.

Taking pity on him, Parker grabbed the little terrorist and lifted her to his face to look at her eye to eye.

She batted at his nose.

He laughed. "Nap time, Destructo." And he dropped her next to her much quieter brother in his lap.

She immediately pounced on her brother with great glee, who opened one eye, gave a mew, and pushed her away.

Not intimidated, she plopped herself down on top of her brother again and began to knead him with her paws like she was making biscuits.

The quiet tabby tolerated the abuse and finally she fell asleep, allowing Parker to work. An hour ago he'd been alerted that the motion detector cams had caught something. He'd accessed the feeds and couldn't believe what he was seeing.

One minute there was a Humvee and the next minute it vanished. Just disappeared into thin air. Parker rewound and slowed things down. This time he could see that the Humvee, colored to blend in, carrying what looked like four men, drove onto the ranch. It was followed by a similarly painted truck, the kind that carries livestock, *large* livestock, and not all that different from the one that had clipped him with Carver behind the wheel.

Parker couldn't see much else as the rest of the daylight faded away. None of them used any lights.

He called Wyatt.

"Yo," Wyatt said. "I've got two minutes

before emergency surgery. A lab ate its owner's lace thong and it's all tangled up in his intestines. She needs to switch to edible undies."

And Parker thought his job was interesting. "You ever hear of Cat's Paw?"

"No, but hang on, I'm putting you on speaker. Dell," Wyatt said, and Parker knew he was talking to the owner and head vet of Belle Haven, whom he'd met the day he'd shoveled shit for two hours. "Parker wants to know what we know about Cat's Paw."

"The town or ranch?" Dell asked.

"There's a ranch called Cat's Paw?" Parker asked.

"Yeah," Dell said, "it's an isolated place out at the base of Rocky Falls."

"We don't service it?" Wyatt asked.

"It's not in business anymore," Dell said. "They lost their livestock not too long after the economy took a shit and they couldn't recover. The place is deserted."

"As in the owners just walked away?" Parker asked.

"Supposedly. The bank took the land back, but like thousands of other properties across the country, the banks are in over their head. Most of those out-of-the-way places are on the back burner."

"So no livestock," Parker said.

"Not unless it's wild and squatting on the land."

The tabby kitten rolled over and his sister, sleepy now, mewed in protest.

"You have a furbaby?" Dell asked.

"I've got two kittens for next week's adoption day."

Wyatt laughed. "Zoe know?"

"Yeah."

"Then you don't have shit for adoption day. She won't be able to let them go by then."

After they'd disconnected, Parker stared at the feeds some more. So if there was no livestock, what the hell was in that truck? If he'd located Carver and the militia he was using to protect himself, the likely answer was that he'd possibly found the storage site for Carver's illegal gains, his holding place before it was sold.

He got up, unintentionally disturbing the kittens, who let him know with their soft mews how unhappy he'd made them. He set them down on Oreo's bed. "Sleep," he commanded.

The kittens climbed all over Oreo.

Oreo gave Parker a baleful look.

"Like you don't love them," Parker said.

And indeed, Oreo licked each kitten from chin to forehead and then, after turning in a very careful circle — three times — plopped down. His hind end caught the gray kitten, who gave a muffled "mew!", crawled out from beneath Oreo's ass, and settled with her brother between Oreo's two front paws.

Oreo smiled down at his babies.

Parker paced for a few moments, brooding over the action he was missing out on. He tried calling Sharon, but either his boss was over him or she was still pissed because she didn't pick up.

When his phone finally buzzed, he answered immediately, thinking it was Sharon getting back to him.

It was AJ. "How are your ribs?"

"Great," Parker said, touching them to check. Maybe *great* was a slight exaggeration, but it would do.

"We're short a guy tonight for our rec league football game," AJ said. "Wyatt says you're the guy we need. You in?"

Parker looked around him, soaking in Zoe's kitchen. It was a great kitchen, warm and cozy and comfortable. And in it, he was shockingly content for a guy who'd always believed he had to be on the go 24/7 to be happy.

But laying low for work was driving him straight up a wall and he had a lot of pent-up energy to burn. He'd like to burn some of that energy off with Zoe.

Naked.

But she was part of his problem. He didn't want to sit around here and think about her, and without her, he didn't have much to do except check the camera feeds. "Who's on your team?" he asked.

AJ laughed shortly. "Worried?"

"I want to win."

AJ laughed again. "Then show up. You won't be sorry, trust me. We kick ass."

Perfect. Just what he was in the mood for.

Several hours later, he was at the park, meeting the rest of the guys on his team. Wyatt. Dell, whom he already knew. Dell's brothers Adam and Brady, both of whom looked very capable of kicking ass. A guy named Grif, whom Parker wouldn't bet against. And Joe, who was filling in for someone, too. They were playing a team of first responders, which included Kel.

Kel grinned at the sight of Parker. "You here for me to wipe the floor with?"

Parker grinned back. "Try it."

In the first huddle, Joe looked over at Parker. "You the reason she hasn't made a decision?"

He assumed the "she" in question was Zoe. "Decision?" he asked.

"I offered Zoe an equal partnership in the FBO," Joe said. "She said she needed to think about it for a while." He paused. "She didn't mention it?"

"No."

Joe grinned. "Maybe you're not the reason after all, then."

Parker wondered about that, about why she wouldn't take such an offer. Assuming the offer was good, it seemed right up her alley, having a stake in the business she loved.

He'd have thought about it some more, but the game was an immediate distraction. It was supposed to be touch football, but Parker learned in the first quarter that touch was more like tackle, and apparently there were no refs and no pussies allowed.

"Jesus," he said, swiping the blood from his cut lip at their first time out. They were tied fourteen to fourteen. "What about personal fouls?"

"No blood, no foul," Wyatt said.

"There's blood," Parker said, jabbing a finger at his own lip, then at Dell's bloody nose, and finally at Grif's arm, which had blood running down it from an elbow gash.

"Nah," Brady said, grinning. "Has to be arterial blood."

■ ■ ■ ■

Zoe had exactly one hour to herself in between two flights. She'd figured she'd go home and find some excuse to banter with Parker, but when she'd landed, she had a text from her brother.

Recruited Parker for football tonight, thought you'd want to know.

Hell yeah, she wanted to know. Rec league football in Sunshine meant sitting with her girlfriends on the stands, eating hot dogs and popcorn, heckling the players — and who in their right mind didn't want to stare at a bunch of hot guys tackling each other for a couple of hours?

She got to the park during the second quarter and found she had a seat waiting for her next to Darcy and the gang, who included Dell's wife, Jade; Dell's brother Brady's wife, Lilah; and two other dear friends, Holly and Kate, all of whom had a significant other on the field.

"How's everyone's man doing?" she asked, biting into the big, juicy hot dog that Darcy handed her.

"Great," Darcy said. "Including yours."

Zoe choked on her hot dog.

Darcy grinned and patted her on the back. "Yeah, and not only does Parker fill out a pair of jeans almost as good as AJ, he can run faster than anyone out there."

"He's not my man," Zoe said distractedly.

"Uh-huh," Darcy said. "Just watch."

"He's not." But Zoe did just that, her eyes drawn to Parker on the field like a moth to a flame.

And holy mother of mercy, Darcy was right.
He did fill out a pair of jeans.
And he was faster than anyone else out there.
And . . . damn. She wanted him to be her man. Bad.

At the half, Parker had found his stride, but they were down twenty-one to fourteen. Dell threw long and Parker went for it with Kel breathing down his neck for an interception. Parker went airborne in the touchdown zone, Kel with him, and by the very tips of his fingers Parker angled Kel out and got the catch.

They landed hard, Parker on the bottom.

A bunch of people landed on top of them both, some cheering, some yelling denials.

Under all of it, Parker, with elbows and knees pummeling him, shoved free and sat up, revealing he still held the ball.

The crowd went nuts and he glanced over at the stands, surprised to find them filled.

"Sunshine takes its football seriously," Kel said, offering him a hand up. "Nice catch. There won't be a second one."

Parker grinned and as he turned away, his gaze caught on a woman in the top row of the stands.

Zoe.

She was surrounded by other women, all of them clearly together because they each had whiteboards and had written various signs:

Go Grif!

Dell Does It Best!

Your mama plays better than you do!

The Other Team Sucks!

Brady's game is tighter than your spandex!

Parker went brows up.

Zoe grinned and wrote on her board and then lifted it:

You've Got This.

Shaking his head, laughing, he joined the huddle.

"New plan," Brady said. "We gotta get the new guy the ball. He knows what to do with it."

Parker listened to the rest of them all agree and realized with some surprise that *he* was the new guy.

The rest of the game was a blur. By the end, they won by one safety — his.

Someone had beer in a cooler and they all sat around after, switching out their cleats, pulling on sweatshirts as the sun sank. Parker felt happily exhausted and realized drinking a beer as the sky slowly filled with more stars than he'd ever seen was a pretty damn nice way to start the evening.

The crowd moved off the stands, dispersing. A group of women moved in. The girlfriends and wives, Parker realized. Giving out hugs and kisses. And for one beat he felt like an outsider all over again.

And then he saw Zoe standing in front of him. She smiled. "For tradition," she said, and as she had that very first time they'd met on her porch, she went up on tiptoe and brushed her soft, warm lips across his.

Just as quickly, she stepped back. "Going back up tonight," she said, and gave him a finger wave. "Nice game."

And he found himself grinning like an idiot. That was the best way to start an evening.

Parker walked out of the shower and into his bedroom, sore in a bunch of new places thanks to the game. But it was a good kind of sore and he felt more relaxed than he had in days.

And then, as he moved toward his duffel bag, pain suddenly shot up his leg from his foot. Hopping, swearing the air blue, he looked down to find he'd stepped on a small wire cat brush.

Zoe had brought it home to groom the kittens, but their resident gray hellion loved to trot it around the house.

Which made him realize the house was quiet.

Too quiet.

He looked around and found her curled up on his pillow, fast asleep. Guess Destructo had finally worn herself out. And of course she had to be on his pillow. Her brother and Oreo were on Oreo's bed, but not her. Figured. It was him she was fond of attacking in her sleep, his ear she purred in when she decided to sleep instead of play, and him she sat on if a calm mood struck her.

He stalked over to the bed and scooped her up off his pillow. She sleepily opened her eyes and at the sight of him, her favorite new toy, she got happy.

And wild.

"Oh no," he said. "It's bedtime. Behave or you'll sleep in the bathroom." That was where she'd started out sleeping, until her offended howling at being shut off from the house-sized jungle gym had kept everyone up.

He dumped her onto Oreo's bed. "Your turn to babysit," he said to Oreo.

Oreo sighed.

Parker slid into bed and sighed, too. Exhausted, he started to drift off.

And . . . heard the kitten climbing her way back onto the bed. "No," he said to the dark.

The kitten bumped her head affectionately to his chin and then tilted her face to his, staring down at him adoringly.

Shit.

He dropped her over the edge of the bed twice before giving up, letting her fall asleep where she wanted, in the crook of his neck. He grumbled about it, but he wasn't fooling the cat and he certainly wasn't fooling himself. He adored her right back. Just like he did the owner of this house.

The truth was he didn't look forward to the day it was time to leave. He was going to miss this damn hellion. He was going to miss Oreo. The house. Playing football.

And most of all, being with Zoe.

EIGHTEEN

The next morning, Parker was again at the kitchen table with his laptop while on his cell phone, through which Sharon had been chewing out his ass for the past five minutes.

He'd used the time to text two pics of Oreo being attacked by the kittens to Amory and was working on a third.

"And now, thanks to you," Sharon went on, "I have to go to the director and —"

"Give him the proof I sent you that Carver's got stuff on the move?" he asked, voice even.

"That's *if* this place is even the right place, and *if* the trucks you saw were carrying the cargo we're looking for, and *if* that even matters because this is out of my hands now and on a different pay grade entirely."

"You ever going to tell me about the deal?" Parker asked.

She was quiet so long he wasn't sure she was still there. "Hello?" he asked.

"You always know what I know," she finally said. "Or you've guessed."

"He's going to give up the militia," Parker said.

"The big cheeses. All of them, and some of these guys have been wanted for years."

"And in return?" he asked.

"He walks."

Parker let that soak in a minute, but no matter how he looked at it, it sucked for him and his team. "Walks," he repeated. "As in goes scot-free? Which agency is he doing this deal with?"

Nothing from Sharon.

Keeping his cool right then was just about the hardest thing he'd ever done. "What about Ned? Where's the justice for his death? Jesus, Sharon, this isn't fair to —"

"— Nothing about life is fair and you already know that. And there's a lot about this deal that neither of us knows."

He was shaking his head even though she couldn't see him. "He can't have died for nothing," he said.

"He didn't. But right now, you have no choice in this matter, Parker. If Carver catches wind of you in the area, you'll spook him and we all lose."

"No, the *other* agencies lose. Our agency is already up shit creek without a paddle since we had to give him up."

"Don't do anything without talking to me first," she said. "I mean it, Parker. If you so much as —"

"Got it," he said, and sensing the conversation was about to deteriorate even further, he disconnected.

And then he turned off his phone. She could kill him later. Much later. He tossed his phone down and realized he had three sets of eyes on him. Or more specifically on the peanut butter toast he hadn't finished.

"Mew," said the gray kitten.

"Mew," said the tabby kitten.

"Woof," said Oreo.

"Hey, I already fed all three of you beggars," he said just as his laptop pinged an incoming e-mail from Amory:

Parker! Loved the pics, send more! And guess what? It's next week now so what day will you be here? I want to put it on the calendar! I tried calling you but it went right to voicemail. You busy? OMG, maybe you're already on your way here!!!!!!!!

Well, hell. Parker e-mailed her back, making sure to tell her that he was not on the way yet but that he'd let her know when. As he hit send, Zoe staggered into the kitchen in another skirt and blazer that made her look like a million bucks, heading directly for the coffeepot.

"Bless you," she said when she found he'd already made the coffee.

He waited as she guzzled the caffeine, and in less than a minute the cobwebs had cleared from her pretty eyes. It was fascinating to watch. She was fascinating to watch. He'd heard her come in at three thirty in the morning and had gotten up to check on her. By the time he'd walked down the hall, she'd been facedown on her bed and out cold. He'd pulled off her shoes and covered her up.

She hadn't budged.

Cradling the mug now, she leaned back against the counter and stared at him like he was a puzzle and she was missing a few of his pieces.

Or maybe that was just how *he* felt looking at her.

"I heard you on the phone," she said.

"Did you?"

"Told you, thin walls." She sipped more coffee. "Same woman?"

"Yes," he said. "My boss."

"And?" she asked with a false casualness.

He took a closer look at her. Was she . . . jealous? Interesting concept, and one he realized he enjoyed the thought of *way* too much. "And nothing," he said. "She's a pain in my ass and I return the favor. She's currently pissed off about the Carver thing."

"Carver?"

"That's the guy I'm looking for," he said. "Tripp Carver."

She blinked.

"What?" he asked.

"That name sounds familiar. I'm sure I've flown a Tripp Carver."

He went still. If so, it was proof positive that Carver was really here, or at least proof he *had* been. "Recently?"

She shook her head. "I'd have to check the logs."

He didn't want to spook her, or ask her to do anything that would compromise her, but Christ. She'd flown the guy? He thought of everything that could've gone wrong and felt his gut clench tight.

"I didn't have any problems," she said. "Or I'd have remembered. The name just sounds familiar, is all."

"Okay," he said, not wanting to make a big deal of it and scare her. "But if you remember details, I'd be very interested in hearing them."

She nodded and refilled her cup.

Not wanting to push, he changed the

subject. "You're not in your pj's this morning," he noted, vividly remembering yesterday morning. Hell, the remembering had gotten him through an entertaining shower just twenty minutes ago.

"Disappointed?" she asked.

"More than you know," he said, and watched the flush cross her face. Good. Now she was remembering it, too, the feel of his hands and mouth on her. Her expression remained calm, but the pulse at the base of her throat began to race and gave her away.

In that moment he wanted more than anything to lay her back on the counter or the floor or whatever surface was closest and finish what they'd started.

"Are you going to get yourself in any trouble today?" she asked.

"No," he said. He'd already gotten in as much trouble as he could. Not that he planned to bother her with that information.

She looked at him for a long beat and then shook her head.

"What?"

"Nothing." She turned away from him and picked up the gray kitten at her feet, nuzzling her to her cheek.

Parker stood and moved toward her. He

took the kitten and gently set her down. Did the same for her mug. Cupping Zoe's face, he tilted it up to his. "What?" he said again.

She hesitated. "Listen, I know we're living in the moment and all that, and I get it. We're not really friends and you're not really on vacay. A job is a job."

"You think you're a job to me?" he asked.

"No. You were a job to me. I flew you, you paid. Just like what I am to you is a convenient place to stay."

Maybe that had been the case in the beginning, but things changed. "I'm more than a job," he said, well aware of the irony of what he was saying.

"I don't think so."

"Then what do you call when I had my mouth on your —"

She reached out and put her fingers over his mouth, giving one slow, serious shake of her head, though her eyes looked like she was fighting a shocked laugh. "That was a . . ." She appeared to struggle to find the right words. "I'm not going to call it a mistake," she finally said. "Because nothing that feels that good could be a mistake."

With her fingers still against his lips, he growled his agreement.

"But we both know where we were going with that," she said.

"Please say your bed," he said. "Or mine. I don't care which."

She stared at her fingers on his lips and then jumped when he nibbled one and then sucked it into his mouth. He was gratified to see her looking a little dazed.

"But it's crazy," she said. "We're not even each other's type."

"I think we do all right," he said.

She looked at him for a long moment. "You're not what I'm looking for."

"Ouch," he said, much more lightly than he felt.

"You know what I mean. You're leaving here sooner than later, and I . . ." She shook her head as if she were surprised at herself. "I need more from you."

From you. "Not Joe? Or any other guy?"

She just stared at him. "You feel different. Scary different," she finally said. "Makes our live-in-the-moment mantra hard for me."

Shit. He was such a dick. She certainly deserved more from him, *way* more than what he could give her. In spite of that, he nearly opened his mouth and said what was on his mind — that all of a sudden he felt damn close to saying fuck the job, he wanted to stick around just to see this thing with her through.

He'd never felt that way before.

Never.

The job was where it was at for him. The job had always been his end-all, the only thing ever waiting for him at the beginning and at the end of every day.

But damn. He'd miss her. He wasn't embarrassed about admitting that to himself, either. The opposite, actually. If he was being honest with himself, he was more than a little relieved to know he was still even capable of feelings like the ones he knew he could have for her if he let himself.

But she was right, about everything. He *was* leaving. It was what he did. He walked away from those he cared about, and he'd made peace with that a long time ago.

He'd come here to Sunshine for a job. Falling for the fierce and sexy Zoe Stone was not in the cards.

Not even a little.

Okay, well, maybe a little, but he'd be the only one to carry that burden.

She was still watching him. "I'm trying to live in the moment," she said softly. "For the moment we have. The three W's and all that, but it's hard for me."

Shit. He wished he'd never come up with such a stupid thing.

"Because that's the way it has to be," she

said. "Right?"

Pull off the Band-Aid and quick, he told himself. *Do it now.* "That's the way it has to be," he agreed, just as softly.

Something crossed her face: disappointment? He couldn't be sure, but he was one hundred percent positive that disappointment was *exactly* what he felt. As well as the certainty that maybe he'd just messed up the best thing that had ever almost happened to him.

"In the interest of those three W's," Zoe said. "I've been asked out on another date for tomorrow night."

This hit him like a sledgehammer. No less than he deserved. "Joe again?" he managed.

"No."

"Did the dentist call you and reschedule?"

"No."

His gut tightened even more. "Who?"

"Kel. He's a local sheriff," she said.

Parker went utterly still as this news hit his brain. On the one hand, he personally knew that Kel was a damn good guy with a solid work ethic and a steady job that wouldn't take him all over hell and back.

On the other hand, Kel was also a man. And as he'd already told Zoe, all men were horndog assholes, even the good ones.

"Is that a problem?" Zoe asked in his silence.

"Of course not."

She stared at him for a beat and then nodded. "Okay, then," she said, and backed away. "Good. See you later."

Parker lasted five minutes before he called Kel.

"Was just going to call you," the sheriff said before Parker could speak.

"She's her own woman," Parker said. "She can go out with whoever she wants." There. He'd said it. Now he just had to believe it.

There was a long pause from Kel.

Hell. "That's not why you were going to call me," Parker said, rubbing the sudden ache between his eyeballs.

"Nope. But if we're talking about Zoe, hell yeah, she's her own woman. Did you really think I was calling you to ask permission to date her? And more importantly, *why* would I call you to ask permission to date her?"

"No reason."

It was Kel's turn to go silent. Then: "You're a shitty liar."

No, he was an excellent liar. Kel just happened to be a damn good silence interpreter. "Let's stick to business," Parker suggested.

"Sure. Right after you tell me what's going on with you and Zoe."

"At the moment?" Parker asked wryly. "Very little."

"Okay, then, what do you *want* to be going on with you and Zoe?"

How the hell did Parker explain that when he didn't even know himself?

"Speak now or forever hold your peace," Kel warned.

"I'm just staying here while I'm in town."

"Tell me something I don't know," Kel suggested.

"I want her to find the right guy," Parker said. "She deserves that."

Kel was quiet a moment. "Why do I suddenly have the feeling that the right guy is going back to D.C. soon?"

"I can't stay," Parker said.

"Can't? Or won't?"

Shit. This discussion was so far out of his league. "You wanted to talk about the case," he said tightly.

"So *won't* then," Kel said evenly. "That's going to cost you the woman, you know that, right?"

"The case," Parker repeated firmly. "Anything new on the case?"

"Actually, yeah," Kel said. "Hang on." A door shut and then Kel was back, all business. "I got a call earlier from my ATF buddy, the one who'd originally told me about the possible militia connection."

"And?"

"And that's been confirmed. So has FBI and Homeland Security interest. The worry now is that with so many agencies involved, someone's going to spook them."

"How is Carver involved?"

"Apparently he grew up with some of them but has been gone for a long time," Kel said. "He's donated plenty of money to their cause to ensure their loyalty, but he's still not fully trusted by the general membership. And the rumor is that he's not trusted for a good reason — that he's going to give them up."

Parker already knew some of this but it corroborated with what Sharon was worried about, and none of it was good news. In fact, it was the opposite of good news. A spooked militia meant that they'd move, and if they moved, that meant so would Carver. He could vanish again and everyone would lose.

A half hour after Zoe went off to work, Parker got a text from her.

I flew Tripp Carver and two others to Coeur d'Alene and back six weeks ago.

He paid cash. The next day I picked up two men in Coeur d'Alene and flew them back to Sunshine and Carver paid for that flight as well. Devon has flown him twice since then, same route.

Parker stared at the text. He wasn't surprised. The Sunshine Airport was the only small airport for five hundred miles. It saw a lot of traffic for its size.

Not much scared him, but the Butcher having been so close to Zoe? That scared him to the bone. He told himself that Carver had no way of knowing Parker was here in Sunshine or his relationship with a woman that Carver had paid as a pilot.

Zoe was in no danger from Carver.

But he still hated it.

The next night Zoe stood in her bedroom in her bra and panties staring at her closet, confused. Something was different and it wasn't the two wild kittens rolling across her floor.

Then she realized what it was. For months, the lightbulb in the closet had been burned out. She'd replaced it twice but it still never worked.

It was working now.

Her throat tightened a little, which was

ridiculous. So he'd fixed it for good, so what?

Except . . . she'd known the man just over a week and yet she felt like he knew her better than anyone else ever had.

But there'd be no crying over the spilled milk. He'd made his feelings clear. He wanted her. But only in the moment. Period.

It was true that disappointment had been sitting like a slug in her gut ever since, but she had to move past that right now. Even if when she'd gotten home last night from work they'd talked about Carver and she knew Parker was far more worried about her than he'd let on. She'd promised not to fly the guy again and to let Parker know if she saw him or any of his men at the airport.

But for now, Kel would be here in five minutes and she had other problems. She'd tried on everything she owned. Not because she was worried about pleasing him. Kel was a great guy: smart, kind, funny, good looking . . . But it wasn't the sheriff she was thinking of while staring into her closet.

Nope. She wanted to pick something to wear so that when she paraded down the stairs and out the front door past Parker, his jaw dropped to the floor.

And not in a *she's off to bingo* way.

She pulled on her little black dress. She'd

bought it on a whim last year after she'd had the flu and lost five pounds in one weekend. She had some really great high-heeled strappy booties to go with it, too. By the time she'd shoved herself into everything, it took her a moment to recognize the woman in the mirror.

"What do you think?" she asked her audience.

The kitties just kept attacking each other. Oreo, square in the middle of the bed, lifted his head and smiled sleepily at her, his tail thumping on the blankets.

"Nice, but you like everything," she said, and snapped a selfie, texting it to Darcy with: too much?

Darcy immediately responded with a phone call. When Zoe answered, all she heard was a wolf whistle.

Zoe let out a low laugh. "Yeah?"

"Oh yeah. So did you finally decide to jump Parker's bones?"

Butterflies erupted in Zoe's stomach. "No," she said, hopefully more firmly than she felt. "Tonight's my date with Kel."

There was a beat of silence.

"What the hell does that mean?" Zoe asked.

"I didn't say anything," Darcy said.

"Your silence spoke volumes. You're the

one who suggested this date with Kel."

"Yes, and don't get me wrong, Kel's a hottie, but . . ."

"But *what*?" Zoe asked.

"Well, my money was on Parker," Darcy said. "What happened?"

"My closet light is fixed," Zoe said.

"Huh?"

Zoe shook her head. "Never mind."

"You two have all that *very* serious chemistry."

They did. They had so much chemistry that he melted Zoe's bones whenever they were in the same room and sometimes even when they weren't. "He's not an option for a viable relationship," she said.

Darcy was silent again. "We're talking about a date, Zoe, and if you're very lucky, also some great sex — not a marriage proposal."

"You don't understand," Zoe said.

"What is it I don't understand? That women have needs? The fact that you're trying to get yourself a life? That you finally realized you need stuff for your own outside of me and Wyatt? I *love* that, Zoe. For so long, for *too* long, you let Wyatt's and my life come ahead of yours. It's your time, babe, and you're looking the part tonight. Just . . ."

"What?"

"Pick the right man, is all."

Zoe's butterflies took flight again. "Like you just said, Darce, it's just a date."

"Well, that's how *I'd* look at it, but you're not wired like I am. Follow your heart, Zoe."

The doorbell rang. Zoe stilled. "My heart's confused," she whispered.

"No, your heart is never confused. It's just rusty from lack of use."

"Dammit," Zoe said. "When did you become the smarter sister?"

"Always have been," Darcy said smugly. "But it's good to finally be recognized."

Zoe disconnected and ran down the stairs. Or, more accurately, did her best to hustle down the stairs without breaking her ankles in her heels. She crossed the *empty* living room — so much for the showstopping entrance she'd imagined — and stood there, heart pounding.

She didn't want to do this, not with Kel . . . "What is wrong with me?" she asked the door.

"You going to open it, or just talk to it?" Parker asked from just behind her.

She froze. Did he like the view? Not sure she wanted to know, she turned and faced him, expecting to see a smug, wry smile on his face.

No smile. And his eyes . . . She swallowed. They were dark, nearly black, and so hot she nearly caught on fire.

Yeah, he liked the view.

He was in a pair of cargo pants and a faded T-shirt that fit him like a second skin.

She liked her view, too.

"You look . . ." He shook his head. "Amazing."

"So not like I'm going to bingo, right?"

Eyes still flaming, he gave a slow head shake. *"Amazing,"* he repeated.

She liked that he didn't sound surprised. She also liked the low, husky quality in his voice, as if he couldn't help but be bowled over by her. "Thanks," she whispered.

And then because they were just staring stupidly at each other, she turned back to the door, drew a deep breath, and whispered to the wood, "Iwanttocancel."

"What?"

She dropped her head to the door and thunked it a few times. *She wanted to cancel. She should've cancelled —*

The bell rang again and she straightened up and shook her head, trying to clear her mind. No. This was what she wanted. And maybe some of that had become cloudy in her mind because of the very hot, very annoying man behind her, but since when did

249

she plan her life around a man? She'd wanted this date. It didn't matter that it wasn't going to be the hot, annoying guy. He'd had his chance.

Now this was hers.

Nineteen

Holding her breath, determined to make the best of the evening, Zoe pasted a smile on her face and opened the door to . . .

Kaylie.

The little girl stood there looking up at Zoe with her huge eyes. "Can I play with the kitties?" she asked hopefully. "My mama said if it's okay with you, I could bring them back to my house for one hour on accounta I cleaned my room real good. So can I?"

Parker went up the stairs and reappeared with the two kittens, riding shotgun on each of his shoulders.

Kaylie laughed and clapped with delight.

Parker carefully handed them over, and then he and Zoe watched as she carried her precious cargo to her house and vanished inside.

Zoe looked at her empty driveway. "Parker?"

"Yeah?"

She heard the huskiness in his voice and would bet her last dollar he was staring at her ass. *Good.* "What time is it?"

"Quarter after seven."

"What the hell?" she said. "Am I wearing a sign that says *Hi, stand me up?*"

"Maybe he called or texted you," Parker said.

"No, I have my phone right here . . ." She pulled the phone from the small cross-body bag she'd thrown on before coming downstairs and stared at the missed call and unread text from Kel. "Well, crap." She accessed the text.

Zoe, I'm sorry, one of my deputies called in sick and I have to go out on a call. I tried to catch you on your cell. I'll try again later. Rain check?

It must have come in when she'd been on the phone with Darcy and hadn't noticed it. She blew out a sigh, pivoted on her heels, and headed straight for the kitchen. Her laptop wasn't there, but Parker's was and she flipped it open.

Of course, he followed.

"By all means," he said. "Go ahead and help yourself."

She tried to access the browser but was

thwarted by a pop-up window asking for the password. "This night sucks," she said.

She felt more than saw Parker lean over her. His scent came to her: warm, sexy man. The inside of both his arms brushed the outside of hers as he reached around her and entered in his password.

"Thanks," she whispered, determined to keep her shit together. Because if she let out *one* single tear she would —

"What happened to Kel?"

"Got a call," she said. "One that was far more interesting than a date with me."

"Zoe," he said quietly. "You know if he's on call and something comes in, he has to take it."

She craned her neck and sent him her best bitch look. "You're defending him?"

"Yes. *No,*" he quickly corrected.

She started typing.

"What are you doing?" he asked.

"I wore my best undies tonight in the hopes of finally getting . . ." She paused. "You know."

A sound that might have been a groan escaped him. "Shit, Zoe, you turn me upside down when it comes to this shit."

She turned *him* upside down? That was rich coming from him. "What, you don't think I should be trying to get a life for myself?" she asked.

"Babe, you have a life. You have a brother and sister you love, you've got a job that you're amazing at, you have Oreo who thinks the sun rises and sets at your feet, and you have —"

"What?" she whispered, turning to look at him.

His green fathomless eyes leveled her. "And you have a roommate who thinks you're the smartest and sexiest woman he's ever met."

Because that made her heart scrunch in on itself, she broke eye contact and turned back to his computer. "You mean a roommate who has an annoying habit of giving a running commentary on my attempts at dating?"

"Just trying to help."

"I don't need your *help.*"

"What are you looking for?" he asked as she typed.

"A hookup site. I heard about one. Grounder or Gander or something . . ."

Parker choked. "Grindr?"

"That's the one," she said, and stood up. "But I need wine first."

"You'll need something stronger than wine for Grindr," he said, and something in his voice — barely repressed humor —

made her look at him.

"It's a site for men," he said.

"Yeah," she said in her best *duh* tone. "And I'm looking for one."

He took the bottle of wine from her hand, poured her a glass, and handed it back to her, waiting until she took a sip to say, "Grindr is a site *just* for men; gay, bi, curious . . . the only requirement is a body part you don't have."

Now it was her turn to choke. "Dammit."

He grinned and took the wine from her before she could drop it.

She forced her nose into the air and strode back to the computer. "Fine. I'll find a site more . . . suited to my needs."

Reaching around her, he shut the laptop. "No, you won't."

She arched a brow at him. "Excuse me? *No?*"

"No. *Hell no.* If you want a connection," he said, "then I'll damn well be the one to give it to you."

"I don't want a . . . *connection,*" she said, and snatched the glass of wine back. She downed it and held out her hand for the bottle.

He held it out of her reach. "Then what the hell do you want?"

"An orgasm," she said. "And that's it."

He didn't blink an eye. "I think we can do better than a single orgasm for you."

"Uh . . ." Her heart skipped a beat, confused in its abrupt switch from temper to arousal as it kicked into high gear. Maybe her brain wasn't so quick on the uptake, but her body sure was and it wanted him. She took a step toward him, but then her knees knocked together as her nerves got the best of her and she stopped.

Parker just stood there, eyes hot, mouth curved in a warm smile as he waited with his characteristic patience for her to get herself together and decide.

"Okay," she whispered.

Unfolding his arms, he reached for her, pulling her in. "Your heart's pounding."

"I think it was the orgasm comment."

He smiled, his jaw pressed to hers, his rough palm stroking up her back while his other hand pushed the hair from her face. "You sure about this?"

She pulled back. "Yes. Are you?"

He laughed and nibbled at her ear, this time his lips lingering, his warm breath caressing her skin. "Zoe, I want you bad, and have since that first kiss on your porch."

"But you said —"

"Never said I didn't want you. Don't ever doubt that I do."

"You were trying to be a good guy," she whispered, marveling over that.

"I have my moments. But now isn't one of them."

She let out a low laugh and buried her face in his chest, trying to get a bearing over this feeling of being out of control.

His hand rubbed in slow circles on her back, giving comfort while spiking up her body temperature. And her need level.

Which was at an all-time high.

But she wanted him in the same state. So she placed her lips at the base of his throat, flicking her tongue out so that she could taste him.

He tasted amazing.

With a groan, he slid his hands down to cup her ass in his palms and pulled her in hard. She couldn't help but rub up against him, smiling in satisfaction when he said her name in a low, gravelly voice.

She lifted her head to gloat and his mouth came down on hers, stealing her breath and urging her on. Better yet, but he was still holding himself in careful control. Nipping his bottom lip, she sucked it in between hers, running her tongue along the edge. "So how about you?" she murmured teasingly. "You want an orgasm, too?"

But he wasn't feeling playful. His eyes

stayed steady and intense on hers. "I told you what I want, Zoe. You."

There wasn't enough air in the room, there just wasn't. *Don't do this,* the smart part of her said. *You'll fall for him, you know you will.*

Too late, another part of her said — her inner ho. *Take what you can get of him.*

He must have seen it in her eyes because he flashed her a wolf grin and then spun her around, away from him, crowding her into the counter.

It had been a damn long time, and maybe this was how it was done these days, but she could admit she'd been hoping for a face-to-face encounter —

Her dress slithered off her and hit the floor, pooling around her heels.

She let out a nervous laugh and gripped the counter with two fists, in a quandary now. She wanted to turn around, but she'd lied before about having her best lingerie on. A bra hadn't been possible with the dress and her panties were so small as to be nonexistent. It had seemed like a great idea when she'd been dressing, but now —

All of her thoughts scattered like the wind when Parker pressed up against her bare back, sliding his hands up the front of her thighs and then nudging them apart. His fingers glided uninhibited northbound until he touched the lace edge of her panties. She was already quivering when he ran a fingertip along that edging. She expected him to slip past the barrier, but instead his hand cupped her over the material, his other sliding to her stomach and then a breast. She arched her back, tilting her head to give him room, and his lips took full advantage, dancing along the column of her throat.

"So soft. So wet," he said in her ear, voice rough, fingers gentle as he tortured her, driving her up, holding her on the edge, his other hand gripping a hip to keep her in place as he teased her until she was panting.

"Parker." She placed a hand over his, grinding back into him.

His hands pushed her legs farther apart, caressing as he did, until she was pushing back against his fingers, wiggling her hips in silent demand, and *finally* he slipped past the lace and touched her skin to skin.

They both moaned at that. Unable to stop herself, she pushed back into him again and turned her face into his neck. As his fingers parted her, her lips latched onto him, alternating tongue and teeth as she threaded her hand through his hair so that she had an anchor.

Every stroke of his fingers had her gripping a little bit harder, back arching, until she was so wet and ready she was begging him to take her.

But he didn't.

Instead he yanked her around to face him, the motion and the rush of cold air puckering her nipples even tighter, needing his touch.

He didn't disappoint, lowering his head to a breast as his hand stretched the lace of her panties, making more room for himself so that his finger could slide in deep. He moved in slow stroking motions, his thumb brushing lazily back and forth in a rhythm designed to drive her right out of her ever-lovin' mind. She struggled to get her hands between them to shove up his shirt and when it caught on his arms, he pulled free long enough to tear it over his head.

He kicked off his shoes and undid his cargos. "Gotta make some room," he growled, and then went back to the task of making her lose herself in him.

It took less than two seconds and she was gone, coming hard. She'd have slid bonelessly to the floor if he hadn't held her up. When she stopped shuddering and opened her eyes, she realized they were on the move. He was carrying her out of the kitchen, smile predatory and just a little smug.

"You liked that," he said.

"Yes." She slid a hand into his opened cargos and wrapped her fingers around his impressive length, which jerked against her palm. "And you like this."

He hissed in a breath and dumped her on the couch. She bounced once before he was on her.

"My shoes," she said. "I've got to take off my shoes."

"Those aren't shoes, those are evil devices designed to blow a man's mind, and they're staying on," he said in a very sexy voice.

She pulled back to look at him. "Yeah?"

He took in the sight of her in the panties and those high-heeled booties and nothing else. "Oh yeah," he said, and made a low, appreciative male sound that sent a shiver of anticipation racing through her. She desperately wanted him inside her, stretching her, filling her up. "Parker, please."

"Kiss me," he demanded, and she lifted her head so that their eyes met for a beat before he met her halfway, claiming her mouth with the same ease with which he'd claimed her body.

Oreo came bounding into the room, looking sleepy, like *maybe* they'd woken him up. When he saw them, he quickly turned playful, galloping over.

"Oreo, sit," Parker said in a deep, firm voice. "Sit and stay."

Oreo actually skidded to a halt and sat obediently.

And stayed.

Zoe understood exactly. Just listening to Parker's commanding tone made her want to do whatever he said.

Then he tugged her panties from her and tossed them over his shoulder. Lacing his fingers through hers, he used her as his guide down her own body, fingering her nipples, cupping their weight, then tracing her belly button and lower, to the V of her inner thighs.

And between.

At the touch, her hips bucked in response.

"I can't take my eyes off you," he said, his lips following their joined hands.

She could only moan in response as he tasted her, sucking her slowly into his mouth as she chased another orgasm. She was still gasping when he brought their joined hands up to his lips. Holding her gaze, he slipped one of her fingers into his mouth. He bit her lightly and she rocked up. Gripping him by the biceps, she tugged him closer and shoved his pants to his thighs, freeing him enough to once again wrap her fingers around his hard length. "Your turn."

"Not done with you yet," he said, and made her tremble in anticipation.

He pinned her hips with his. She reached for him but he eluded her, coming up with a condom to protect them both. He took his sweet-ass time about getting it on, too, pushing against her so that she could feel every solid inch of what waited for her.

Finally he lifted her just enough that he could slide into her, inch by slow aching inch. Closing her eyes, she reveled in the sensation of him filling her. When he was as deep as he could go, he dipped his head, his hair falling over his forehead as he watched himself move inside her.

He rode her slowly, letting it all build to an incredible height again. He had her desperate in moments and she ground her hips against his for more, harder, faster. When she whispered her plea, he groaned her name and gripped her hips, thrusting deep, giving her everything she wanted, and unbelievably she peaked again.

This time he came with her, burying his face in the crook of her neck and shuddering hard in her arms. It was exquisite and absolutely the most erotic experience of her life.

When they both fell back against the couch together, Parker shifted so she didn't bear all his weight, turning them so that they lay on their sides facing each other.

Stroking a stray strand of hair from her face, he brushed a kiss over her damp temple. Her jaw. Her lips. He lingered there, tasting her until he lifted his head and met her gaze.

He smiled.

"What?" she asked, her voice all raspy, reminding her that not only had she lost track of how many times she'd come for him, she hadn't exactly been quiet about it, either.

"Was going to ask if you were okay," he said with a low laugh. "But your dazed expression says it all."

"Hey." She poked him in the chest. "You look pretty sated yourself."

"Mm-hmmm." And then his arms tightened possessively on her, the message being *you're not going anywhere* . . .

Which was nice since she didn't want to. She wriggled to settle in comfortably and was surprised to feel him stir against her, going hard. "Already?" she asked in disbelief.

"It would have been sooner but I don't have another condom."

She trailed her fingers over his chest. "I'm on the pill," she said softly. "I'm safe . . . if you are."

Tipping her chin up, he met her gaze. "I am."

She smiled. "Okay then."

"Okay then," he repeated, matching her smile, his own wicked enough to make her quiver. "I want you to do that again," he said.

"What?"

"Call out my name."

She looked at him. His eyes were hot, his body even hotter still.

He'd given her everything she'd asked of him and she intended to do the same. So she gave him a smile. "Make me."

He proceeded to do just that.

Twice.

TWENTY

When the knock came at the front door much later, Parker was sprawled spread-eagle on the living room floor staring up at the ceiling trying to get his breath back.

Holy.

Shit.

He'd never lived his life like a monk, but he couldn't remember ever feeling like this after time spent with a woman, like maybe he'd been both hit by a Mack truck and also taken to heaven and back.

Barely managing to turn his head, he found Zoe. She was face down and unmoving.

And deliciously naked.

Unable to stop himself, he reached out and palmed her sweet ass, giving it a squeeze.

Nothing.

He gave it a light smack. It jiggled enticingly and she squeaked but still didn't budge.

Laughing, he tugged her to him. Not easy when she was completely boneless and unmoving. "You breathing?" he asked.

Her eyes stayed closed but her mouth curved. "Don't know. Can't feel any of my parts."

Huffing out a laugh, he stroked her damp hair from her face and leaned down to kiss her just as the doorbell rang.

This accomplished what Parker hadn't managed. Leaping to life, Zoe jumped up and whipped around in circles looking for her clothes.

Damn, the view was fine. Enjoying it, he put his hands behind his head and remained on the floor as Zoe ran around looking for her clothes. She found her teeny-tiny pant- ies — which, for the record, he loved — and hopped into them, nearly falling over, elicit- ing a bunch of creative swearing from Zoe.

He arched a brow, impressed. "You could just not answer the door, you know."

She stared at him as if he'd lost his mind. "I can't find my bra!"

"You weren't wearing one."

"Oh yeah." Clearly also unable to find her dress — which he happened to know was on the kitchen floor — she grabbed his sweats and yanked them up. And then grabbed one of his shirts and pulled it on

267

over her head.

She looked so sexy-adorable he gave her a finger crook. "C'mere."

"Oh no," she said. "I have rug burns on my knees because of that very smile —"

The doorbell rang again.

"Ohmigod," she whispered, waving her hands at him. "Get up, get up! Put some clothes on!"

He laughed at her but got to his feet. "Babe, you're wearing my clothes."

She looked down at herself, made a sound of frustration, and gave him a shove toward the stairs. "What if it's one of my nosy-ass siblings?" she hissed. "They have a key!"

"Then they would've already walked in on us."

When her mouth fell open in horror at the thought, he shook his head. "It's probably Kaylie again. With the kittens."

"Oh yeah." She put a hand to her heart and let out a big breath. "Right." She gave him the once-over, her gaze stuttering to a stop at his groin area.

He flashed another smile. "Say the word," he murmured, reaching for her.

"Word," she whispered, and then sagged against him like he made her knees weak. Liking that way too much, he pulled her in.

"Wait, no," she gasped, pulling back. "Oh

my God, all my brain cells are gone. Go get some more clothes!"

Holding eye contact, he cupped her head and kissed her. He'd meant it to be a light kiss, a thank-you for the most amazing evening kiss, but the wires got crossed in his brain and before he knew it he was in deep and completely lost.

She pulled back first, eyes glazed. She blinked a few times. "Um. Where were we?"

He had no idea.

She shook her head and suddenly her eyes were solemn. She touched her kiss-swollen lips. "That felt . . . serious."

Yeah. It had.

"Did you mean it to be serious?" she asked.

Did he? Christ, he was confused. Not a comfortable state for him. When he didn't answer, couldn't because he had no idea what to say, she blew out a breath and held up a hand. "Never mind. Strike that from the record. In the moment, right?"

He looked into her eyes, saw how much she regretted her question, saw so many, many things, all of which pinched his heart. "Zoe —"

"Right, then," she said.

He opened his mouth, undoubtedly to say something stupid, but she tilted her chin up, nodded once like her decision was final, and . . . headed toward the front door without another word.

Which reminded him he was bare-assed. He took the stairs at a quick clip, and at the top he glanced back down at her.

She had one hand on the door handle but was watching him move with just the slightest bit of a smirk on her face.

And that was when he knew. She'd been okay before him, and she would be okay after him. She was a survivor. And hell, maybe he'd overthought his impact on her life or his importance to her.

Maybe it was *him* who was going to get hurt.

On that uncomfortable note, he went to his bedroom and met his reflection's gaze in the mirror over the dresser. Yeah. He was the one who was going to get hurt. "You're an idiot," he said.

His reflection didn't disagree.

He hit the shower, the entire time thinking of the tough, beautiful Zoe, looking at him, waiting for him to say they could make a go of this, her gaze filled with what he knew was a rare vulnerability.

Because of him.

And then how easily she'd seemed to decide to move on. That thought was so deeply disturbing, he started to go find her, but his phone buzzed. A text from Amory.

You're not here yet.

With a sigh, he called her.

"Parker!" she yelled in his ear. "Are you on your way?"

"No," he said regretfully. "Listen, it's not going to be soon."

"But it has to be. You said a week and I got everything ready so you have to come."

Uh-oh. "I never said a week, Amory. What did you get ready?"

Silence.

And silence when it came to Amory was never a good thing. "Am? Talk to me."

"No! You don't love me, either!"

And then she hung up.

He tried calling her back, but she didn't answer. He left her a text and an e-mail.

More nothing.

Shit. For anyone other than his sister, he might've just given it a few days and tried again. But this was Amory, and though her moods were pure and one hundred percent genuine, they were also mercurial. He stared at his phone for a while, trying to talk himself into letting it go. But the last time he'd let it go, she'd run away from home

271

and managed to get herself on a bus to D.C. to come see him, where she'd gotten herself mugged.

Shit.

He called his dad. His dad was usually more reasonable than his mom.

"Son," his dad answered. "Been a long time."

Two months. Parker had called on his mom's birthday and caught them in the middle of dinner with friends. It had been a good call as far as these things went mostly because with their friends listening, neither his mom nor dad had wanted to reveal any rift. "Dad. How are you? How's Mom?"

"She's right here, son. I've got you on speaker."

Parker grimaced. "Great," he lied. "Hi, Mom."

"Did you know?" his mom asked. "Did you know what Amory was up to?"

He scrubbed a hand over his face. "That depends on what she's up to. She just told me she'd had something planned for when I came but I'm not able to leave right now —"

"Right, so now she's decided to go see you."

Damn. "No," he said. "I was just talking to her and —"

"Parker, how could you?" his mom asked. "She can't travel on her own, you know that, and yet you persist in putting these crazy ideas in her head. After last time —" She broke off and started to cry.

Parker closed his eyes. "Mom —"

"We're going to have to get a court-ordered conservatorship to protect her now that she's a legal adult," she said tearfully. "We didn't think we'd need one, but now with you tempting her at every turn to do the wrong thing . . ."

"It's not the wrong thing for her to want to get out and see and experience new things," Parker said.

"No," his dad said. "It's not, of course it's not. But *you're* the one who wants these things, not her."

Parker pinched the bridge of his nose. This was a very old argument. "Dad —"

"No, Parker, you don't understand," his mom said. "You never have because you think what you want is what everyone should want. But everyone's different, Parker. And Amory happens to be very different. She's happy here and you need to see that and stop trying to make waves. It makes her anxious to think she disappoints you. So now she's determined to make you happy. And we've all seen what a determined Amory can do."

Parker inhaled a deep breath. "Mom, that was three years ago, and we both know that the whole D.C. thing could've been avoided if you'd let her off the leash once in a while. With some supervision and practice, she'd have the experience to travel more —"

"She was *mugged,* Parker," his dad said. "Mugged on the street waiting for the bus. What is this world coming to when a handicapped little girl can't even be safe in broad daylight?"

"She's not a little girl anymore," Parker said. And actually, Amory had been mugged while showing a perfect stranger the picture of him in her wallet, which she'd held open, revealing the wad of cash she'd "borrowed" from their parents. "She needs experience handling herself in the real world," Parker said. "She can do this, she just needs some help. I could —"

"What?" his mother interrupted to ask. "Continue to fill her head with ideas of traveling and living her life the way you do?"

"Not the way *I* do," Parker said. God no. He worked 24/7. Hell, he worked even when he was on "vacation." He lived and breathed the job and didn't have much of a life outside that job. And he'd made that work for him.

But the fact that he'd run so far and hard away from his workaholic parents and the life they'd chosen, only to also be a workaholic in his own field, didn't escape him.

The apple, in spite of its best efforts, hadn't landed all that far from the tree.

But he didn't want *his* life for anyone, especially his sister. He sighed. He knew they thought he was being too hard on them, that they were doing the best they could. "All I want for Amory is happiness," he said. "That's the bottom line, the most important thing. Thanks to you both, she has a good life. You've always been there for her."

"We're not the only ones," his mother admitted. "You've given her as much of yourself and your time as you can; we know this. But she's getting the wrong idea."

"Mom," he said as gently as he could. "You're underestimating her. You're holding the reins just a little too tight. You're asking for her to rebel —"

"She was *hurt,* Parker," his mom said. "A concussion. A broken arm. She was hurt and devastated, and it nearly killed her spirit to know what the real world is like. Next time it could be worse; next time she . . ." She broke off with a shuddery breath.

"You keep sending her pictures of every

place you land," his dad said. "Son, she looks up to you. You have so much influence over her, I don't know if you realize how much. She wants to be like you, she wants to do all that you do."

Which wasn't mining.

Or staying near the family.

"Please," his mom said. "She's impulsive. You have to fix this before something else happens."

Parker shook his head. "And how do you expect me to fix it?"

"Talk to her," his father said. "Tell her that you and she aren't the same, that she can't live the way you do. That she can't run off just because she doesn't like the answers we give her."

"Please," his mom said. "Before it's too late."

When they ended the call, Parker tried Amory again. She didn't pick up, so he left her a voice mail and said the only thing that would fix this. "Amory, I'm coming to see you soon as I can. I promised you, remember? But now I need something from you, okay? Now that you're eighteen, you're a grown-up. And grown-ups understand that things don't always happen as fast as they want."

Yeah, he was ruthlessly manipulating her

feelings, but his mom was right on one thing — Amory was incredibly impulsive. "I'm finishing up a job here shortly. I'll be there right after," he promised.

One way or another. "You don't need to go anywhere. I'll see you soon."

He disconnected and prowled the house. He was looking for Zoe but told himself he was just making sure the house was all locked up and that the occupants were okay. Zoe's car was in the driveway but her room was dark. Hand on her doorknob, he stilled, debating with himself for a long, tense moment there in the hallway. But in the end, he didn't open the door.

If she'd wanted his company, she'd have left it open.

He checked the kittens next, who'd been brought back by Kaylie. They were not only okay, they were wild. He sat on the bathroom floor and played with them for a few minutes, interrupted when his phone pinged a notification.

Once again, the cameras in Cat's Paw had been activated.

He went to the kitchen to check his laptop.

A convoy of five trucks, empty by the looks of them, drove into the ranch. Only one reason for it that he could think of. They were there to load up and move out.

Seemed that what he'd told Amory was correct — this job would indeed be over soon, one way or the other, and he'd be free to go home. He'd leave Sunshine, and all that was in it. Normally at this point on a job he felt a driving need to get out.

He felt a driving need, all right.

To *not* go.

Twenty-One

Zoe stayed up late visiting with Manda, who taught her how to make the most amazing blueberry muffins she'd ever had. She knew it was likely that most of the love and adoration for them might be attributed to the bottle of wine they'd shared, but Zoe had crawled into bed with a smile on her face.

Okay, so maybe the smile was also from all the earlier orgasms she'd had with Parker. Good Lord. She'd actually lost count. But once her mind went down that path, she lay in bed remembering some of the things Parker had done to her, and there in the dark she blushed.

And ached for more.

She'd done things to him, too, and reliving some of them got her hot and bothered all over again.

Maybe he'd realize they could really have something.

She got halfway to his room before she

came to her senses. Even if he did realize
their potential, he wouldn't give in to it or
do anything about it. He'd been nothing
but crystal clear that they weren't going to
entertain having any kind of relationship
past his time here in Sunshine, which put a
pretty quick damper on her libido. Right
there in the hallway she stilled. Then turned
away.

And that was when Parker's bedroom
door opened, backlit by the moonlight slant-
ing into his bedroom and across a wedge of
the hallway.

He stood there looking disturbingly awake
in nothing but forest green knit boxers riding low on his hips, like maybe he hadn't
been able to sleep, either.

"What's wrong?" he asked.

She stared at him, fighting the urge to lick
him from sternum to the waistband of those
boxers.

And beyond.

And she wanted him again. *Why fight it,* a
voice inside her head asked — the slut
again. *Live in the moment.* "I'm cold," she
lied. "I can't get warm."

"It's summer. It's a warm night."

"Parker?"

"Yeah?"

"Do you really want to argue with a

woman who's trying to seduce you?"

He went from sleepy to hot, aroused male complete with the slow and easy smile in a single heartbeat. "You're trying to seduce me," he said.

"*Trying* being the key word here," she said, starting to feel a little put out that he was still standing way over there.

With a low laugh he reached for her, but she evaded. "I think I'm warm enough now," she said, giving him a push.

He didn't budge, just hauled her into his arms. "No, you're right, you feel pretty chilled to me," he said, his voice one-hundred-percent sex. "Can't have that, not on my watch."

She wrapped her arms around his neck. "If you're sure it's not a bother."

"No bother at all. I'm your man."

The words put a little thrill into her heart even though she knew he didn't mean it.

"First, I'm going to warm you up. I'm going to share my body heat," he murmured against her ear. "And I have lots of body heat, Zoe."

She shivered in anticipation.

"And then," he went on, carrying her to his bed, "I'm going to make sure you stay warm, even if it takes all night."

And then he made good on his every word.

■ ■ ■ ■

Zoe woke first and slipped out of Parker's bed. One more night of erotic pleasure like the one she'd just had and she didn't think she'd be able to walk away.

No, she was *sure* she wouldn't be able to walk away. Falling asleep in his arms had probably been a mistake because that had felt even more intimate than the lovemaking.

In the hallway, Oreo nudged her toward the stairs. He wanted food. She crouched low and hugged the dog. "Listen," she whispered into Oreo's fur, "I know he's super sexy and he smells good and his smile makes us stupid, but he's leaving. We need to remember that and be strong. No falling for him, okay? Promise?"

Oreo didn't promise, and she sighed. Then she headed to the kitchen in desperate need of caffeine. She intended to wake up fully and get herself to work. She didn't have any flights scheduled, but there was a staff meeting she had to attend. Joe, annoyed by the exorbitant maintenance cost of the aging Caravan, wanted to sell it and get something newer and bigger, and she wanted in on that discussion.

But mostly she wanted to keep busy so she could think about something other than Parker. His moan of appreciation when he'd tasted her French toast. The sound of her name on his lips when he'd been buried deep inside her. The look on his face whenever he touched her, a look that conveyed something his words never did, that he was every bit as into her as she was him . . .

Damn. She had it bad.

Hey, it's not all doom and gloom, her little voice said. *You learned to bake kick-ass blueberry muffins last night.* Somehow, in spite of herself, she'd opened her life a little and was having some fun.

Actually, if she factored in all the sex, she was having *lots* of fun. After Wyatt and Darcy had moved out, she'd really thought all her fun was behind her, but she was happy to be wrong about that.

And there was a lot more fun out there to be had, she told herself. When Parker was gone and the glow of all the orgasms wore off, she'd still be going for life, one hundred percent.

Or at least seventy-five percent.

Determined to be fine, she decided it was a blueberry muffin sort of morning. While waiting for the coffee to brew, she carefully re-created a batch from the recipe Manda had written down for her, doing everything from the night before — except drink a bottle of wine — and stuck them in the oven.

Waiting was not a strong suit of hers, so she ran upstairs to shower and dress for the day, and then, because she'd forgotten last night, she started to switch her laundry from the washer to the dryer. But she got distracted by the kittens, whom she'd let run free while she was in the shower.

Massive mistake.

Wild woman was hanging from the curtains in the living room, swaying back and forth like Tarzan. The tabby had vanished completely. It took Zoe fifteen minutes to find the thing. Eventually she found him in the dryer she'd left open — snoozing on her fresh, clean whites. She scooped him up in her hands and he lifted his little fuzzy head to give her a sleepy "mew," looking so adorable she couldn't find her mad.

That was when she remembered the muffins.

A few minutes later she'd tossed out the burned muffins, run across the driveway to get a bag of muffins from Manda, and then corralled the heathens in the kitchen with her, and was opening the bag of muffins that Manda had given her. It took only a minute to decide that last night's muffins would be better warmed.

Five minutes later, the room no longer smelled like burned muffins but instead like perfectly baked and warming muffins, and Zoe nodded in satisfaction. *This* was more like it.

She needed a Manda.

She looked up when Parker came into the room, dressed in jeans and a button-down, keys in hand. His hair was still damp from a shower. As she took a deep breath, her nose filled with the essence of Parker: soap, deodorant, and delicious, sexy man. Her body practically vibrated with unbidden memories: Parker in his bed, inside her body, his mouth hot at her throat, his hands positioning her as he wanted as he'd moved within her, driving her wild.

"Hey," she said.

"Hey." He smiled and her heart hurt. "I thought I'd wake up with you."

She ignored the way her heart squished at that.

"What smells so good?" he asked.

She looked at the oven, where the muffins were warming. Manda's muffins. But hey, Zoe had helped make them, so technically that meant they were half hers, right? Maybe more than half since she'd done the reheating all on her own. And if she'd decided to make breakfast casserole or breakfast burritos or something like that, she would have rocked it because she could so totally cook, dammit. "Blueberry muffins," she said, and nonchalantly pulled the pan of perfectly made blueberry muffins from the oven.

Both man and dog locked eyes on them and licked their lips.

"Did you make 'em?" Parker asked, not making a move any closer.

His wariness was more than mildly annoying. "Why?" she asked. "Are you afraid?"

He looked pained now, like he was in a quandary.

"Guess you are," she said, taking a muffin from the tray and slowly peeling back the paper, breaking the muffin in half, watching as the steam rose. Mouth watering, she took a bite and closed her eyes. "Mmmm," she moaned.

When she opened her eyes, Parker had moved into her personal space, his eyes dark with heat and more than a little bit of trouble. He'd skipped a shave this morning and his jaw had just the right amount of scruff on it so that if he rubbed it against her she'd probably orgasm on the spot.

Her inner thighs trembled.

"Good?" he murmured, his gaze locked in on her mouth.

"Very." She stared up at him, out of breath. Why was she out of breath? *Because you want him. Just one more time* . . . "Parker?"

"Yeah?"

Deciding to show, not tell, she ran a finger down his chest to the button on his jeans.

His eyes heated, but he remained still.

So she let her finger slip beneath the waistband of his jeans.

He caught her wrist. "You chilly again?" he asked, amusement in his voice.

"Don't play hard to get now," she whispered, and he laughed.

"Zoe," he said in that early-morning sexy guy voice, "with you, I'm never hard to get. I'm just hard."

She snorted and pulled him down to kiss him.

He kissed her back and then looked deep into her eyes.

She did her best to look like something he couldn't live without. At least for the duration.

"When you sneaked out of my bed this morning, I figured you'd come to your senses," he said.

"If I'd come to my senses, I'd have kicked

you out days ago." To soften the words, she once again pulled his head down to hers.

"Be sure," he said, voice low, calm, even though the hunger and desire in his eyes gave him away. "No regrets."

"Of course not," she said. "The three W's, remember? No wondering, no worrying, no wishing for things I can't have." Okay, so she'd added on those last few words, but it sounded like a good policy.

"I don't want to hurt you —"

"You can't." She put her finger over his sexy lips when he didn't cave. "I get it now," she promised. "I want to enjoy this, enjoy you, while I can. I need this, Parker. I need you."

She waited a beat for him to deny her, to be stoic and strong and hold her off because that was what he thought was best for her. But doing what perhaps was the most incredible thing any man had ever done for her, he assumed she was an adult and capable of making her own decisions. His hands settled on her hips and he pulled her in. "Zoe?"

"Yeah?"

He slid the pad of his thumb over her lower lip and then let his fingers sink into her hair so that he could tilt her face up to his. "I'm going to kiss you," he said in that sexy, gravelly morning voice.

She nodded eagerly, her breathing already shallow and rapid. "Yes —"

Before the word was all the way out of her mouth, he lowered his head and kissed her hard, pinning her to the counter. She sucked his tongue into her mouth, greedily savoring the taste of him while he appeared to do the same. "Here," she said.

Demanded.

And he made it so. He stripped her quickly, murmuring hot praises in between kissing and stroking everything he exposed, and when she was naked, he set her on the counter.

"Hold on," he said.

And she did. She held on, feeling his muscles bunch and release as he slid into her and began to move, pushing in and out in a rhythm that took her from zero to sixty in a heartbeat. She held on, her ankles linked at his backside, moving with him, sensation after sensation pummeling her until she was so close to coming she could hardly breathe.

And then Parker gripped her hips hard and yanked her in so that their torsos were plastered together, so that she could feel the weight of him leaning into her, the carved muscles of his chest and arms working. And in the sensual haze of her preorgasmic state, she looked up. His face was an erotic mask of pleasure and that was all it took. She came with his name a mantra on her lips, came so hard she was barely cognizant of him burying his face in the crook of her neck and doing the same.

When he pulled back, Zoe realized she had a two-fisted grip on his shirt and was still letting out helpless little whimpers as she came down. "Sorry."

He eased her to the floor and held her still when she tried to turn away. "Don't ever be sorry for your passion. It's beautiful. I love it."

"I . . . got a little wild."

He tightened his grip and kissed her until she forgot what they'd been talking about. "I love it," he repeated against her mouth, and finally let her go.

Flushed, she resisted the urge to stick her heated face into the freezer. Instead she dressed — again — and poured them both a coffee and tried to act like this, having a man in her kitchen in the morning, one she'd slept with, was an everyday occurrence.

Except that until he'd shown up, it was a *never* occurrence.

He'd inhaled three of the muffins and

praised her baking after each one before her conscience got the best of her. "Parker?"

"Yeah?" He was eyeing yet another muffin and she realized that when he left here, she wanted to leave her mark on him the same way he'd left his mark on her.

She wanted him to remember her as great in bed — or in this case, great on her kitchen counter, the couch, and the floor, and his bed . . . She wanted him to remember her house and her damn amazing blueberry muffins. "Nothing," she said.

He smiled and popped another muffin into his mouth, and she had to close her eyes because the sight of him eating with such pleasure made her ache. *Dammit.* "Ididn'tmakethem," she said.

"What?"

She kept her eyes closed because if she didn't look at him, he couldn't turn her upside down.

Then she felt his warm, large hand along her jaw. "Look at me."

She grimaced because her body had a serious problem with ignoring a command from him, but she opened her eyes.

"I know," he said, and flashed her the sexiest of all his smiles. Holding her gaze, he went for his fifth muffin, breaking it in half to share with Oreo, who was sitting on

Parker's foot.

Both man and dog ate with pleasure, Oreo nudging Parker's hand with his nose for more.

"You know?" Zoe repeated.

"Yep." Parker licked crumbs off his thumb and then sucked his forefinger into his mouth to get that one clean, too.

The sound made her nipples hard.

Damn misbehaving nipples! "How did you know?" she demanded.

He shrugged his broad shoulders and captured the naughty gray kitten before she could tumble headfirst into Oreo's empty bowl.

"Parker."

He glanced up at Zoe. "When you say my name like that, I want to make you say it again. While I'm inside you."

Her legs quivered, but she put her hands on her hips.

"Yeah," he said, nodding. "I think it's the 'tude combined with the tone. And the way you're dressed, too. Like you're a pissed-off teacher. Want to play teacher and deviant principal?"

"No!" she said indignantly, for women everywhere, even as a part of her — a shockingly big part — wanted to say *YES!*

He was watching her face and laughed.

"You're a pretty liar, Zoe. Maybe *I* should be the teacher and you the naughty student."

She felt ground zero twitch and get damp at the thought. "Both of those things put *you* in charge," she noted.

"Yeah. So?"

"So maybe I want to be in charge," she said.

His eyes darkened. "Say the word."

She took a big step back. Damn, she should know better than to play with him. "We just did it," she said with a low laugh. "On the counter! And then like a hundred times last night! Aren't you tired?"

With another laugh, he hauled her into him and nuzzled his face into the crook of her neck. "You smell so fuckin' good," he murmured. "Like blueberry muffins. I want to eat you up."

"I have to go."

With a sigh, he released her. "Be safe today."

She met his gaze. "I will if you will."

Zoe ended up with an unscheduled late flight. By the time she got home, it was past midnight. Parker wasn't there. She checked.

Or rather, her hormones checked.

She fell into bed after setting her alarm,

which went off what felt like only a few minutes later. She showered in a bit of a fog and hit the kitchen, desperate for caffeine.

Parker was there with the kittens and Oreo, looking like he belonged in her life, the four of them having a breakfast party. His sharp eyes met hers and he wordlessly got up and poured her some coffee.

"Thanks," she said gratefully, refraining from mentioning how good he looked in her life — oops, her kitchen.

Her heart hitched, a little warning that she was in over her head. Big-time. She ignored it and when Parker pulled her in, she wrapped herself up in him willingly.

He held her for a moment, his arms comforting and warm. She wasn't exactly sure when the embrace changed, heating up, but she welcomed it, clutching at him as his mouth forged a hot path along her jaw and down her throat.

With a helpless moan, her head fell back to give him more room and she clutched at him. "This can't happen right now," she said weakly. "I've only got ten minutes to get out of here."

"Ten minutes works for me." His hands ran along her hips, down her thighs, and back up again, beneath her skirt to cup her ass.

"It doesn't work for me," she managed to say. "I need at least twenty."

"Hmm," he murmured, kissing his way down her throat like a man on a mission. "A challenge." He flashed his badass grin and slid her blazer off her shoulders, laying it across the back of a chair. "Accepted."

"No, I didn't mean —"

Her cami was no match for him. In two seconds he'd nudged the straps off her shoulders and down her arms, where he left them so that her hands were bound at her sides. "Um —"

Her bra, a front clasp, came undone with a flick of his wrist and her breasts spilled into his hands.

He let out a low, appreciative breath and bent his head, using his tongue to flick one nipple, and then the other before pulling it into his mouth and sucking hard.

Her knees wobbled and he picked her up, setting her down on the kitchen table between his laptop and her coffee and some flight files she'd planned to go over. "The computer —" she whispered. "My files —"

"They'll be fine if you stay still. Can you stay still, Zoe?" he asked between nibbles, and when she didn't answer, he gently closed his teeth around a nipple.

"I don't know," she managed. Panting

now, she spread her legs and wrapped them around him, pulling him in close, needing him right up against her. Her coffee nearly sloshed but he caught it, steadied it, all without taking his eyes off her.

"Hold still," he reminded her.

She had no idea what it was about his soft commands that turned her on so much, but there was no denying that she was very, very turned on.

Her skirt was snug and a stretchy material that Parker had no trouble sliding up to her hips. He took in her plain black bikini panties and smiled. "I like."

"You like everything."

He chuckled but his eyes stayed hot as he leaned her back on the table, dropping kisses across her shoulders, her breasts, her belly. "You always taste so good," he whispered against her hip now.

"Parker . . ." Freeing her arms of the cami's straps with some arm flapping, she reached down and entangled her fingers into his hair.

He lifted his head, eyes glittering. "I'm starving for you, Zoe."

"First of all, that can't be true," she said. "I can see you finished off the muffins. And also it's been less than twelve hours since we did this."

"I always save room for dessert, and it feels a lot longer than twelve hours." He had his fingers spread wide on her legs, his thumbs brushing over the heated skin of her inner thighs, moving higher and higher with each stroke.

"Do you want to know what I'm going to do to you?" he asked, his voice so low as to be nearly inaudible.

With each brush of those callused pads of his thumbs she whimpered and writhed and rocked her hips up for the touch that wouldn't come. Did she want to know what he was going to do to her? *Hell yes.* She desperately wanted to know, but she couldn't formulate a word.

"Still, Zoe," he warned, and then went on with his story. "First," he said, "I'm going to make you come with my mouth. Lift up."

When she did, he slowly pulled her panties down her legs, letting out a low, sexy growl at what he'd exposed.

"Then I'm going to bury myself in deep," he said, "until you want to rock into me and thrash around, maybe try to claim the control for yourself."

If she'd had a breath left in her lungs she might have laughed. Or grabbed him down onto the table with her.

"But you're not going to," he said, his

mouth working its way south. "You're going to stay still, very still because of your files and my laptop." He sat on a chair and ran his hands up her thighs again, almost getting all the way to the top this time before stopping.

She slapped her hands down to the table, desperate for something to hold on to.

"Don't move," he said. "Not an inch. We're on borrowed time here and I don't want to have to stop before you cry out my name."

"I'm not going to" — she had to pant for breath — "cry out your name. I don't do that."

He didn't argue with her, nor did he talk again for a few minutes. Instead he licked his way to her center, doling out sucking little kisses that drove her wild, but ignoring The Spot until she started to sit up.

The coffee mug next to her, the one so close to the laptop, sloshed a little. Parker's hands tightened on her thighs, a silent warning. With great effort, she stilled.

Parker went back to his ministrations.

And then he made her cry out his name.

Twenty-Two

As Zoe left for work, Parker mentioned he'd be out that night late, and though he didn't say and she didn't ask, she knew it was job related. And for a minute, just a minute, she'd let herself entertain the thought of them meshing their lives together. The realities of his job were fairly terrifying, but she could work with that.

What she was starting to realize was that what she couldn't work with was being without him — a problem. A big one.

At the airport, Joe was all business for their weekly production meeting, but as soon as the room cleared out, he asked Zoe to stay.

They hadn't had a single spare moment to talk one on one since their date. She didn't know if he wanted to discuss that, or the offer to partner in with him on the business — which she still wasn't sure about — but she blew out a breath and faced the music. "I'm sorry," she said. "I know I ended our date abruptly."

"No," he said. "I wanted to thank you. My mom and sister saw me with you and they are now officially satisfied that I can get my own dates. They said I did good, finding a ten to my six."

She laughed. "I'm no ten," she said.

He grinned and gave a playful tug of her hair, leaning in close to say huskily against her ear, "And I'm no six. In bed, I'm an eleven. Your loss, sweet cheeks."

She smiled. "An eleven, huh?"

"Want to change your mind about me now, don't you?"

She opened her mouth, but before she could figure out how to let him down gently, he shook his head. "Too late," he said. "You'll have to forever live with the fact that you moved too slow to catch me."

"Is that right?" she asked.

"I've been after my sister's best friend, Stacey, for five years. She's never given me the time of day — until she heard about my hot date with you. Suddenly she's all into me." He chortled and rubbed his hands together. "She asked me out for tonight. Good times ahead for Big Joe *and* Little Joe — not that Little Joe is little, if you know what I mean."

She grimaced. "How about we not talk about Little Joe?"

"Sure, how about we talk about you making me some money today?"

"I'm not ready to talk about the business offer, either. But soon," she promised. "I'm not being coy —"

"Zoe," he said with a laugh. "I've known you for years. You don't have a coy bone in your body. Nor have you ever rushed a decision."

True. Until the one where she jumped into bed with Parker . . .

"Take your time," Joe said, serious now. "I'll be here. But for now, you've got a lesson and two flights scheduled. What do you say about getting outta here and bringing in some dough today?"

Parker spent the better part of the day up at Cat's Paw, stealthily replacing batteries in his cameras. It wasn't easy. There was a new set of guards and these guys were better than the other shift.

He'd had to park the Jeep two miles back and hike in, dodging the surveillance team when he could, waiting them out when he couldn't.

Halfway through, twenty-five feet up in the air, stretched out on a branch to reach one of his cameras, he heard an engine coming his way. Several vehicles.

There were four, with a Land Rover in the lead, the top off.

He'd been made, he thought, and remembering what had happened the last time he'd had a run-in with one of Carver's trucks, he froze and did his damned best to be the tree.

No. Not made. They were leaving the ranch, en masse.

He'd bet his last dollar Carver was among them.

The convoy came through the brush with the Land Rover in the lead, weaving to steer clear of the growth. They were about a hundred feet away from Parker when he heard an ominous little creak from the branch he'd balanced himself on.

And then a *CRACK*.

Shit. Now the convoy was at fifty feet.

And then twenty-five. There were two men in the front seat of the Land Rover, both heavily armed by the looks of them.

Another crack from his branch and Parker started to sweat. Fuck, he was too old for this shit. He couldn't move or he'd be seen, but if the branch broke, he'd fall to the ground practically at their feet, and that was going to go over like a fart in church.

Just hold, he prayed to the damn tree. *Just for another thirty seconds.*

But then the convoy slowed. And stopped.

Sweat dripped into Parker's eyes, but he didn't dare even blink. He focused in on the men in the Land Rover and realized they were on their comms, communicating with the other vehicles.

Parker literally held his breath. Any second now he was going to fall right on top of them.

Finally they hit the gas, passing almost directly beneath him, one vehicle at a time. They were no sooner out of sight when Parker took his first deep breath — just as the branch creaked and cracked one last time and . . .

Dumped him to the ground.

It was the end of the day before Zoe decided she needed something to keep her mind off Parker, so she'd stopped at the hardware store on the way home from the airport and had purchased a new lock mechanism for her back door, which had been broken forever.

The guy in the store had sworn that even an idiot could handle the installation, but that he'd be happy to make a house call if she needed him.

Since he'd accompanied this with a brow waggle and a wink-wink elbow jab to the ribs, she'd decided she'd need a house call from him *never*. Yes, he had a job but he was lacking her core requirements — and that wasn't even counting the fact that he'd been chewing tobacco and may or may not have been in possession of all of his teeth.

And of course there was the real problem — she was now using Parker as a ruler to measure all the other men up against. Which meant she was certainly setting herself up for failure.

But she didn't care at the moment. She had other things to worry about. Such as the new lock on the back door. She worked on it for an hour before sitting back on her heels and admitting defeat.

Replacing the lock — like falling success-fully in love — wasn't in her wheelhouse.

Shaking that off, Zoe moved to the counter next to the fridge, where she'd left herself some banana bread she'd been given by a client.

It was gone.

She looked at Oreo.

Oreo held her gaze but his ears went down.

"You didn't," she said.

He gave one thump of his tail and tried to

look innocent.

He failed.

She sighed and turned away, her gaze catching on the motion detector camera on the far counter, the spare that Parker had said she could use. "Okay, big guy," she said to Oreo. "It's time to put you to the test."

She set up the camera on top of the refrigerator, relieved to find it easy to use. "There," she said when she was finished, and turned to Oreo. "I've got eyes on you, buddy."

Oreo pretended to be asleep.

Around her, the house was quiet. Or as quiet as it could get with two wild, batshit-crazy kittens on the loose. She told herself she liked quiet, but she missed the comforting presence of a man in the place.

And not just any man. She missed Parker. She wondered where he was.

She cooked herself her favorite dinner — which was breakfast. She put on her pj's. She tiptoed down the hall and peered into Parker's room.

Yep. Empty.

Get used to that, she told herself, and got into bed. She snuggled with Oreo and the silly kittens, whom she'd decided to name after all — Bonnie and Clyde.

She woke up at some point around midnight and knew she was going to have to read to make herself tired enough to go back to sleep. She picked up her phone to search for a new book to download, but realized she had a notification on the app connected to the motion detector camera.

This wasn't good. Hugging her phone to herself, ready to call 911, she waited for the feed to load and reveal her kitchen.

Not dark as one would expect at midnight. This was because the lights were on. In stunned disbelief she watched as Parker fixed the lock on her back door.

In like five minutes.

"I don't know what to do about that," she said to Oreo. "Or him."

Oreo had no answers, either.

Parker slept like shit, and not just because he hurt from fucking head to fucking toe thanks to falling out of the fucking tree up at Cat's Paw.

Luckily he hadn't broken anything but his own damn ego. He did have a new slice through his eyebrow, and okay, his left thigh had been nearly stabbed straight through by a branch, but he considered both of those things collateral damage. He'd live.

Nope, what was keeping him up were some unusual concerns, at least for him. As he'd proven today, keeping his head in the game was hard. Harder than it had ever been, and the reason why didn't reassure him.

For the first time he didn't want a job to end. He realized he wasn't officially on any job at all, was in fact actively jeopardizing his job, but he'd started this and he intended to finish it. He just wasn't in a hurry to move on.

In fact, he didn't want to move on at all, but he knew his lifestyle wasn't good for the people he cared about.

Not that caring was all that good for him, either. It distracted him, and being distracted could get him killed, like it had nearly done up at Cat's Paw.

He needed to focus. Not easy when he felt all twisted up over Zoe. He knew damn well it was going to come down to choosing her or the job. He couldn't have both and he knew it.

When dawn finally hit, he showered and dressed and then walked — okay, maybe limped slightly — into the kitchen to find Zoe pacing. Whirling to face him, she put her hands on her hips, her pissy look firmly in place.

He knew it couldn't be the cut above his eyebrow, because he'd worn a baseball hat to cover it for exactly that reason. He had no idea what had crawled up her ass, but that look on her face only made him want to kiss it right off her. It made him want to drag her off to his bed, where he'd put her into a different mood entirely. "We out of caffeine?" he asked mildly.

"What's this?" she asked, gesturing to the back door and the shiny new lock he'd installed.

"Huh," he said. "You did a nice job."

She narrowed her eyes. "Like I did on the fireplace? And the electrical? Or on any of the other millions of things that have suddenly gotten fixed?"

"I'll pour you some coffee," he said, heading to the pot.

"Do you ever just answer a question?" she asked his back. "No, you don't. *Ever.*"

"Overexaggerating much this morning?" he asked. "And I answer your questions to the best of my ability."

"Yeah? Well, then answer this one — how do you nicely tell someone that sometimes you want to hit them in the head with a brick?"

He poured a cup of coffee and added a healthy serving of vanilla creamer — her favorite — before holding it out to her. "You could say that you'd like to rearrange their facial features with a fundamental material used to make walls," he suggested. "That does have a certain ring to it. Drink, Zoe. Fuel up."

She took the proffered mug, drank generously, and sighed. "Probably I shouldn't talk before I've had caffeine."

He refrained from agreeing.

She sighed again. "I'm sorry. I'm a morning shrew."

Again, he thought his restraint was remarkable and deserving of a medal.

Her lips twitched. "How many live-in girlfriends have you driven right out of their minds by being so morning perfect?" she asked.

He choked on his coffee and very nearly snorted it out his nose.

"So all of them?" she asked.

He smiled. "You're fishing."

With a shrug, she went back to sipping her coffee, but it didn't take a genius to see that she was trying so hard not to push him. "I've never had a live-in girlfriend," he admitted.

"Never?"

"Never."

She considered this for a long moment. "Well then, women the world over are missing out. You're a good roomie. Thanks for fixing the lock, Parker. And for all the other little fixes, too. I appreciate it."

"What makes you so sure it was me?" he asked.

She gestured to something above the refrigerator.

His motion detector camera.

He stared at it and then her and cocked a brow. "You're spying on me?"

"As I told you when I borrowed it, I meant to spy on Oreo. You were an added bonus," she said.

For a guy who guarded his privacy, this admittedly threw him. "You've had the camera for days," he said. "Where else have you set it up?"

She stared at him, looking surprised at the question.

"The shower?" he asked.

"No," she said, looking horrified that he'd think so. "I swear." But then her curiosity apparently got the better of her. "Why?" she asked. "What do you do in the shower?"

"Well, this morning I jacked off to the memory of you crying out my name."

She swallowed hard and looked like she might be having trouble breathing. "You . . . *really*?"

"Really."

Abruptly setting down her mug, she

walked out of the kitchen.

What the hell? Not nearly finished with this conversation, not even close, he followed her out, through the living room, and up the stairs to the bathroom he'd been using. It was still a little foggy from all the hot water he'd used.

She stood in the middle of the room and stared through the glass.

"Zoe?"

"Shh. I'm picturing it," she whispered, like it was too naughty a conversation for a normal speaking voice.

Behind her back, he found a smile. "Seems only fair since I picture you all the time. You have a handheld in there. Do you ever use it when you think of me?"

She gasped. "I don't . . . I don't use it like that — and I don't even use this shower."

He turned her to face him and found her blushing and biting her lower lip. "But you do think of me in *your* shower, where you also have a handheld." Leaning past her, he flicked on the water.

"What are you doing?" she asked, sounding more than a little panicked.

Smart woman.

"I want to see you do it," he said. "I want to see you doing yourself while you think of me."

"I'm not going to — I have things to do, I have a flight later this afternoon —"

"Plenty of time, then." He smiled and tugged off her blazer. "And besides, all you need is twenty minutes, remember?" He started to unbutton her blouse and leaned in to kiss her. "Which we both know I can cut down to seven if I'm on my game," he whispered against her lips. "And I'm feeling *very* on my game at the moment, Zoe."

She stared at him for a beat through the steam filling the bathroom and then kicked off her shoes. "All right, fine," she said with gracious defeat, "but only because you got me all hot and bothered and I have to be able to concentrate today."

"Duly noted," he said, his mouth watering as she shimmied out of the rest of her clothes.

"Less staring and more stripping," she said, nodding her chin toward his clothes. "We're on the clock here."

He was laughing as he did her bidding and stripped, completely forgetting his injuries.

She gasped at the gash on his forehead and then her attention drifted southbound, right past his favorite body part, and locked in on the gauze he'd wrapped around the wound on his thigh.

She dropped to her knees and set her

hands on either side of his leg. "What happened?"

"You got on your knees in front of me," he said, voice unintentionally gravelly.

She stared up at his erection and choked out a laugh.

"It's not polite to laugh at a naked man, Zoe."

"I didn't mean —" She closed her eyes for a beat and then opened them. "Tell me why you have a cut on your head and you're bleeding through a bandage."

"Later," he said, and scooped her up and stepped into the shower with her.

She turned to face him, letting her heated, appreciative gaze run down his body again, slower this time, and not in alarm but arousal. She smiled. "You like me."

"Hard for a man to hide it," he agreed, smiling back.

She bit her lower lip again. "Show me?"

He arched a brow. "You mean —"

"Yes," she said. "Show me what I missed this morning. If you're . . . up for it."

He snorted and reached for the soap, running it down his body while she watched avidly. When he was good and soaped up, he wrapped his hand around himself and stroked.

All laughter gone, Zoe's eyes glazed over.

She might have drooled, it was hard to tell, but her expression was gratifying to say the least. It had been a long time since he'd had this kind of intimacy with a woman. He'd not even realized how much he'd missed it.

Damn, he had it bad. He'd never meant to put himself at risk with her, but he had. He'd put his heart on the line and he hadn't even realized it.

So much for being aware of his surroundings.

He let her watch for a minute and then, tired of playing solitaire, reached for her. "Your turn."

She was breathless. "But you're not done."

"Ladies first." To ease her sudden anxiety, he pulled her in and spent a few minutes nuzzling and touching and kissing her, and when she was kissing him back, breathless and frantic, he turned her away from him so that the warm water cascaded down her front.

"What are you doing?" she asked.

"Helping." He soaped up his hands again and slowly massaged her shoulders and arms until she sighed and let him support her weight, leaning her head back so that it rested on his collarbone.

With his height advantage, this gave him a

great view of her slicked, soapy body, and he watched her nipples tighten even more as he nuzzled into the crook of her neck. When she was as loose as he could get her, he took her hands in his, guiding them over her own curves and then to those gorgeous breasts. He used both their fingers to lightly tug and tease her now-straining, wet nipples until she was moving of her own accord, rocking her sweet ass against his erection.

Damn. She undid him, completely, and he had no idea how the fuck he was supposed to walk away from her when this was all over.

Don't go there. Not now. Don't borrow the heartache sooner than you have to.

"Parker . . ."

The need in her voice fueled him on. Kissing the column of her neck, her shoulder, distracting her with his mouth, he turned her toward the corner of the shower, placing her left hand flat on the wall, her right still caught in his. Pushing a thigh between hers from behind, he bent his leg and lifted one of hers until her foot rested on the edge of the tub.

Perfect.

Now he slid their still-joined hands down her beautiful breasts, her quivering stomach, and lower — right between her thighs. Their fingers traced her every fold and then circled back and started again.

And then again.

Neither of them spoke; the only sounds were the thunder of the water and their equally harsh breathing. Leaning over her shoulder, Parker took in the sight of them both driving her up. "Watch," he murmured, and nipped her shoulder until she dipped her head. She sucked in a breath and her entire body began to tremble.

With his leg beneath her bent one, his foot on the ledge next to hers, he could feel her body pressed against him like they'd been hot-glued together, the softness of her skin tempting him as he held her in place, still watching while their fingers swirled and dipped and teased. He was harder than he could remember ever being, his erection nestled between her ass cheeks, straining like a homing beacon, trying to work its way inside her however it could.

She tensed and he turned his head to whisper in her ear. "Relax, that's not where I'm headed."

She let out a half laugh, half moan and tilted her head back for a kiss. He gave it to her. Hell, he wanted to give her everything and anything she wanted, always, and to distract that thought from creeping in, he took the handheld massager out of the wall cradle and put it into her hand.

She squirmed. "You do it," she whispered, closing her eyes.

Laughing softly, he kissed the sweet spot just beneath her ear. "After all we've done to each other, Zoe, you can't possibly be embarrassed."

She didn't answer, so he covered her hand with his and guided her. She moaned and started to relax again now that he was in charge.

"Am I doing it the way you do?" he asked.

Still no verbal response, though her body was telling him everything he needed to know. *Stubborn to the end,* he thought with a surge of lust and affection and hunger. But in a clash of wills, he never lost. When he misdirected the spray of water by about an inch, she whimpered in distress and tried to guide his hand back to where she wanted it, but he held firm.

"If you want it some other way," he murmured in her ear, taking the lobe between his teeth, "you'll have to hold it yourself."

She tried to arch her hips to force his hand but he couldn't be budged. Finally, with a huff of great frustration, she yanked the handheld from him and shifted it right where she wanted it. It took her another

317

thirty seconds to find her groove, but he knew when she melted against him again, her hips rocking, her breath coming in sexy little pants, that she'd lost herself in the game.

And God, she was the sexiest thing he'd ever seen.

When she started to tremble, a punch of lust went straight to his gut. Again he slid his hand between her thighs and while she aimed the pulsing water, he stroked with his fingers.

She came with a cry and a racking shudder. He held her through it until with a soft sigh, she leaned her head back against him and closed her eyes, making him want to crush his mouth to hers, fit his lips to hers, suck her tongue, suck every part of her.

Then she turned to face him. "Your turn," she said, holding the handheld like Annie Oakley with a gun.

"It doesn't work that way on me," he said with a smirk.

"Well, I know that." She put the massager back in its cradle so that the water once again rained down on them from above. With a naughty smile she dropped to her knees and wrapped her hand around his erection. "Luckily for you," she said, looking up at him, "I know what *does* work."

And then she sucked him into her mouth.

A groan shuddered through him as she teased him, and he slid his hands into her hair because he needed an anchor on his spinning world.

That was when she got down to serious business.

Parker let her dictate the pace as long as he could, but then she did something magical with her tongue that took him nearly to the point of no return. He tried to pull back, tightening his hands in her hair, but she wasn't having any of that. She took him all the way and he came hard, his groan echoing between the shower walls. Unable to stand, he sank to his knees in front of her and dropped his head to her shoulder while he tried to drag air into his lungs.

TWENTY-THREE

Wrapping her arms around Parker, Zoe held on while the shower kept them warm as they both struggled to come down. When the water turned cold, he stirred. Reaching past her to flick it off, he wrapped her in a towel and then himself.

"Holy crap," she said, feeling dazed. "That just gets more intense and more intense. Can you imagine what it'd be like a month from now? We'll be dead. Death by orgasm."

"I won't be here in a month," he said quietly. "Maybe not even next week."

He was right, of course. Horrifyingly right. They didn't have a future, and damn.

She'd almost forgotten.

Wishful thinking, she knew. Just as she knew something else. She met his gaze and found him watching her, following her train of thought, and God, her chest hurt. Afraid to make this too serious, she forced herself to go with a light tone, the lightest she could get as she gestured to the space between them. "Maybe we should keep some distance until you go. A foot seems about right."

He rubbed the scruff on his jaw, clearly working up a smile, trying to match her tone. "You think a foot of space is enough?"

She smiled. "I think anything over about nine inches should do it."

Parker laughed and she laughed, too, but it faded quickly.

The air between them crackled with tension.

"It's all my fault," she said as she searched out her clothes. "I started this."

"It's not your fault at all. I'm pretty irresistible when I want to be."

Knowing he was trying to keep the light-and-easy thing going for her, she let out another laugh and shook her head. "And even when you don't want to be," she said. "The truth is I'm out of control when it comes to you."

"Giving information to the enemy, babe."

She clutched her towel to her chest and heard the truth escape her. "It'd help if you stopped."

"Stopped what?"

She'd let her smile fade. "Looking at me," she whispered. "Touching me, smelling so good . . . and breathing." She offered a half smile, acknowledging the ridiculousness of the suggestion. "That would be really great."

The corners of his mouth quirked slightly. "I'll work on that." He handed over her panties.

She shoved her feet into them and wriggled them on. Then she attempted to put on her bra, but it took two tries because it was tangled in her blouse. Frustrated, she tugged and tugged until Parker took them both from her fingers, righted everything, and handed them back to her.

Dammit. He was standing there quiet and utterly at ease in his own skin, and why shouldn't he be. He was smart and sharp and funny and . . . perfect.

And he was leaving.

He was really leaving.

She kept telling herself that worked for her. She always had carried a bit of a trust issue, and she certainly hadn't been looking for anything with him. But somewhere along the way, she wasn't sure when, maybe when he'd hugged her silly dog for the first time, she'd started to trust him.

And now, as a direct result, she was falling for him. Only he had this expiration date, one that was flashing big, bright red warning signs at her with every breath.

Knees weak, she sank to the edge of the tub, unable to keep up any sort of pretense of having her shit together. "I'm sorry," she whispered. "I thought I could do this, I really did. But I can't."

His smile vanished and his eyes went serious as he crouched in front of her, his hands on her knees. "I know," he said just as softly.

"I mean, it's good between us." She gathered his hands in hers and let out a small, watery laugh. "Actually, it's great. Which is what keeps tripping me up. I get all confused because my body's emotionally invested and so my brain thinks it should be, too. It's how I work, you know? But not you, which means you're not The One. I wanted you to be, but you're not, and I should've known from the very beginning because you weren't the things on my list that The One was supposed to have. You're all these other things like sexy and —"

He put a finger on her lips. "I know," he said again.

She just stared at him and realized he wasn't going to say anything else. He wasn't going to dangle a carrot, or try to talk her into setting aside her needs for his.

Or tell her he couldn't live without her.

Damn. She'd really sort of hoped for that, ridiculous as it seemed. Rising, she dropped his hands and dressed in silence, her throat getting tighter and tighter with each breath.

When she'd finished, he pulled her around to face him, waiting until she met his warm eyes.

"I wanted to be okay with this," she said quietly before he could speak, and damn, her eyes threatened to fill.

Parker held her gaze. "I'm sorry, Zoe. You deserve better; you deserve someone who can give you what you want for the long haul."

And that someone wasn't going to be him. Unable to hold eye contact with him without dissolving into a sniffling mess, she dropped her head to his chest. She wanted to be mad, but he'd been open and up front and honest about their future — or lack of one — from the beginning.

And anyway, he was right. She needed to move on. She needed to go back to her plan. Lifting her head, she looked into his warm eyes and promised herself she'd do just that. She'd go back to the plan.

Tomorrow.

For now, she simply breathed him in before gathering her strength and heading toward the door.

Parker let her go. What the hell else could

he do? She'd been so genuine and earnest, so sweetly apologetic, so absolutely positive they had to stop this madness.

It had just about killed him. Because against all the odds, he'd liked the idea of them being a . . . well, *them.*

But she needed him to stop messing with her. Except he hadn't been messing with her at all. He'd been as shocked as she at their easy chemistry.

But it was a lot more than chemistry. He knew that now. And yet the reality was that he was leaving, and he had to find a way to do that without further hurting her. That was a priority for him. She'd set the boundaries and he'd honor them.

Even if it killed him.

He could have changed her mind. There'd been a beat there when she'd hesitated, as if waiting for him to say something. And he'd known what she wanted him to say, that this didn't have to end when he left.

Just as he knew what he wanted to say — *Let's take this thing, this really great, hot, sexy, wonderful thing as far as we can before I have to go.*

No, that was a lie. That was what he'd have wanted to say when he'd first arrived. But things had changed. He no longer wanted to go — not that it mattered. His job was his life and he was going back to it.

So even though she'd looked at him like maybe she wouldn't argue if he made a good case for continuing their relationship, he wouldn't. She'd been hurt enough in her life; no way would he add to it, ever.

TWENTY-FOUR

Parker slept like shit, his dreams mocking him with images of Zoe smiling at him, making his life better just by being in it.

At some point before dawn, he was woken up by a notification on his phone. When he accessed the app, he couldn't see much in the dark but there was definite movement. Trucks on the go, leaving the ranch just like the other day but more. Like all of them . . .

Shit. He sat up and called Sharon. "He's moving his stash," he told her. "He's got a buyer or he's going to auction, or maybe he's been spooked and is changing locales."

"Parker —"

"Look, I'm working on accepting that this asshole got a deal even though he shouldn't have been allowed one," he said. "Just tell me you have someone on him, that he's not getting away."

There was a beat of silence and there in the dark, Parker swore. "You don't."

"It's not my responsibility," she said quietly. "He's not our responsibility anymore. It's out of both of our hands."

"Do they have eyes on him?"

"A deal is a deal," Sharon said. "He gave up intel and evidence on the militia that was needed, and in return he agrees to stay in Idaho and retire from his business of choice. You know this."

"And you believe him? You really believe that he's not going to pull up stakes and simply move off the radar to continue his extremely profitable business somewhere else?"

There was a long pause. "Not my call," she finally said.

So she didn't believe it, either. Which didn't make it any easier to swallow. Parker disconnected. He knew what he'd seen on the feeds, and it didn't look to him like Carver had stayed behind. It looked to him like the entire operation had cleared out, and there was nothing to stop them from finding another isolated spot in another state to start all over.

He called Kel, who answered with, "Was just calling you."

"What's up?" Parker asked.

"I think you know."

"Yeah," Parker said. "There's movement.

Where is he going and why is he being allowed to go anywhere?"

"Complicated," Kel said. "Back before Carver landed on the FWS's radar, the FBI had him with enough charges to put him away for a long time."

"So what happened? Wait, let me guess. The bastard was slick enough to make himself a sweet deal."

"Jackpot," Kel said. "He remains free as long as he helps the FBI indict a large slice of the evasive militia group he funded, most of whom are wanted for a multitude of other crimes as well. The problem has been that Carver makes new deals, promises that are always juicier than the current evidence."

"So he keeps getting an extension on his lucrative deal," Parker said. "Fucking unbelievable."

"It gets worse," Kel said. "Every time he gets into trouble — like he did with your agency — the FBI has no choice but to step in and bail his sorry ass out of the sling or they lose their ground."

"Perfect setup for an asshole like Carver," Parker said, impressed in spite of himself. "He's got us over a barrel and knows it. And he's extended his base of operations from illegal antiquities to funding the militia, so now what?"

"The FBI and the ATF are in way too deep to back out," Kel said. "Everyone thinks they're in control, but it's a political and red-tape nightmare, leaving Carver as the only winner. There are piles of charges that the FBI keeps promising all the other agencies that they'll get to pursue, but they're being strung along just as Carver is stringing them along."

"So what's his endgame?" Parker asked.

"Anyone's guess," Kel said.

Yeah, well, Parker intended to find out.

Zoe got up early, ready for her day. Or so she told herself. She'd had a flight scheduled, but according to a text from Joe, it had been moved to another day. He said the Caravan should be fixed this morning and needed a test flight. He'd put it up for sale and had an interested buyer up north that he wanted her to go show the plane to after the test.

She would miss the Caravan, but she'd do just about anything to keep her mind off Parker and all that they were no longer going to be doing together. Her eyes on her phone, she headed out of her room and . . . right into Parker.

He'd come out of the bathroom, hair wet, body damp, one of her towels wrapped indecently low on his hips.

Damn. Looking that sexy should be completely illegal. She nearly said *I want to recant my statement, the one where I said to stay at least nine inches away from me. I spoke too hastily.* Instead she said, "Sorry! I need to learn to walk and read my phone at the same time."

"You can get a ticket for that these days," he said.

She laughed, relieved that they were going to be grownups about this. It was a huge effort not to step close and run her finger over the cut on his forehead and demand to see his leg, but she managed by shoving her hands into her pockets. "So, where are you off to this early? More . . . sightseeing?"

"Yes, actually." He met her gaze. "I'm going up to Rocky Falls."

Her own hair was wet, too, still in a ponytail. She could almost feel his hand curl around the back of her neck, wrapping the strands of her hair up in his fingers as he slowly deepened their kiss. She had to shake the memory off. "Your cameras not working?"

"Saw something that I didn't like," he said.

"But aren't the good guys watching, too?"

"Yes, but as long as Carver feeds them the intel they want, they're happy."

"And you're worried that happy equals complacent or sloppy?" she asked.

"Exactly. Carver's cagey as hell. He's a master at vanishing like smoke."

She marveled at his courage, at the strength of character it took to put what was right ahead of what was easy, even if it meant risking his job. Zoe's job meant everything to her — *flying* meant everything, and she wondered if she could put the right to do that on the line and be willing to walk away from it if she had to.

But that was just it; she'd never have to. It wasn't her job to make those kinds of decisions. It was Parker's, and she was beginning to understand what he had at stake.

Everything.

All the time.

It was little wonder that he lived the way he did, with few to no distractions, no ties, and no real home base.

"I'll fly you," she heard herself say.

He started to shake his head, but she said, "The Caravan's been repaired and Joe wants to sell it. I'm taking it up north today so the buyer can get a look at it. Rocky Falls is a barely there detour. You can come along and get a look at what you need to see on the way."

"No."

"No?" she asked, surprised.

"I'm not going to ask this of you."

"Well, that's the thing," she said. "You didn't ask. I offered."

He didn't respond, and given his expression, he wasn't going to change his mind, either. And suddenly she realized what she'd given up, because just yesterday he'd have moved toward her, taken her into his warm arms, and pulled her in tight like he'd done so often since he'd come to Sunshine.

God. Had it really only been a little over a week ago?

"Not happening," he said, sounding different to her. A little cool, a little distant, and she found her mad.

"Why?" she asked. "Because I'm not going to sleep with you anymore? We aren't even friends now, is that it?"

"Not what I said." He paused. "And there's been very little sleeping involved."

"You know what I mean!"

He looked at her for a long moment, as if wrestling with himself. And given his overactive sense of privacy, he probably was. God forbid he just come out and say something about himself without being arm-wrestled for it.

"When I first came out here," he finally

said, "I thought this case was about one thing."

"Yes," she said. "The antiquities dealer making a boatload of money off his illegal gains, right?"

"Right. But now it's something else, something bigger, and I won't drag you into it."

"How would me flying you around on a sightseeing trip drag me into anything?" she asked.

"Maybe it wouldn't, but you've already flown me over Cat's Paw once. I'm not going to risk Carver noticing you for the second time. He might get suspicious and investigate, and realize he knows you. And if Carver found you, I'd never forgive myself."

"It's not even the same plane as before," she said. "It'll be the Caravan today. It was the Cardinal last time."

"And when you flew him before," he asked, "or his men, was that always the Cardinal?"

"Yes, I'm pretty sure."

Parker ran a hand down his face, and she knew she had him. She also knew nothing bad would happen to her while she was with him; he'd protect her, body and soul.

The real question was, how to protect her heart?

Their flight was quiet and — at least in Zoe's case — a little awkward. She had no experience with this, falling for a guy, having sex — and not just any kind of sex, but the fantasy kind, where orgasms happen in a shocking blink without having to strain for them — and then having to act like they hadn't.

Parker didn't seem to be having the same problem. He was calm, quiet. Focused. Like maybe she was pretty damn easy to get over. Her attitude deteriorated a little at that, but she was a professional, she reminded herself. She'd keep it bottled up tight.

And for the most part, she thought she was successful with that as she handled the testing on the plane and then flew them over Rocky Falls, specifically Cat's Paw.

Parker had both his laptop and long-range camera, quietly scoping the place out.

"Anything interesting?" she asked.

"Yeah," he said, dividing a gaze between the scope and the laptop screen, but he didn't elaborate. He did, however, take out his high-powered binoculars as well and had her make a second pass.

And then a third.

She had no idea what he was looking for as he took a long careful look at the surrounding area before finally indicating that he was satisfied.

After that, she flew onward, landing at the private airstrip of the Caravan's potential buyer. That detour, the meeting, and the potential new owner's inspection took the better part of the afternoon.

When they finally landed back in Sunshine, Zoe turned to a very quiet Parker. "Everything okay?" she asked.

"If anyone were to come into the airport asking for the flight logs from today, would they be able to get them?" he asked.

"Why?"

Face blank, he looked at her for a long beat. His expression was a visceral reminder that they were practically strangers.

Except they weren't. He'd helped her fix up her house. He'd rescued two kittens for her neighbor. He'd kissed her like she hadn't been kissed in too damn long, making her feel sexy, wanted . . . "No," she said. "No one should be able to get the flight logs without some sort of court order."

"Which doesn't mean that they can't," he said. "They could get stolen. Or leaked."

"Well, yes," she said. "But it hasn't happened before, that I know of." She paused.

"Sorry about the bad day and all the dead ends."

"Nothing where I get to be with you is ever bad."

The man had a knack for saying things that hit her right in the heart, and she had to swallow past the lump in her throat.

They exited the plane, Parker moving with the same easy confidence with which he did everything, when he turned to her.

She couldn't see much behind his mirrored sunglasses, which only served to make him appear even more badass. "It wasn't a dead end," he said.

She waited for more and when it didn't come, she blew out a sigh. "You're pretty damn annoying sometimes; anyone ever tell you that?"

"Every woman in my life," he said without hesitation.

This caught her off guard. "I was trying to insult you, but you don't seem insulted in the least. And just out of curiosity's sake, how many women are currently in your life?"

"Too many," he said a little grimly, and when he saw her expression at that, he reached for her hand and squeezed.

Their first physical contact all day, something she'd yearned for, but all she wanted to do was smack him.

"There's my boss," he said. "Sharon's pretty certain I'm the most annoying man alive. And then there's my sister. Amory loves me, but I annoy her big-time. It's a special talent of mine."

"Hard to believe," she said, hoping the teasing note in her tone served as an apology for sounding like a shrew.

He brought their joined hands up to his mouth and brushed a kiss to her palm. "And then there's you," he said with one of his panty-melting smiles.

She tugged her hand free. "Okay," she said. "No more of that, because my clothes tend to fall off when you look at me like that."

He laughed, but his smile slowly faded. "Cat's Paw has gone cold," he said quietly. "They've moved out."

She took in the tight look in his eyes, the grim set to his mouth. "You're frustrated."

"Frustration is a useless emotion. Goes against productivity."

"So you never let frustration get to you?" she asked.

His gaze dropped to her mouth. "I didn't say that."

She sucked in a breath and then another one when he pulled his sunglasses off and let her see the heat in his eyes. And then he slid a hand to the back of her neck and drew her in and kissed the ever-living daylights out of her.

When he pulled back, he slid his glasses back on.

"What was that?" she managed.

"Me, letting my frustration get to me."

And then he was gone, heading inside to wait while she did the postflight check and tie-down.

It didn't take long. Within thirty minutes she was done and entered the airport reception hangar.

The open greeting area had a few people milling around and there were several more up front, not a single one of them Parker.

Joe was behind the front desk. "You sell our baby?" he called out.

"Did my best," she said. "I think they'll be calling you. Have you seen Parker?"

Joe gestured toward the hallway. Zoe headed that way, taking a quick side trip toward the restrooms, when suddenly she was stopped and pushed up against the wall. In the next beat, a mouth covered hers.

Parker. She'd have recognized his kiss blindfolded but her heart still leapt into her throat at the feel of his bigger, harder body pressing hers into the wall, holding her there for his kiss.

Not that she wanted to escape. It felt so good, so heart-stoppingly good that she struggled to free her hands just so that she could get them on him.

Instead, he growled — *growled!* — and grabbed her hands, pinning them on either side of her head as he kissed her deeper.

And then deeper still, so that escaping was just about the furthest thing from her mind. As for the *closest* thing on her mind? Finding a place to break her promise to herself and get them both naked as soon as possible.

Parker couldn't believe it when he'd seen Tripp Carver coming through the front door of the airport. He'd had a single heartbeat to realize that the guy was about to see him and Zoe — who was coming toward him with a smile on her face — and he reacted.

He pushed Zoe up against the wall and kissed her, hiding both of their faces.

He had no idea why Carver was here right now, but he could guess. He was heading out, never to be seen again. And if that was true, the very last thing Parker wanted was to get caught spying on the Butcher with Zoe anywhere near him.

She could kick his ass later, but for right

now this was about getting out of here without her being seen.

When he heard Carver pass by them and head down the hallway toward the private lounge, Parker broke off the kiss but left his mouth against hers. "Zoe."

She blinked slowly, dazed. "Yeah?"

"I need you to go to Joe's office, lock the door, and stay there until I come for you."

"What? Why?"

"I'll explain later, move now." And when she just stared at him, he added a quiet but hopefully urgent "Please, Zoe." Having no choice but to believe that she trusted him enough to do as he asked, he took off after Carver.

TWENTY-FIVE

Parker's urgency had Zoe moving instinctually to Joe's office, which was right off the hallway and only ten feet away. She shut the door and hit the lock and then stood there for a second, trying to gather her wits.

Didn't happen.

When several minutes passed — okay, maybe thirty seconds — and Parker didn't come for her, she was driven by a need to make sure he was okay. She cracked open the door and peeked down the hallway. It took a ninety-degree turn so she couldn't see around the corner. She closed herself back in the office and once again locked the door just as her phone buzzed in her pocket. She whipped it out. "Parker, where the hell are you —"

"It's Darcy," her sister said. "You didn't look at the ID screen?"

"No, I —" Zoe swiped a hand down her face and let out a low laugh. "Sorry. Parker

just told me to stay and I got all discombobulated."

"No man tells me to stay and lives through
it," Darcy said. A beat went by. "He give
you a reason?"

"No," Zoe said. "One minute he was kissing me and the next he got all weird and
told me to stay, threw out a 'please,' and he
took off."

"You should definitely stay," Darcy said.

"But you just said that if a man told you
to stay, he wouldn't live through it."

"Yes," Darcy said. "But you have sharp
instincts. Remember that time we were in
Budapest and I was hungry and you
wouldn't let me eat because you had a weird
feeling?"

"Because what you wanted to eat was
some bad-looking fish."

"It looked fine to me and everyone else in
the market," Darcy said. "Remember I
asked around?"

"God, you were a spoiled brat that day,"
Zoe said. "And everyone but us got sick. I
saved you."

"No, your *instincts* saved us," Darcy said.
"Which is my point. What do your instincts
say now?"

"That something's up." Zoe's heart was
beating heavily, although there was a solid

argument to be made that it was from the kiss. She felt anxious, especially when she once again peeked out and peeked around the corner of the hallway, past the restrooms and pilots' lounge to the side exit and saw not a single soul. She moved back to Joe's office.

Still no Parker. "I've gotta go."

"Follow your instincts," Darcy said firmly.

Zoe disconnected and tried calling Parker. No answer. Dammit. Darcy had suggested she follow her instincts, but her instincts were tied. She needed a tiebreaker. So she called the most logical, reasonable, straight-headed person she knew — her brother.

Wyatt answered sounding harried and rushed. "Yeah?"

"You mean 'Hello, sister, lovely to hear from you,' " Zoe said.

"Hello, sister, I'm about to go elbows deep in a cow. Literally," Wyatt said. "State your emergency or hang up."

"Parker told me to stay," she said.

"Then stay," Wyatt said without missing a beat.

"What?" Zoe asked. "You don't just tell a woman to stay and expect her to do it blindly."

Wyatt sighed. "You're calling me again why?"

"Because this is all your fault, he's *your* friend!"

"And I think he's something far more to you," Wyatt said calmly. "Or you wouldn't be calling me all bent out of shape because someone bossed you around, when we all know *you* have to be the boss."

"I don't —" Zoe pressed a finger to her twitching eye. "I just . . ." She didn't know. She'd called an end to things and she'd already been conflicted about that *before* the kiss. "I'm a little out of my league here," she confessed.

"Well, join the club," Wyatt said. "Falling in love isn't for the weak, that's for damn sure."

"I'm not falling in love."

"You sure?"

Dammit. She'd never been so unsure in her entire life. "I've got to go."

"Yeah," Wyatt said. "But Zoe? Do him a favor and give him the benefit of the doubt. And then if you care about him like I think you do, hear him out before you shut him out."

"What are you talking about?" she asked. "I don't shut people out."

"Mom. Dad. Me when I went to under-grad in New York. Every man you've ever dated. Should I go on?" Wyatt asked.

345

She disconnected. And then blew out a breath as she looked around. Out the side wall of windows she could see Devon preparing the Lear for flight. He must have caught a flight she hadn't heard about.

Biting her lower lip, she stared at the door for a beat before deciding she needed one more peek. She unlocked the door and stuck her head out.

The door at the other end of the hallway opened, only the man who came inside wasn't Parker.

It was Tripp Carver. He was over six feet tall, midthirties, and built like he'd once been a football star and had let himself go a little soft.

But there was nothing soft about his face. His expression was dark and mean. He eyed the row of three metal chairs against the wall between the men's and women's restroom, snatched one, and jammed it under the door handle.

Zoe gasped and he turned to her. A gun had materialized in his hand. "Get over here."

Could he see her knees knocking together? She hoped not. "I don't think so."

"Look, I'm not fucking around. I've got a scheduled flight in five minutes, and now Parker James is here, breathing down my

346

neck. So you're my leverage out of here."

"Me?" she squeaked, finding her voice. "Why me?"

"I saw him with his tongue halfway down your throat. You mean something to him. So get your sweet ass over here or I start shooting."

Well, hell. Next time Parker said stay, she would absolutely do just that.

Twenty-Six

Parker had followed Carver down both legs of the hallway and out the side door.

Nothing.

He moved around the side of the hangar toward the front and scanned the lot.

More nothing.

Hearing running footsteps back the way he came, he followed, retracing his steps, past the door he'd used, where he came face to face with a fence lining the tarmac. No one could have climbed that fence; it had barbed wire across the top and was electrified.

He moved back to the door leading inside the hangar. The handle readily turned beneath his hand but the door wouldn't open.

Something was blocking it from the inside.

Shit. Whipping around, he went running back toward the lot and the front door, forcing himself to slow to a casual walk as he entered the front reception area of the hangar. There was a small crowd still milling around, a group that had just come in on a private charter. Devon was inside looking for his next charter client, calling out for a . . .

John Smith.

The confident asshole Carver had chartered a jet and used the most common alias in the world to do so.

Parker stopped at Joe, who was at the front computer looking distracted. "Where's Zoe?"

"Shit, man, I can't keep eyes on everyone," Joe said. "She's probably in the can; give her a minute."

Parker's gut was screaming now and he strode down the hall, making the turn to the end, to the door he hadn't been able to get back into from the outside. It had a folding chair shoved under the handle, blocking it from being opened.

Fuck.

He whipped around. No way had Carver jammed that chair beneath the door and then just vanished into thin air.

And where the hell was Zoe? Certainly not where he'd left her . . .

He didn't want to put a name to the emotion trying to choke out his common sense.

An emotion shockingly close to panic.

He never panicked.

He strode back down the hallway and right into the women's restroom. He pulled the gun from the small of his back as he entered, hoping like hell he wasn't about to scare some woman to an early grave.

Zoe was in the corner between the sink and a bathroom stall, hands up, facing . . .

Carver, who had a gun on her.

"About time," Carver said. "What did you do, take a nap?"

"Let her go," Parker said. "She has nothing to do with this."

"Too late for that," Carver said. "Get in here, shut the door quietly behind you, and lock it. Now."

Parker looked into Zoe's eyes and felt his heart seize when he saw something besides terror.

Regret.

He stepped into the bathroom and, with his gun still trained on Carver, shut and locked the door. "What do you want, Carver?"

"Are you fucking kidding me?" Carver asked. "I want what was promised. A life free of looking over my shoulder for you, asshole. Thanks to you nosing around, people got jittery. My people. They found out about my deal."

"You mean they discovered you ratted them out," Parker said, gun still on Carver.

"I had no choice," Carver said, voice hard. "But you do. You're going to choose to let me walk out of here without a fuss. I'm going to get on that plane I chartered in good faith, or your cutie pie here is going to pay the price. Not today, maybe not tomorrow. She won't see it coming, but you can count on me to make it happen."

"Parker, don't do it," Zoe said. "Don't let him go."

Carver smiled grimly. "A *tough* cutie pie. I should've hired you instead of Devon for today. Three seconds to decide," he said to Parker. "And take your gun out of my face."

Deep down, Parker knew that Carver wouldn't risk taking a shot in here. He didn't have a silencer on his gun and the report would make a huge noise that people wouldn't mistake. It would bring a lot of unwanted attention to Carver. And this might be a small airport, but it was an airport with rules and regulations. If a gunshot was heard, no planes would be landing or taking off for a good long time. Carver would be grounded and quickly arrested. This was logic, and it went through Parker's head in a nanosecond.

But so did something else: the knowledge that Carver was a desperate man, and desperate men did stupid things.

Parker should know. He was a desperate man about to do a very desperate thing. "If you come back here," he said to Carver, "if you so much as lay an eye on her, *ever,* all bets are off. I'll find you. So you'd better make sure you're going somewhere far and you stay off the map."

Carver slid one last look at Zoe and then met Parker's gaze again. "Deal."

"Get the fuck out of here, then," Parker said.

Carver's eyes lit with malice and greed and triumph as he backed to the door. But one last time he aimed his gun at Zoe. "If you change your mind," he said to Parker, "if the authorities stop me now or when I land, all bets are off. She will pay for your mistake."

A month ago Parker wouldn't have been able to fathom this, letting Carver walk. His need for vengeance wouldn't have allowed it, but he had something to live for now. And it wasn't the job. Fuck the job. He stepped in front of Zoe so that Carver's gun was aimed at him instead. He looked at the son of a bitch with cold steadiness. "Go."

Carver nodded once, and then he was gone.

Parker turned and pulled Zoe in, wrapping her in his arms as close as he could get her. Then he pulled back, taking her in with one quick sweeping gaze, not seeing any injuries.

"I'm okay," she said.

He lifted her chin and looked straight into her eyes.

"Really," she said.

"You're shaking."

"Like a leaf," she agreed. "But I'm not hurt."

He nodded and yanked her back in, holding her too tight and he knew it, but he couldn't make himself loosen his grip.

"Parker? You heard me, right? I'm fine."

"I'm not," he said, and buried his face in her hair.

She let out a watery laugh and squeezed him back just as tight. Christ. If anyone had asked him an hour ago how he reacted to stress, he'd have shrugged and said stress wasn't one of his problems.

That had changed in a blink. He had little experience with the level of terror he'd just experienced, and he didn't want to ever feel it again. Far more importantly, he didn't want Zoe to ever feel it again.

■ ■ ■ ■

It was hard to see past the little black dots floating in Zoe's vision — a side effect from holding her breath so long — but she didn't need to see in order to absorb the feel of Parker's arms around her.

She could've stayed right here forever.

But eventually Parker pulled back, keeping one of her hands in his as he kicked in the doors of the four bathroom stalls.

"There was no one with him," she said. "At least n-not that I saw." Great, now she was shaking *and* stuttering.

"Only a few more minutes, Zoe," he said with quiet understanding.

She started to say she was still fine, but her teeth were chattering now. As if from a great distance she felt Parker tighten his grip on her hand and pull her from the bathroom. He led her down the hall, slowing his long-legged stride to match hers.

In the front reception area, he pushed her into one of the chairs and squatted in front of her. "Take a few deep breaths," he said quietly. Calm steel.

As she did just that, he kept one hand on her and with the other pulled out his cell. "Sharon," he said. "Carver just took an outbound flight from Sunshine Airport. Tell me you got everything you needed from him — Yeah, I do realize you would have rather I called you *before* he took off, but there were extenuating circumstances — Such as? Such as I had to make a deal to keep someone I care about safe. We can't tail him. Now did everyone get what they needed from him or not?" Eyes on Zoe, he let out a breath and briefly closed his eyes. "Okay, good. Yes, I'm sure you do want to talk to me. Later." He disconnected and hit another number.

Zoe couldn't imagine who he was calling now, but the mystery was immediately solved.

"Kel," Parker said. "Incident at the airport. You'll want to come down here and get it on record personally." He disconnected and slid his phone away. It was already ringing, but he didn't pull it back out or take his eyes off Zoe. "Joe," he said in his normal speaking voice, and how he'd known Joe was heading his way, Zoe would never know. "I need a soda for Zoe."

Shocking the hell out of Zoe, Joe did an about-face and headed for the soda machine against the far wall without a word. "Can you teach me how to do that?" she whispered.

Joe came back and handed Zoe the soda.

"Sip it," Parker said. "It helps with shock." He rose to his feet and said a few quiet words to Joe that she couldn't catch — undoubtedly telling Joe some version of a story about what had just happened and that the authorities were on their way.

She closed her eyes a moment and then Parker was back, crouched in front of her, his face a mask of concern.

"You told me to stay," she said. *"Stay."*

"Which, by the way, you didn't do."

"Because I'm not a dog," she said.

He dropped his head and studied his feet a moment, whether to control his temper or resist strangling her, she had no idea. "If there's danger and you're with me and I ask you to do something like stay, then I have to know you'll do just that."

"You didn't ask," she said. "You told. And even if two out of three siblings agree with you, I would've liked to be asked."

He just looked at her. "Drink the soda."

"I'm fine!" And pissed to boot, it seemed. "And define 'with you.' "

"In a relationship."

"You don't do relationships," she said. "And it's no wonder, you can't even have a real conversation. Asking me to stay would have meant a question mark at the end of your sentence. Like, 'Hey, Zoe, could you wait here a sec?' Or how about 'I'm about to go jump right into harm's way, don't worry your pretty little head about a thing, the big bad caveman's got it all covered.' "

He wrapped his hand around hers holding the soda can and brought it up to her lips.

She took a long sip, and then as the sugar eased into her system, she sighed. "Okay, so adrenaline rushes tend to make me cranky."

"Understandable," he said with only a very small lip twitch. "But you need to understand something, too. When it comes to your safety, I'm never going to take a chance."

She opened her mouth, but he shook his head. "Never, Zoe."

Saying anything more to that would be like talking to a brick wall. "I don't know who in their right mind would want a relationship with you," she grumbled.

Except she *did* know who. Dammit. *She* wanted a relationship with him.

She'd told him he wasn't The One, that he didn't have her basic requirements. But she'd just watched him handle a volatile, violent, dangerous situation without blinking. He'd have done anything to keep her safe, including stepping in front of a gun, no questions asked. He'd put his life before hers.

And right then and there she mentally rewrote her requirements in a man, and those requirements all added up to Parker James.

Too bad he wasn't available.

She drew in a deep breath and she realized she was thinking clearly again.

"Better?" he asked.

"Yeah."

He didn't smile but his eyes did, with a light that said he was proud of her. Still, there was a grim set to his features as he rose.

"You're going to figure out how to stop him now, right?" she asked. "Find out where Devon is flying him to and have him followed and arrested?"

"No."

"But —"

"*No,*" he said implacably.

She heard all sorts of things in his voice and had no idea what any of it meant. "Parker, I am not going to be the reason you don't do your job."

Nothing.

"Dammit, Parker, say something."

He didn't, and in the next minute the lobby was filled with cops, including Kel.

She was given a blanket and hot tea, and tucked into a corner like a damn victim. And then asked a million questions by the police.

And by Kel.

And then a million more by others whom she guessed were FBI and ATF, and a few more alphabet agencies she didn't know.

But not Parker.

She was seen by medics who fretted about shock, but she wasn't in shock. She was in the damn dark. She refused to go to the hospital and was reluctantly cleared at the scene.

Parker was the one to collect her, reappearing after too long a time where she hadn't been able to see him in the chaos. He ushered her out to her car and into the passenger seat.

"I can drive."

"I know," he said, but he got behind the wheel.

"Let me guess," she murmured. "You've got this."

"Yeah," he said quietly. "I've got this. I've got you."

And on that, she was going to have to trust him because she was suddenly so exhausted she couldn't lift her own head.

■ ■ ■ ■

Zoe opened her eyes and gasped in horror.
Once again she was in the airport's bathroom, panic flowing through her veins
instead of blood. She watched in slow motion as Parker stepped in front of her so that
Carver's gun bumped him in the chest.

Parker's gun had vanished. He had no
protection at all — not that she could tell
by the way he stood there still as night and
deadly calm, like maybe he faced down
maniacs on a daily basis.

Not Zoe. Her skin felt too tight for her
body. She was both sweating and shaking.
And her heart thundered against her ribs so
hard she was sure they'd shatter before this
was over.

"Drop the gun," Parker said.

Carver laughed maniacally and emptied
his clip into Parker's chest.

Zoe screamed as he crumpled to the floor.

"Zoe."

She jerked awake to the feel of Parker
undoing her seat belt. They were parked in
front of her house and he was outside the
car, crouched at her side. "Easy," he said.
"Just me."

Breathing like a lunatic, she'd have fallen

right out of the seat if not for Parker. "You're safe," he said softly, his hands on her thighs.

Because he had her. And no one had ever made her feel so good. She let out a shaky breath and shoved her fingers through her hair. "I'm awake now."

He nodded and rose to his feet, holding out a hand for hers. Night had fallen and so had the temperature. He wrapped her in his sweatshirt and led her to the house. Inside, he took her straight through the living room to the kitchen, where he sat her at the table.

"I have questions," she said.

"I know." He let Oreo out the back kitchen door to do his business and then fed the kittens, who were wild and unruly and climbing up her legs. He pulled them free, set them on the floor with a few of their toys, and put water on the stove to boil.

"What are you doing?" she asked.

"Making you tea."

"I don't want tea," she said. "I want answers."

When the tea was ready he set a hot mug in front of her and leaned back against the counter, arms crossed. Clearly not exactly open to talking, but he hadn't refused her, either.

She'd take it. "At the airport," she said,

"Kel told me you'd done the right thing, which was a lot harder than the easy thing, and that it was going to cost you, which *wasn't* the right thing."

Parker's face was blank, giving nothing away of his thoughts. He didn't speak.

Shock.

"What's today going to cost you?" she asked.

He slid his gaze away.

"Your job?" she asked.

He shrugged.

"Oh, Parker," she breathed. "But I don't get it. In the end you did what your boss had asked you to do. Honor the deal with Carver and let him walk."

"They meant for him to stay in Idaho, in a known place where they could keep an eye on him. I sent him packing."

"But Joe told the authorities that Devon only flew Carver to Coeur d'Alene."

"We lost him from there," he said.

She bit her lip, refusing to cry for him because he wouldn't want her to, but it was all so unfair. That he'd ended up doing what he had was all her fault, her doing. He'd had to react to keep her safe and if she knew one thing about Parker, she knew that he'd never even weighed the choice. "Surely they'll understand —"

"Don't worry about it. It's my problem, not yours."

Right. She'd nearly forgotten. Her problems were his problems. And his problems were his problems. It infuriated her all over again. God, she was such an idiot. Because she was still falling for him, even now. Hell, she'd already fallen. She dropped her head to the table and thunked it a few times, but it didn't help.

"Okay," he said, and pushed away from the counter. "Bedtime."

She lifted her head when he wrapped a palm around her arm and pulled her out of the chair. "I'm not in the mood."

His lips quirked. "To sleep."

"I knew that," she muttered. Tugging free, she headed to the door and then stopped. "I need something from you," she said to the wood.

"Anything," he said from behind her. *Right* behind her.

He'd followed and was close enough that she could take in his scent. They'd been gone for hours, in an incredibly tense situation, and he still smelled amazing.

She could hate him for that alone. "I need you to be strong here, because I don't think I can be, not after today. I need you to keep the space invasions to a minimum until you go, which I assume you're doing sooner than later."

Parker paused. "I have to be in D.C. to face the music on Monday," he finally said.

Today was Friday. She swallowed hard and nodded, and walked out.

TWENTY-SEVEN

Parker walked through the house, checking windows and locks, turning off lights. He'd put off going to bed because he knew sleep wasn't going to come for him.

He spent a few moments with the ridiculously energetic Bonnie and Clyde, who'd gotten bigger this week, their strength finally matching their courage and bravado. They were now insane heathens who climbed and destroyed everything in their midst.

And he adored them every bit as much as he did Oreo.

When he finally went upstairs, he passed by his bedroom, heading to Zoe's, needing to check in on her just to make sure she'd been able to fall asleep without any trouble, that what had happened wasn't bothering her.

He had no intention of letting her know he was there, but the sight of her soothed an ache he hadn't even realized he'd had.

In the center of her bed she was curled up around Oreo, the two of them huddled together and lit by only the moon's glow.

Oreo's nose wriggled. Then one bleary eye pried open. At the sight of Parker, his tail thumped the blankets.

"Stay," Parker mouthed to him, pointing at the bed, but Oreo, hopeful that he'd brought food, abandoned his mistress and hopped off the bed.

Zoe turned restlessly, reaching out for the dog in her sleep with a soft sound of distress.

Stay the hell away from me.

Okay, so that wasn't exactly what she'd said, but it was what she'd meant. And then she made the sound again, like her dreams were dark and chasing her, and he couldn't, he just couldn't leave her to face the demons — his demons — on her own. Lying down beside her — on top of the covers — he stroked a hand over her arm to her fingers, which he entwined with his. "You're safe," he whispered.

He'd made sure of it. There was a watch on this house, and would be for as long as he thought it necessary to make sure Carver kept his word.

Zoe immediately curled up into Parker, pressing her face in the crook of his neck and inhaling deep, like she needed his essence to breathe, like maybe he could chase away all the bad in the world.

And then she made a sound of frustration at the covers caught between them, yanked them free, and wrapped herself around him like an octopus. He was still fully dressed but she wore her pj's, which tonight consisted of a teeny, tiny pair of shorts and an equally tiny, snug tank top. He had to close his eyes and do math problems in his head. When that didn't work, he tried to count sheep. Hell, he told himself, think of the job he'd probably screwed himself out of.

But all he could think was that there was nowhere else on earth he'd rather be than right here, holding Zoe. And knowing it, he buried his face into her hair.

"Parker?" she asked sleepily.

"Shh," he said. "Go back to sleep."

There was a beat during which he held his breath, but then her arms came around him and she did just that, went to sleep.

Even more amazingly, so did he.

Zoe came awake when her blanket moved and let in the cold morning air.

Except it hadn't been a blanket, it had been Parker. She opened her eyes as he reached over her to the nightstand and grabbed his phone, which was vibrating across the wood.

He slid his thumb across the screen and listened for a long moment. "I'll be there," he said. "Yes, as in today, so stay right where you are. Don't move until I get there."

He disconnected and, silent as a cat, slid out of the bed.

He was shirtless and shoeless, wearing low-slung jeans, unfastened.

He looked delectable.

Not that she was going to bite. She might be a little bit slow in the man department, but she did learn from her mistakes.

Eventually.

He pulled on his shirt and met her gaze, something passing over his face. Regret? Whatever it was, it put a hard fist of anxiety in her throat, one she couldn't swallow down. And it got worse when he grabbed his shoes and started to walk out of her room.

"Did you get called to D.C. ahead of schedule?" she asked.

"No." He turned to look at her. "I have to go fix a problem in Vegas."

Zoe tossed her covers back and stood.

"What are you doing?" he asked.

She thought of how he'd held her all night long, a solid, warm, steady presence in a world that had gone a little topsy-turvy on her. There'd been no strings attached to his comfort, one of the things she admired about him and one that also frustrated her half to death.

The three W's again, which equated to no price. There was no price on their friendship, no price on what they gave each other.

Or received from each other.

"You need to get to Vegas," she said. "I can fly you."

His face was impassive, giving nothing away. "I was going to catch a commercial flight out of Coeur d'Alene. It's not a life-and-death kind of emergency," he said. "This isn't work. You don't have to —"

"Say that again and I'll make you fly in the luggage compartment," she said.

One brow rose.

She knew what he was capable of and that his life should scare her. And it did, a little. But in that moment she felt it was important to stand toe to toe with him and show him she wasn't afraid of him or his life.

An hour and a half later they were wheels up and she had them nosed in the right direction before she glanced over at Parker.

He was watching her.

"What?" she asked.

"You didn't ask me any questions, you just had my back."

She smiled a little grimly. "You've certainly had mine enough times."

He held her gaze. "This trip is personal," he said.

Trying not to react to that even though it hurt, she nodded and kept her gaze straight ahead in flight. "So you said."

"No." He put his hand over hers. "I just meant it's not my job. And because it's not, it's going to be tricky."

She found a laugh. "In case you haven't noticed, Parker, life is tricky."

He let out a wry smile. "Not at work, it's not."

"Are you kidding me?" she asked with more than a whisper of incredulous disbelief. "You were nearly shot yesterday. You've been run over by a truck!"

"I'm talking about emotionally tricky," he said. "At work, things are black or white."

She paused. "So you're saying that work is easier than real life?"

He let out a low, wry laugh that was answer enough.

She'd always known his stance. He'd never been anything but honest about that. Which meant she had no one to blame for her heartbreak but herself. But she really wished she had some of Manda's muffins.

"Zoe —"

"Don't," she said quietly, and took a deep breath past the pain in her damn heart. The damn heart she'd told not to get involved.

He opened his mouth but she shook her head, sending him her best death glare. "I mean it, Parker. I'll pull this plane over and kick your ass out."

The look on his face said he wished things were different, and for just a second she allowed herself to believe it. But in the end, it didn't matter what he was thinking. If he truly wanted something, he'd make it happen. That was who he was.

"Different subject," he said a few minutes later. "I told you this trip was personal. Before you jumped to conclusions and decided I was shutting you out, I was about to tell you that I meant personal as in personal to *me*. It's about my sister. Her name is Amory. She's eighteen and flexing her independence muscles for the first time. Problem is, she's a bit of a wild spirit and hard to contain. People love and adore her, but she doesn't always understand the real world."

Surprised at this unsolicited glimpse into his world, Zoe glanced at him. "She lives in Vegas?"

"No," he said. "She lives with my parents. She took a bus to Vegas from Arizona."

She glanced over at him. "She ran away?"

"Worse." He shook his head. "She wants to get married."

"So young?"

"Yeah," Parker said, and scrubbed his hands down his face. "Last time I talked to her, I said she needed to be a grown-up. I think this is her way of showing me she's doing just that."

"Who's the guy?"

"Henry. Also eighteen. He's quiet and shy and utterly guileless. This is all Amory's doing."

When they landed a short time later, Parker arranged for a rental car and drove them straight to Elvis's Wedding Chapel.

Zoe stared at it. "You're kidding me."

"It's where she called me from," he said. He parked and turned to Zoe, who was torn between horror and laughter. "She loves old movies, especially Elvis," he explained.

"Not judging," Zoe said. "Do you want me to wait here?"

Parker actually looked uncertain at that. She'd never seen this look on his face before; he'd never been anything but one hundred percent sure of himself.

Which settled it. She unhooked her seat belt and got out of the car.

Parker did the same. With his dark sunglasses and a pair of dark jeans with a white button-down shoved up at the elbows, he looked movie-star handsome.

And tough and impenetrable.

Unapproachable.

She walked right up to him. She pulled off his glasses. "Better," she said, and cocked her head, studying him. "Don't take this personally, okay?" Sliding her hands up his chest and around his neck, she tugged his head down and kissed him.

Not one to be a passive participant in anything, Parker kissed her back, hard and more than a little bit rough, and a whole lot desperate. She was breathless when she pulled back and stared into his face.

Much more relaxed, she decided, and nodded. "Better. You don't look nearly so intimidating or scary as hell now. You look almost . . . sweet."

"You think I'm sweet?" he asked in disbelief.

"No, I think you're intimidating and scary as hell." She smiled and patted his arm. "And okay, maybe a little sweet." And kind. And decent. And loyal. And . . . shit.

He *was* everything on her damn list.

They walked into the wedding chapel reception area, which was bright white with flowers everywhere. Wedding pictures were plastered across one entire wall. Next to the reception desk stood Elvis.

In drag.

"Hubba hubba," the guy said. "We got a live one, folks." He grinned at Zoe. "You want your groom to dress like Elvis, too, darlin', or just me?"

Zoe opened her mouth and then managed to close it. "We're not . . . getting married."

Elvis sized up Parker. "He not getting the job done? Do we need to put more men on the job?"

Parker started to speak, but Zoe quickly put a hand in his and squeezed, talking hurriedly before he could. "We're looking for someone. She's —"

"Ah," Elvis said, understanding crossing his face. "So you're who they're waiting for. The two mentally retarded kids, yeah?"

"Down syndrome," Parker said. "They have Down syndrome." He spoke quietly. Calmly.

But Zoe knew him now, knew the tells, and he wasn't feeling quiet or calm.

"Whatever," Elvis said with a shrug. "They're inside." He gestured with his chin to the open door to the chapel.

Back in charge, Parker took Zoe's hand and pulled her along with him. At the back of the chapel was one guy. A kid, really. He was sitting on the back row bench, head bowed, but when they entered, his gaze went straight to Parker. With an audible gulp, he stood up and shuffled his feet a little bit, his dark hair falling into his sky blue eyes. "You made it," he said with what sounded like great relief.

"Where is she?" Parker asked.

The kid pointed to the front of the chapel. "They don't have any other weddings today. The lady — er, the guy — um, Elvis said we could stay as long as we wanted."

Parker nodded and strode down the aisle. Zoe watched him head toward a girl sitting huddled in misery on the front pew.

Zoe turned to Amory's boyfriend. "I'm Zoe," she said. "And I'm guessing you're Henry?"

Henry nodded. "We didn't do it." He shoved his hands into his pockets. "Parker said to wait. So we waited."

Zoe smiled. "That's good."

He gave her a tentative smile back. "Yeah. Except probably it'd be even better if we hadn't come at all. Everyone's upset."

"How about you and Amory?" she asked. "Are you guys upset?"

"No," he said. "We're in love."

Zoe's heart squeezed at the sincere honesty in the kid's voice, and she smiled.

"Then everything else will work out," she said.

Henry nodded, and when his glasses slipped down his nose, he shoved them up again. "I told her that. And I told her we have time, too. But Parker wanted her to be a grown-up and stuff, and so yeah . . . here we are."

"I don't think Parker meant she should get married to show she's an adult," Zoe said carefully.

Henry nodded. "Sometimes she gets mixed up between her parents and Parker, and confused on what they want her to do." Poor Henry immediately looked stricken and guilty as soon as the words were out, like he felt awful saying anything bad about Amory's family.

Zoe looked down the aisle, at the two heads bent together. Parker had pulled Amory up to a seated position and was next to her, his arm around her shoulders, speaking quietly.

Amory was listening carefully and then speaking in return, the polar opposite of the body language of her brother. Her arms waved, her face became animated, and her voice got high and excited. She was seriously adorable.

And though Parker wouldn't like to know

it, so was he. Cocking his head, he listened to everything she said without interrupting her. When she'd wound down, he spoke again and Amory clearly hung on every single word with rapt adoration.

Zoe's heart sighed. She knew the feeling. She suspected that she'd often looked at Parker the same way. "What was the plan after getting married?" Zoe asked Henry.

"She wanted to see snow," Henry said. "But I don't think we have enough money to get all the way to Glacier Park."

"Montana?" she asked, surprised.

"Yeah, they still have snow, right?" Henry asked. "I searched it on my phone and couldn't find any other place that had snow at this time of year." He looked uncertain. "But Montana's pretty far from here."

"It sure is." Zoe whipped out her phone, sent a text, and then waited.

In the front row, Parker pulled his phone from his pocket and eyed the screen, and then craned his neck and stared at her.

She smiled.

He smiled back and shook his head, like maybe she was a complete nut. Well, that or she was annoying as shit, but she was really hoping it was the former.

Parker murmured something to Amory, who squealed so high-pitched that Zoe's eardrums nearly burst. She was looking around to see if the windows had shattered when Amory bolted up the aisle and threw herself at Zoe.

"You would do that? Really?" Amory shrieked. She was much shorter than Parker and also a little bit wider, but they had the same irresistible smile.

Zoe hugged her back. "Yes. And hi."

"Hi!" Amory grinned. "I'm Amory, nice to meet you, you're the best girlfriend Parker's ever had!"

"Uh . . ." Zoe looked over Amory's head at Parker. "I'm not Parker's girlfriend."

Amory's head came up. "But you're a girl and you're his friend."

Well, when she put it like that . . .

Amory skipped over to Henry. "Guess what?"

He smiled helplessly at her, like she was the best thing he'd ever seen. "What?"

"We're going to Glacier Park!" Amory yelled. "Where there's snow! Parker's girl-friend's going to fly us! In an airplane! She's a pilot!"

Henry slid a look at Zoe before looking back to Amory. "So we're not getting married today?"

"Let's do this instead!" Amory jumped up and down in excitement. "Does that work for you?"

Henry smiled sweetly at her. "Whatever works for you works for me."

Zoe felt her heart melt.

"Can we leave now?" Amory asked. "Can we? Can we?"

"Yes," Zoe said. "Well, as soon as I can get a flight plan filed and arrange for a rental car in Glacier Park. In under an hour, certainly."

Parker slid an arm around Amory's shoulders. "Yes, but —"

"Uh-oh," Amory said, smile fading fast. "You didn't mean it?"

"You know I always mean what I say, Am. Always."

Amory stared at him and then slowly nodded.

"Just like when I tell you I'm going to do something, I do it," he said.

Again she just looked at him and then nodded.

"So now I want the same from you. I want you to tell me you're going to do something — actually two somethings — and then follow through so that I can trust you as much as you trust me."

Again Amory gave this some thought and then nodded. "What things?"

"Call Mom and Dad," he said. "Tell them

379

where you are and where we're going. That's what a grown-up does, Amory; they act responsibly."

"Did your girlfriend have to call her mom and dad first?" Amory looked at Zoe. "Did you?"

"No," Parker said, answering for her. "Because we're already grown-ups."

"And I'm not his girlfriend," Zoe said again.

Amory looked at Parker. "Did you forget to ask her to be your girlfriend? You know you have to ask, right? Henry asked me a long time ago."

"We're talking about you," Parker said firmly.

"It'd be more fun to talk about you," Amory muttered.

"Be a grown-up," Parker said, ignoring her pout. "And when you start doing that, you'll find people much more willing to trust you to live your life the way you want to."

She blinked. "What's the other thing I have to do?"

"Promise me that you and Henry will just enjoy being eighteen for a while. There's no reason to rush anything. I promise to come see you more often. And when the time is right, I'll help you guys get married, if that's still what you want."

Amory was still staring at him, her mouth open a little as she took it all in.

"Anything you don't understand?" Parker asked.

"I understand," Amory said. "But I don't like some of it."

Parker smiled. "Welcome to grown-up land."

Amory executed an impressive eye roll that would've made Zoe laugh in a normal situation. She really loved watching brother and sister, loved the easy rapport, the obvious love and affection between them.

Loved him . . .

TWENTY-EIGHT

It was difficult for Parker to play travel guide for his sister with so much on his mind, not the least of which was Zoe and how for every minute he spent with her he wanted more minutes.

Hours.

Days.

Weeks . . .

For most of his grown-up life he'd gotten through the demands of his job by living one minute to the next, not looking back and not looking ahead either, at least not past the current case.

And now he couldn't see any cases in his future, which brought on a whole new level of what-the-fuckery because his job had been his life so long he wasn't sure he knew how to live without it.

But once Zoe flew them to Glacier Park and Amory and Henry got their first sight of snow, everything else sort of faded away.

He knew he would never forget the sheer jubilation in Amory's face as she scooped up a handful and threw it at Henry.

Henry, much gentler than she, simply pulled her in for a cold, icy hug that had Amory laughing out loud and tackling them both to the snow.

"Make snow angels!" Amory yelled, commanding everyone around her. "Henry, make one for your nana who's sitting on a cloud watching us!"

"Henry's aunt died a few months back," Parker explained to Zoe. "She was his caregiver."

"Who watches after him now?" Zoe asked.

"He has no other family."

"No one? He's got no one?" Zoe asked, clearly dismayed by this. "Who helps him if he needs it?"

"He's hanging in there," Parker said. "He got his GED and is thinking about taking some night classes at the local community college."

Zoe turned from the sight of Henry and Amory making snow angels and laughing like children and stared up at Parker. "It's you," she said softly. "He has you. You've been looking after him, haven't you?"

Parker lifted a shoulder. So he had a soft spot for the kid and helped out monetarily, making sure he was okay in the home he shared with other disabled adults and that he had food and everything he needed. "He's a good guy. And he's good to Amory. He makes sure she's got what she needs and I do the same for him. It's no big deal."

"It's a very big deal," Zoe said softly. "You love someone, you take care of them. You don't walk away and move on. You keep in touch. You let them know that even though maybe you can't be with them, they're on your mind. It's called caring, Parker, and whether you want to admit it or not, you know how to do it, and in fact you do it better than most."

He inhaled a deep breath. "Zoe —"

"No," she said. "I know what you're going to say, and I don't need to hear it again." She looked at him for a long time, her eyes shining with emotion that wasn't all that hard to read and made his heart squeeze painfully.

She had no idea what he was going to say; she couldn't. Because he didn't know, either. Still, intending to try, he opened his mouth —

And a snowball hit him right in the face.

Amory grinned wide. "Parker and Zoe standing in the snow," she said in a singsong voice. "K-I-S-S-I-N-G . . ."

384

Parker crouched down to make his own arsenal while above him he heard Zoe say, "I'm not his girlfriend."

For the third time.

Not that he was keeping track or anything. Hoisting two huge snowballs, he threw one at Amory as she squealed and tried to outrun it — she couldn't — and then used his second snowball to nail Zoe.

It was the last thing he did before being jumped by both of them and tackled down to the ground, where he got snow in places that no one should get snow.

They landed in Sunshine fairly late. The plan was to keep Amory and Henry until the morning, when Parker would drive them to the Coeur d'Alene airport and put them on a plane home.

When they all walked into the reception hangar, Parker saw Kel standing at the front desk looking tense. He had another officer with him. Both locked eyes on Parker.

Parker slowed and pulled Amory aside. "Remember when you told me you called Mom and Dad?"

"Uh-huh."

Amory was a lot of things, and guileless was one of them. She didn't have a poker face and she couldn't lie worth shit. She just didn't have the conscience for it.

Which was why he knew he'd been had; it was all over her face. "You didn't call them, did you?"

"I did," she said, and then her face crumpled with guilt. "Just not today."

"What's wrong?" Zoe asked quietly, eyes on Kel.

"I don't know." Parker ruffled his sister's hair. "Stay here, Am, with Zoe and Henry." And then he walked toward Kel.

Kel came forward to meet him. "Hey, turns out you were right about Carver going back to the scene of the crime. Only it wasn't Carver himself. He'd sent back two of his militia to see if the coast was clear and we nabbed them. They squealed like good little pigs and gave up the rest of the militia's scattered whereabouts and we found Carver with two of them holed up."

Parker let out a relieved breath. "Damn. They got him."

"You got him," Kel said.

Parker knew his agency wouldn't see it that way, but he was still more relieved than anything else because with Carver locked up, Zoe would truly be safe.

"I've got something you might be interested in," Kel said.

"Yeah, what's that?"

"A job. The way you handled yourself with Carver got around, your under-the-radar investigative skills, how you dealt with him here, which could've ended so badly. My buddy at the ATF says if your agency's stupid enough to let you go over what happened, they want you. They have a supervisory position open in the county office about forty-five minutes from here." He glanced over Parker's shoulder at Zoe and then met Parker's gaze again. "Something to think about if you were feeling the urge to stick around," he said, reaching out his hand to shake Parker's.

"No!" Amory yelled, and suddenly she was standing in front of Parker, arms spread wide, blocking him off from Kel. "You can't take my brother, I won't let you!"

Kel was tall, so tall he had to bend down to look into Amory's panicked eyes. "You're his sister, right? I'm a friend of your brother's. Where do you think I'm taking him?"

"Jail!" she wailed.

"I'm not taking him to jail," Kel said. "I'm not taking him anywhere."

Amory blinked. "You're not?"

"Nope."

"Pinkie-promise?" she asked.

Kel solemnly held out his pinky finger.

Just as solemnly Amory shook it with hers.

Then Kel's gaze met Parker's over her head. "Think about it," he said. He looked at Zoe then and smiled, and then he walked away.

Parker looked at Zoe and realized she'd either heard what had happened or figured it out because her eyes were warm and relieved and . . . shit. Full of pride. For him, which he wasn't sure he deserved. He gave her a smile and then turned Amory around to face him.

Her eyes filled. "I'm sorry I lied," she said. "But Mom and Dad would've made me come right home and I wanted to see the snow, Parker! They don't understand that you want me to have adventures."

"Amory," he said softly. "The adventures are for you, not me. You don't ever have to do anything you don't want to, especially with me."

"But I love it when you're happy," she whispered.

Chest tight, he found a smile. "Same goes."

"I know they think you're an influence on me, but they're wrong, Parker. You're not an influence at all, and even if you were, you're my favorite influence."

And then she flung herself into his arms and sobbed.

He sighed. "Amory, do you know what *influence* means?"

"No, and I don't care," she sobbed into his shirt.

He stroked her back. "It's when someone has a special advantage over you and has the ability to change your mind on something."

She stopped crying and stared up at him. "Oh," she breathed, swallowing hard. "Then they're right. You *are* an influence on me, Parker!"

"And you're one on me," he said. "And because you are, I know you. I know you pretty well." He tweaked her hair. "I called Mom and Dad, Amory."

She blinked slow as an owl as she absorbed this. "So you're not in trouble?"

"Not any more than usual," he said.

She winced with guilt all over her face. "I didn't mean to mess anything up. I just wanted —"

"What?" he asked.

"To make you see me as . . . normal."

"Normal is overrated," he said. "You're perfect just the way you are. I just don't want you to be limited, or accept the path that others put you on. I want you to live the life you deserve."

"I know." She looked down. "Sometimes

the people who stare at me," she said quietly. "They say mean things, like I'm never going to be smart. You're not like them, but sometimes you look at me all sad. You're sad for me. But, Parker, I feel sad for you."

"Why?" he asked, completely baffled.

"I know that you think my life isn't good, but it is," she said earnestly. "It's good because I have Henry. But all you have is work and you won't even let Zoe be your girlfriend and she likes you so much. And you like her back, too, I can tell."

Well, she had him there. He turned to look at Zoe and found her watching them, her eyes suspiciously shiny, which made his chest hurt. "Want to know something?" he asked Amory softly.

"Yes!"

"I think you're smarter than me."

She grinned.

Adoption day dawned bright and warm. Parker got up early to take Bonnie and Clyde to Belle Haven. He had them in the kitchen, where they were busy tormenting Oreo on his bed while Parker made coffee.

He was leaning back against the counter watching Bonnie climb onto Oreo's head while Clyde cuddled between the dog's two massive front paws when it hit him. This was the kittens' last day.

And his. He was going back to his life, just as he'd wanted.

Zoe did her usual morning stagger into the kitchen. She wore a big T-shirt that fell to her thighs — his, he realized, his coffee mug frozen halfway to his lips. She had on one sock, the other foot bare. Her hair was . . . everywhere.

She looked like a shipwreck survivor and she'd never seemed more adorably sexy. With a moan that reminded him of how she sounded when he was buried deep inside her body, she headed straight for the coffeepot.

He held his tongue while she poured herself a cup and then sucked half of it down before sighing.

"Better?" he asked.

She slid him a look.

"What?"

"I told myself I wasn't speaking to you," she said. "I'm pretending we're strangers. Which, really, we are."

"You're wearing my shirt," he pointed out.

She looked down at herself and blinked, as if baffled to know how that had happened. "Yes, well, I guess we're not total strangers then."

He smiled.

She started to smile back and then caught herself. "Dammit, no. Don't do that, don't look at me like that. You make me forget that I'm trying to keep my distance. Space bubbles and all that."

"Fuck space bubbles," he said, and hauled her in. Turning them, he pinned her against the counter, lowering his head to nuzzle at the warm, soft crook of her neck.

With a gasp she locked her knees and tightened her grip on her coffee, which she held between them like a chastity belt. "What are you doing?"

Getting in as much time as I can get with you for my last day . . . He nipped her warm skin and she gasped again. "Where are Amory and Henry?" she asked, taking one hand off the mug to fist it in his shirt, holding him to her.

"Out back picking flowers for my mom and dad," he said. "Amory wanted to bring them home some Sunshine flowers." With great reluctance he pulled back. "I'm going to drop the kittens off at Belle Haven on the way to Coeur d'Alene airport."

"Why?"

"Because Amory and Henry have a flight."

"No," she said. "I mean why are you taking the kittens to Belle Haven?"

"It's adoption day."

She froze and pushed him from her so that she could move to Oreo's bed. Sitting right there on the floor, she pulled Bonnie and Clyde into her lap. "No," she said, lifting Bonnie to kiss her on the nose.

Bonnie batted adorably at Zoe's finger, making her laugh. "They can't go to adoption day," she said, snuggling Clyde next.

"Why not?"

"Cuz they've already been adopted. By me." Clyde was falling asleep in Zoe's hands, and she cuddled him in for one last kiss before setting him between Oreo's two huge front paws.

Oreo tipped his head down and gave the sleepy kitten a lick, his tongue bigger than Clyde's entire head.

"Mew," the kitten said without opening his eyes, and then he pressed his little face into Oreo's fur and began to purr.

Parker crouched in front of Zoe. "You don't have to take these two heathens on. I'm the one who —"

"I don't have to do anything," she said, lifting her chin, meeting his gaze, her own stubborn. "I want them. Just like I want you."

Her words, laid bare, were bold and simple, and stunned him. "Zoe —"

"I just wanted to be clear," she said. "In case you weren't sure of my feelings. You're leaving, I know that, but I wanted to put it out there before you go. The three W's and all that —" She shrugged like it didn't matter, but it did.

He pulled her up and into him.

She went without hesitation, wrapping her arms tight around him, tucking her face into the crook of his neck. "You're leaving today with your sister," she accused. "I saw your duffel bag by the front door."

He stroked a hand down her silky hair, closing his eyes as he breathed her in. "Yes," he said quietly. "I'm leaving today."

He had to. He had his orders. Be back in D.C. by Monday to face all that had gone down, and in spite of the fact that it had all worked out, it most likely wasn't going to be pretty.

Still, he wouldn't change a thing he'd done.

But before he could do that, he needed to go home with Amory and Henry and try to repair the relationship with his parents.

Zoe stared at him. "I heard Kel said something about a job here —"

"I'm not walking away from my job," he said.

"No." She pulled free and stared at him.

"Of course not. You're just walking away from me, and pretty damn easily it seems like."

He let out a breath and shook his head. "If you think that, you haven't been paying attention."

"I'm paying attention," she said. "I'm paying lots of attention. Staying here, taking on a job that would keep you in one place, allowing you a personal life, would be settling. Your biggest fear — turning into your workaholic parents. Well, open your eyes, Parker, you've already become them."

That she was right didn't help any. "You want to go there?" he asked. "Fine. Go ahead and weigh in on my life while ignoring that your own is just as much in flux as mine."

"It is not!"

"Really?" he asked. "Is that why you spend your spare time attempting to fix up the house instead of going out and getting a life for yourself now that your brother and sister are gone? Or why you haven't accepted Joe's invitation to become an equal partner in the FBO? Or why you say you want a real relationship, when the truth is that you'd turn the right guy down flat?"

"The right guy?" she asked in disbelief. "And who's the right guy, Parker? The dentist? Joe, who sleeps with anyone with boobs? The guy who wanted me to take pole-dancing lessons? In his basement?"

This stopped him cold. "Who the fuck was that?"

"Never mind! And the FBO thing is none of your business. *I'm* no longer any of your business." She turned away.

He knew she had a point, a big one, but she sure as hell *felt* like his business. "Kel," he said.

She turned back to face him. "What?"

"Kel. He's got a steady job, doesn't have to travel for it, and he's into you."

She stared at him, hurt swimming in her eyes, making him hate himself.

"You want Kel to be the right guy," she said flatly.

No. Christ, no. Just the thought of Kel pulling her in and kissing away the pain in her eyes made him want to wrap his hands around the guy's neck. But she wasn't for him and he knew it. Forcing himself to keep his expression even, he said, "I want you to do what works best for you. Kel's steady. Solid. He'll give you a good life. A diamond ring. A white picket fence for Oreo. Tricycles in the yard for the kids. You could become partners with Joe and have a stake in the business you love."

"And what makes you think I want any of those things?" she asked.

He met her gaze and found the hurt gone, replaced by a fiery temper. "Why else were you on the serial dating spree in the first place?"

"Oh my God," she muttered, and pressed the heels of her hands into her eye sockets. "Listen, I need you to do me a favor."

She asked it in such a reasonable voice that he said, "Sure," before he could think.

"When you go today, don't look back," she said. "I don't want to see you again."

TWENTY-NINE

A week later Zoe was in her bedroom, once again staring at herself in the closet mirror.

"Not bad," her sister said, eyeballing Zoe carefully over her shoulder. "That top makes your boobs look really good. I'm going to need to borrow it."

Zoe eyed her boobs, which did look good if she said so herself. "It's the bra."

Darcy slipped her arms around Zoe, smiling at their reflection in the mirror. "No, it's you. And combined with your long legs and your new status as a partner at the airport with Joe, well, I'd have to hate you if you weren't my sister."

Zoe slid her a look. She'd taken Joe up on his offer with little fanfare and a whole lot of unexpected pleasure, and hadn't realized it would give her brownie points with her sister. "What do you want?"

"What, a girl can't give her favorite sister a compliment?"

"You need money, right?"

Darcy laughed. "Stop. I'll have you know that for the first time since my accident, I've actually got a savings account now. Thanks to all those years of you nagging."

"Okay," Zoe said. "Who are you and what have you done with my sister?"

Darcy sighed. "I just think you might want to reconsider tonight."

Zoe turned to face her sister. "Kel's going to be here to pick me up any second. I didn't wear the bingo dress. I thought you'd be excited about that most of all."

Zoe also hadn't worn the little black dress. Because if the bingo dress reminded her of her failures, the LBD reminded her of the first time she'd been in Parker's arms, and at the thought her resolve to go through with this nearly crumbled.

She wasn't ready to go on a date, and she knew it. But Kel had asked her to dinner and she needed to eat anyway, so she'd said yes. But she was determined to keep this casual, hence the dark jeans and a cute little knit top that gave her the aforementioned good boobs.

"I'd be more excited," Darcy said, "if the date was with the guy you fell in love with."

Parker had been a constant in her thoughts, but she'd made peace with all that had happened. She'd let it go.

Okay, so she was pretending to let it go, but sometimes a girl had to fake it to make it. Easier said than done. She'd seen the cops drive by, checking on her, and she knew that was Parker's doing. They were watching, making sure no one from Carver's world came after her.

She appreciated that but felt it unnecessary. She'd only been targeted because she meant something to Parker.

And now that was no longer true. "We've been over this," she said.

"Right. You told him not to contact you, and that makes perfect sense." Darcy nodded and then shook her head. "Wait — how does it make perfect sense again?"

"His job —"

Darcy snorted. "Screw the job. The job doesn't matter. It's about a guy's character, his heart. And nothing says character and heart like a big, tough badass softening his hard edges for the woman he loves." She spoke firmly, clearly knowing of what she spoke.

And she did. She had AJ, a guy who loved Darcy for exactly who she was, warts and faults and all.

Zoe loved that for Darcy, but she didn't know if she'd ever be lucky enough to find such a thing for herself.

The doorbell rang and she froze. Kel was here a few minutes early.

Darcy gave her a long look. "Problem?"

"Nope. Of course not. I'm just about ready . . ." Zoe looked around for something to do. Aha! Bonnie was struggling to get out of one of Zoe's boots in the closet. Zoe rescued her, setting her on the bed next to where Oreo was snoozing. She then turned around, looking for the other heathen, and found him asleep on her T-shirt in the hamper.

Parker's T-shirt . . .

Oreo lifted his sleepy head and licked his kitten with one huge tongue lap.

Bonnie fell over.

Oreo licked her again, and a rough, rumbling purr filled the room.

"Good boy, Oreo," Zoe said. "Watch the baby."

Darcy snorted. "You need real kids in the worst way," she said.

"Why would I need kids?" Zoe said. "I have you and Wyatt."

"You're stalling," Darcy said.

Yes. Yes, she was. Determined, Zoe grabbed her purse and walked out. Her steps faltered as she passed the room where Parker had stayed. If she stepped inside and inhaled deeply, she could almost catch his scent, see him sprawled on the bed, smiling. Beckoning her with a finger crook . . .

Closing her eyes, she turned away. They'd said all they had to say. Still, she had to rub the physical ache in her chest as she walked by. She hit the stairs, crossed the living room, and plastered a smile on her face.

Then she opened the front door.

Not Kel.

It was Parker, hands up on the jamb above, looking tough and badass in mirrored lenses and no smile.

Her heart skipped a beat. And then another. Not able to deal with what she was seeing, she placed her hands on his abs — rock hard, of course — and gave a little shove so that she could step out onto the porch and look around him to check the driveway.

No Kel.

"Looking for someone?" Parker asked her back.

Her eyes drifted shut. She hadn't seen him in a week, hadn't heard his voice, but she was reacting to him as if he hadn't left. "What are you doing here?"

He didn't answer until she turned to look at him. "Turns out, I forgot something," he said.

THIRTY

Parker's heart had taken one good, hard knock against his ribs at the sight of Zoe, a punch to the system.

"So what did you forget?" she asked, cool as a cucumber.

Clearly she didn't intend to make things easy on him. Zoe was a lot of things. Easy wasn't one of them. Not that he deserved it, anyway. Nope, Zoe was tough on the outside, and though she'd deny it, on the inside she was sweet and warm and capable of such staggering emotion that she scared him to the bone. Right now, *way* on the inside. She wasn't going to give an inch; she never did.

He loved that about her. "You," he said. "Zoe, I forgot you."

Not looking impressed, she crossed her arms. "I don't buy it. You never forget a damn thing." She looked at her watch. "And I don't mean to be rude, but I've got plans."

"I get that. I had plans, too," he said. "But things change."

She just stared at him. "What are you doing here, Parker?"

It was a legitimate question, one that he'd asked himself only every hour or so since he'd last seen her.

He'd gone home. Spent time with Amory. And with his parents. Things were going to be okay there; he'd been shocked and surprised. He'd been welcomed, and together they'd come up with a plan to allow Amory to have some more freedom. They'd all spent a whole twenty-four hours together and no one had raised their voice.

Progress.

From there it had been onward to D.C., where he'd gotten the shock of his life to find out he wasn't fired. His job was still there if he wanted it. A month ago, hell yeah, he'd have wanted it, but he wasn't that same guy. He'd never be that guy again. "I didn't lose my job," he said.

She softened slightly. "I'm glad it worked out for you," she said genuinely.

"I resigned, Zoe."

She blinked. "What?"

He'd walked away and then taken the job with the ATF. Right here in Idaho. He'd have cases much like he'd had for the FWS, but it would be regional. Close to home.

He'd gone his entire adult life not wanting to be like his parents and yet in the end, that was exactly what he'd become. He'd visited with them for a day and realized something else — they had each other, always. He'd realized how much he wanted that, wanted to let someone in.

Zoe.

The job here with the ATF would challenge him and keep him on his toes, but there was a balance to be found between work and a personal life.

And he'd found it.

And then walked away from it.

He'd been a boneheaded dumbass, and all he could do was hope that he wasn't too late because when it came right down to it, all he really wanted was for Zoe to be his.

And for him to be Zoe's.

The sound of a vehicle coming down the street had Zoe giving him another push. "You've got to go," she said quietly. "I've got a date —"

The car drove right by.

"Kel's not coming," Parker said.

"Why not?" She narrowed her eyes. "You messed it up somehow, didn't you?" Giving up trying to push him away, she poked him in the pec. "You know that I manage to mess up these things all on my own. I don't need your help. Dammit, I needed that date tonight, Parker. I needed it to get you off my mind. You had no right to —"

"I'm your date, Zoe."

She blinked. "What?"

"I'm your date tonight," he repeated. And if things went okay in the next few minutes, he was hoping to be her date until the end of time.

But she was shaking her head. "We don't date. We just f—"

He hauled her up to her toes and covered her mouth with his. He kissed her until she sagged against him, until she sank her fingers in his hair and wrapped herself around him with a soft moan that went straight through him. Only when they were both breathless did he pull back, just a fraction of an inch, because he needed to see her.

"You walked away from me," she said softly, her pain like a knife to his gut.

"I'm sorry. I'm so fucking sorry." He dropped his forehead to hers. "I wanted you to have the life you deserve, Zoe, not a guy who would come and go at the mercy of his job, who might not be reachable for long stretches of time or be able to help you if you needed him. I wanted you to have a guy whose job doesn't come with the potential of criminals tracking him down and threatening the people he cares about."

"So you gave up the job for me?" she asked. "No. No, I can't live with that, Parker, I —"

He kissed her again, more softly this time. "I gave it up," he said against her lips, "because I realized that without you in it, my life means squat."

She let out a low breath and poked him in the chest again. "But the job made you *you.*"

"Maybe I don't want to be the job anymore," he said.

She took that in. "What do you want to be?"

"Yours." Cupping her face, he stroked her jaw with his thumbs and looked her in the eyes. "I took the ATF job. I'll be working right here in this county."

She sucked in a breath.

"I was hoping you could live with that," he said, wishing she'd say something. Anything.

"What I want is to be with a guy who can let *me* decide what I can live with and what I can't."

"I know," he said. "And I intend to be that guy."

Another poke, this one even harder, but he manfully held in his wince.

"Really?" she asked. "Because if you were that man, you'd already know that I could live with the travel that comes with a job you love. You'd know that I can live with being more security smart if that takes a weight off your mind. You'd know that what I *can't* live with —" Her voice caught and she swallowed hard before sliding her fingers into his hair and fisting them there, holding his face to hers, "is being without you."

"I hear you," he said softly. "And I can't live without you, either."

A few tears spilled from her eyes and he felt like she'd stabbed him. "Zoe." He reached for her but she backed away, swiping at the tears angrily before whirling on her heels and vanishing inside the house.

He stared at the still-open door. What had just happened? He started to follow her, but suddenly Darcy was there blocking his way.

"You're back?"

"How much did you hear of our conversation?" he asked.

"All of it."

"Then you know I'm back," he said.

She studied him for a long beat. "So, you going to stand here all night or go after her?

Wyatt said you were a sharp one, but I gotta say, not sure I see it."

Zoe turned on the oven and was heading straight for the freezer for the lasagna she'd made the day before when two big hands snaked around her. She was pulled into Parker. "Hey," she said. "I need some cheese and trans fat, stat."

Parker whipped her around to face him and then proceeded to melt her brain with a blistering kiss. "I've got something better than trans fats."

She rolled her eyes.

He smiled and pushed her hair back from her face in that warm, familiar gesture she loved. "I'm all in with you," he said. "You know that, right? The good, the bad, the ugly, all of it." He stared at her like he'd never get enough. "All in," he repeated. "I love you, Zoe."

Oh God. Those words. She'd wondered if she'd ever hear them directed at her. Wyatt and Darcy loved her, to the bone, she knew that. But the three of them had grown up with parents who hadn't used the words, and as a result none of them were all that good with them, either. She closed her eyes. Closed her mouth, too, because she was afraid to let anything out, afraid she'd humiliate herself.

Parker merely adjusted, shifting so that his mouth slid over her earlobe to press a kiss there in the spot that he knew damn well melted her bones every single time. "You're gonna have to talk to me eventually," he murmured.

"I'm confused on your need to talk at all," she managed. "It's unlike you."

"You're right. But as I said, things change. *I've* changed." He tipped her face up to his and looked into her eyes. God knows what he saw there. Most likely a good amount of stubbornness because his gaze lit with wry humor . . . and damn. She'd missed him so much. She had to bite her lip to keep the words. He wasn't getting her words, none of them, not a single one.

"Okay," he said gently. "How about this instead — I'll talk, you listen."

She lifted a shoulder, as if to say: *Look at me not caring,* even as her pulse pounded as though she'd been running uphill.

He smiled; she could feel it against her jawline where he bent to nuzzle her, making her knees weak, damn him.

"You're right," he murmured. "I'm not an open book, not even close. You're not the only one who carefully guards their heart, Zoe. It's my default mode and it's going to take me some time to get this right. I'm going to need some patience here, and you might even have to smack me upside the back of the head once in a while."

"Only once in a while?" she asked.

He set a finger on her smart-ass lips. "No, you're just listening now, remember? I'm being as open and honest as I know how here, babe. With you more so than I've ever been with anyone else."

At that, she felt her heart melt more than a little. She stared into his eyes and saw that he spoke the truth. While her mind was spinning over that, he reached over and shut off the oven.

"Hey," she said.

"Just making sure we don't burn the place down while we figure this out," he said, and while she scrambled for something appropriately scathing to say, he apparently decided he was done standing. He kicked a chair away from the table and sank into it, pulling her down on top of him.

"There's nothing to figure out," she said, the words not quite having the impact intended since she was straddling his lap. "I threw myself at you. And you shut yourself off from me. You were gone for a week. Seven damn days, Parker, and I spent every last one of them pining away for you."

A full, genuine smile curved his mouth at this. "Pining? You?"

She crossed her arms, feeling pissy. "I didn't mean that. Forget I said that." She huffed out a breath. "I just missed you, dammit. A little."

He was still grinning when he gripped her hips in his big hands and yanked her in closer so that not even a piece of paper could fit between them. "You going to run scared?" he asked.

She gaped at him. "*You're* the one who let *me* go! You took off! You're the big, fat baby here, not me."

He went very serious. "And I'll regret that to my dying day, Zoe. I was an idiot, a complete dumbass. I know that now. I want to be a part of your life. If I'm being honest, I want to be the most important part."

"My life is in Sunshine," she said.

"I get that. I'm interested in having a home base, too, but you've got to know that the home base I'm thinking of is you. Not a house. Not a town. *You.* As long as you're with me, I don't care where we live. Now it's your turn. You've got to give me something here, a crumb, anything. I'm a desperate man, Zoe."

She blew out a breath, feeling the last of her fear drain away as her heart bloomed and opened, warming her from the inside out. "You're a better detective than this," she said quietly. "I've managed to sabotage every single relationship that's come my way except for the one I have with you. You're the one I want. I love you back, Parker. Don't ever doubt that."

"God, Zoe." He touched his forehead to hers. "I don't know what I ever did to deserve you, but I plan on spending the rest of my life proving to you I'm worth it."

It was the Parker James equivalent of begging on bended knee. She drew in a deep breath and then nearly had heart failure when Darcy stuck her head in the kitchen.

"Sorry," she said, not looking sorry at all. "But I have to get home and I don't want to leave before the show's over. Can we fast-track it to the ending?"

Zoe stabbed a finger at the door and Darcy flashed a grin. "Fine. I'm out." She took the time to point at Parker and then back at her own two eyes, mouthing *I've got my eyes on you* . . .

When she was gone, Parker looked at Zoe. "My sister has nothing on nosiness compared to yours."

"Nope."

He gave her a little smile. "She loves you."

"Yep." Zoe squeezed him tight. "Where

were we?"

"You were about to spill your guts to me," he said.

"I'm glad you came back," she said. "Took you long enough."

"I tried not to come back," he said with a low laugh. "Christ, I tried."

"I know." With a little laugh of her own, she rested her head on his chest so she could admit this part without having to hold his gaze. "And I tried not to care."

His voice had a wry smile in it as he hugged her into him. "We deserve each other."

"Yes, we do." His hands slid down her back to cup her ass, and she felt her body rev. She lifted her head. "Maybe we should go upstairs and give each other what we deserve."

They made it as far as the stairs before Zoe dragged him down on top of her, reaching for his zipper. "Thank God my sister left," she said, freeing a most impressive erection.

He was in the middle of stripping her naked, his hands everywhere. "Yeah, maybe we could not talk about your sister right now."

She smiled coyly. "What should we talk about?"

He pulled her over him and shoved her hair from her face. "How I've been yours since the second we met."

She felt her throat tighten, but still she tried to make light. "You mean when I mistakenly kissed you on my porch?"

Poised to enter her, he stopped and cupped her face, staring into her eyes, not letting her joke this away. "Best damn mistake to ever happen to me, Zoe."

Oh, he was good. So very, very good. "So what now?" she asked in a whisper.

He kissed her softly and then not so softly. And then he pulled her down so that he could thrust up into her. "First, I'm going to take you on these stairs."

Her breath caught and she found herself nodding her head like a bobblehead. "And then?" she asked eagerly.

"And then we'll move to the upstairs landing. And then your bed. And then maybe the shower, if we can still walk."

She pressed her mouth to his gorgeous lips. "And then?"

"And then," he said, voice rough with need and emotion, God, so much emotion, "I want to hold you while I sleep. All night, Zoe. I want to wake up with you in my arms. And then we do the same thing all over tomorrow night. And the night after that."

Her heart had swelled up against her rib cage. "For how many nights?" she asked.

"All of them," he said, and mended the last rift in her heart.

EPILOGUE

Six months later . . .

A warm breeze settled around Zoe and Parker as they watched a just-married Wyatt and Emily sway to the music together in Zoe's backyard. The plan had been to do the reception in the house but the day had turned out so unseasonably perfect they'd moved the party outside. They were still dressed as bride and groom, though Emily was barefoot and on tiptoes, wrapped in her husband's arms as they stared at each other raptly.

"You look so beautiful tonight," Parker murmured, coming up behind Zoe, pulling her back into his strong, warm arms. "You outshine even the bride."

She felt herself flush a little and wriggled, gratified to feel Parker's body respond.

Mouth nuzzling her ear, he laughed softly, naughtily. "Keep that up and I'll drag you inside."

"Not yet, you won't." She laughed breathlessly. "AJ and Darcy went inside an hour ago for more booze and never came back out."

"Lucky bastard," Parker murmured, and dragged her out to the dance floor, where he succeeded in heating her up and making her look longingly at the house.

He laughed at her. "Not yet," he teased.

It was two more hours before Zoe stood in the middle of the street, finally watching Wyatt and Emily drive off in his truck, the *Just Married* graffiti all over it.

Behind her, the rest of the gang cheered loudly and migrated back to the yard, where the wedding reception would carry on, probably late into the night.

Parker slid an arm around her. "They grow up so fast."

She laughed and turned into him, her breath catching at the sight of him, as it had all night. "Did I ever tell you that the sight of a man in a tux makes me wild?"

He flashed a very wicked smile at that. "How do you feel about a man stripping off his tux?"

"Even better." She laughed when he nudged her toward the house instead of the party. "We can't yet," she said. "We have guests."

418

"They'll never even notice," he promised.

Inside, the house was dark and quiet. Parker didn't turn on any lights, leading her by the hand into . . . the kitchen? "Not that I'm complaining," she said. "But I'm tired. I'm going to need a bed to do my best work —"

He flipped on the light.

Oreo lifted his sleepy head from his bed by the stove. Bonnie and Clyde, both cuddled with him, lifted theirs, too. At the sight of Zoe, the Food-Giver-Outer, they came running and tumbling toward her and she gasped.

Each of the kittens had a ribbon around their neck and from the ribbon hung a sign. Clyde got to her first, and his sign read:

Marry our daddy?

And Bonnie's read:

Will you . . .

Parker sighed. "The one night that he's faster than she is . . ."

Zoe turned and threw herself at him, both laughing and crying as she squeezed him tight.

Parker's arms came hard around her. "Is that a yes?"

Speechless, her chest tight with emotion, she nodded.

Oreo, sensing the escalating excitement,

lifted his head and barked.

Zoe laughed through her happy tears and kissed Parker. "Yes," she said against his lips. "We'll all marry you."